KING PENGUIN

BEACHMASTERS

Thea Astley is the author of nine previous novels, including *A Boatload of Home Folk* and *An Item from the Late News* (both available from Penguin). She has won the distinguished Miles Franklin Award in Australia on three occasions, as well as several other literary awards. A retired professor of English and creative writing, she now lives in Kuranda in Queensland, Australia.

Beachmasters

Thea Astley

A KING PENGUIN
PUBLISHED BY PENGUIN BOOKS

PENGUIN BOOKS
Published by the Penguin Group
Viking Penguin Inc., 40 West 23rd Street,
New York, New York 10010, U.S.A.
Penguin Books Ltd, 27 Wrights Lane, London W8 5TZ, England
Penguin Books Australia Ltd, Ringwood,
Victoria, Australia
Penguin Books Canada Limited, 2801 John Street,
Markham, Ontario, Canada L3R 1B4
Penguin Books (N.Z.) Ltd, 182–190 Wairau Road,
Auckland 10, New Zealand

Penguin Books Ltd, Registered Offices: Harmondsworth,
Middlesex, England

First published in Australia by Penguin Books Australia Ltd 1985
First published in the United States of America by
Viking Penguin Inc. 1986
Published in Penguin Books 1988

LIBRARY OF CONGRESS CATALOGING IN PUBLICATION DATA
Astley, Thea.
Beachmasters.
ISBN 0 14 01.0946 3
(King Penguin)
I. Title.
[PR9619.3.A75B4   1988]   823   87-7213

Printed in the United States of America by
R.R. Donnelley and Sons Company, Harrisonburg, Virginia
Set in Goudy Old Style

Acknowledgements:
Impulses from Maggie Paton's Letters and Tom Harrisson's *Savage Civilisation*.
The Literature Board of the Australia Council for a writing grant.

Notes:
The pidgin used throughout generally follows the South Pacific French spelling. Dialect words and custom references are drawn from a number of areas in the one island group.

While the revolution in this novel may have recent historical parallels, the islands and the characters are fictional.

There has been only one peril in the Pacific, the white one.

— *Tom Harrisson*

I know what happens
I read the book
I believe I just got the goodbye look.

— *Donald Fagen*

Mifala i man.
No animol. Okey!!

— *Banner slogan at a Pacific island demonstration*

In the waters of these islands there is a certain fish whose eyes, like the eyes of the chameleon, are able to look in opposite directions at the same time.

Like aeland Kristi.

Kristi last winter and the summer before that, while the wind off the Channel was munched by the wooden teeth of the shutters.

Like man Kristi – man bush or man solwata.

Like the colons and the British ex-patriates and the rag dolls District Agent Cordingley with his wife Belle and French District Agent Boutin and Madame Boutin and Planter Salway and his grandson Gavi and Gavi's maman, Lucie Ela, and Madame Guichet and Chloe of the Dancing Bears and a beach bum from the big land, man blong Australia, whose real name was never known, with a lifetime of small riots behind and more in his blood like bubbles.

And, too, oh in this litany, pray, your eyes east-west, pray for Hedmasta Woodful, now and at the hour of the changing, and for the Bonsers, mechanics of more than boat engines, for Planter Duchard and family, and above all, for the big man, the yeremanu, Tommy Narota, part Kristi, part Tongan, part Devon, who has taken on his new native name, abandoning that of his sea-faring adventurer daddy, along with his ceremonial dress of Bipi fringed tablecloth and lace antimacassar loin-wrapper. Send your prayers east-west or north-south for the vanikoro to pluck up with its swoop of a beak.

And pray in three tongues: in Seaspeak, in English, in French; for there are three ways of praying.

The eyes move two ways. The voice moves three. Two-eyed. Triple-tongued. While the wind is eaten by the shutters and the small canoes move down the thick blue waters of the Channel towards Trinitas or Emba.

The sea rocks. The palms shake out clicking scales of music drier than sand. There are only silver scars left behind the little boats that

1

soon no one at all will be able to see – scars, boat, water are all one. As man and land are one. Man ples. And therein, in that unity of land with man, lies the trouble.

It is time to storian.

Fifteen days after they locked the *yeremanu*, Tommy Narota, away in Mataso town gaol for seven years on the grounds of treason and inciting to rebellion against the state, a young boy shoved his way through the clutter of bad-wishers and the merely curious outside the gates and, calling through the bars, held his hands out to be taken. '*Metuan*,' he kept calling. 'Uncle.'

Tommy Narota, stripped of his military second-hands and wearing only a Chesty Bond singlet and too big white underpants, looked around bewildered, as all his moments were bewildered now, an attempt at a smile on his plump daddy yam face.

There was no one he knew outside the gates; only a few ni-Kristi there to gawk and shout rage sounds, a couple of followers who had escaped the military net, none of his women and a knot of abusive children on their way to school. He limped over to the gates and took the boy's hands and then one of the guards hustled him along and another one grinned and the gawkers, the prison forecourt, the gates, the block shadow of the mango trees blue in the butterscotch morning, were the last sharp photographs he took with him to his cell.

But he had many other sharp-edged memories going back, going back, to his white daddy, one of those island knockabouts that Europe spewed out in the Pacific, a big bugger of a man, bearded ginger, with pale Anglo-Saxon skin and blue eyes, his appetite for sun and women, liquor and the sea, making him a force all those years ago, *longtai'm bifor*, when he traded and peered for landfall along the black sand coasts.

And how many *hapkas* did papa sire?

Some said ten.

Some twenty.

There were six before him, Tommy Narota knew, grown up and gone away into yam gardens on other islands by the time he and a

3

younger sister, Seruwaia, were conscious of the roaring patriarch and the brown-skinned woman who were their parents. Tommy had thrown white, as they said in those parts; well, in some respects. Like Seruwaia. Clad in a blander skin, their features boned differently, but the hair a giveaway.

Papa, playing at custom, drinking kava in the sacred ground with the other men, listening to stars sing earthwards, stars moons galaxies dropping from the skies as they contemplated the stones. Papa not believing the stone magic or the star magic or the crazy *klevas* raving above the *navilahs*, but drinking, none the less, passing the gourd as they storied on and numbing old-world yearnings that leaked from dropping stars into drooping ragged beard when he sang later on the *nasara* ground as the dancers clicked nut anklets, 'Tom's gone to Hilo', ironic with 'I've never seen a sight since I be born, like a big buck nigger with his sea-boots on' or – and or – just that. Papa in the heavy dark stippled with fireflies.

And older, ten, eleven, hunting with pig clubs through the *mori* trees out beyond the village gardens where jungle billowed down the mountain slopes in waterfalls. But mainly with papa on his boat, harvesting the waters out beyond Buala and learning another language of wind and current.

From his hot cell he could hear hooter blasts from boats in the Channel beyond Mataso and the blasts became all those *stima* days and the women broad-lapped along the quay with the fish strung nicely or spread on plantain leaves, the yams, the taro, the woven baskets of dragon plums and Malay apples displayed for the *wai'tes* from the ships. His big day, this, coin-cadging from a *misis* with scarfed hair and little biting heels, from others who squealed with cameras to their eyes, *tekim piksa*; or making a nuisance of himself at the wharves, rope-hauling, canoe-paddling, diving, giggling, circling, watching the *gavman* men.

The mission school, where there was too much singing, taught him to pray, to read, to draw a map of his own island like a vast green mitten and mark on it Pic Kristi, the rivers Quiros and Tasiriki and a big dot for Mataso town.

At twelve he went to the *nakamal*, became a man, drank kava and watched his papa cough himself to extinction, saw his mama waste

4

from the lack of the big blusterer and ran off from his fishing village to the black dot on the map where he odd-jobbed for Bipi and the Chinese trading stores, light-skinned enough to show promise but too dark, of course, to get anywhere on an island with a long white memory of planter picnics and drinks on verandahs and the cocktail gabble of the ruling classes.

The two worlds did not touch, could not touch, except through feelers of resentment and envy.

People kept saying 'war' in Mataso town. There was big-eyed talk of great explosions and burning planes and ships like islands sinking to the north, *long wé*, *long wé*, past the yam gardens and the fish tides and the dusty stores of the Boulevard d'Urville. And then the war came in the shape of thousands and more thousands of American troops who planted a town overnight and watched buildings sprout like stinging-vine. And more came and more and buildings clustered like turtle eggs and there were blacks as well as whites wearing *masta* clothes and handling guns and radios and army trucks.

He'd never seen such cargo.

Hanging about the camps, an attractive *hapkas*, smiley, gentle, obliging, he'd run errands, let them josh him, watching their wastefulness with food and equipment and begging throw-outs. There were official buried caches of radio and engine parts wrapped in rubber and lead. He made a small living from selling off the stuff he dug up later when no one was around, selling back, sometimes, to Yankee privates who kept their mouths shut because they were going to sell off in their turn. Mataso town became a city of Quonset huts and hospitals, PX stores, cinemas and canteens on newly constructed roads that jammed up with jeeps and trucks and carloads of men with strange accents; and later there were planes flying in and out, in and out, from the coral landing-strip at Kapi and bomber landing-fields higher up in the hills.

His sixteen years hadn't stretched his frame much but he had a strange dignity in his grubby alertness that ignored ragged shorts and mission issue singlet. Too old now to care that the succour of family was gone, even Seruwaia gone now across the Channel to Emba as house-girl for a red-mugged planter; but wrung, even while unaware of the cause, by the furies of mixed blood. He found

5

shelter outside Mataso town where a group of ni-Kristi drawn like copra beetles by American cargo had made an abandoned drying shed a sorting house for scrap, the expensive detritus of these wry-mouthed newcomers.

They were a sad little group.

Strutters with cast-off forage caps, wind-breakers with colour patches, army shirts and loincloths. There was a stack of canned food and a fancy opener whose working no one had solved yet, a battery radio, a pile of comic books no one could read except Tommy and an army cot with broken legs. They took turns sleeping on it.

The army used some of them to help coast-watchers camped on rocky scarps about the island. Tommy Narota spent three months with a British planter from Thresher Bay, stationed on the seaward slopes of Pic Kristi watching American bombers thunder north into wet dawns.

The war didn't mean much.

When the planter sickened with malaria, Tommy got him down, somehow, bushmen from the hills helping, to the mission at Port Ebuli. Only Père Bonnard thanked him. The war still meant little. He understood nothing of the loyalties of these intruders. He understood only the excitement of their possessions.

In the weeks before the last troops pulled out as the war ended, or they said it had, some giant bomb *long wé long wé*, bringing it all to an abrupt close, he watched horrified and close to tears as Yankee bulldozers shovelled tons of food ammunition guns tractors jeeps still in their crates demountable buildings radios, oh everything, *olting*, off a southern point into the deep running tides of the Channel. The water hissed and sucked and swallowed army furniture, road-making equipment, rescue boats and generators with blue indifference. The Channel ate and ate and the trucks kept going and coming, crammed with gear and the bulldozers kept shoving until even they, and then the carrier trucks, were propelled driverless into the Pacific on a mound so high that the driving cabins of the monster waste-heap could be seen at low water.

Tommy had stood staring with a group of islanders as machines disappeared into the sea and he had run forward alongside the second last of the trucks, pleading with them not to do it.

He yelled in French, in English, in Seaspeak.

'Shift your goddam ass!' the driver had roared, revving up and preparing to jump from the cabin.

The G.I. was fed up with the place, the stinking heat, the black stupes who got in the way. He'd picked up a dose somewhere, too, and the drugs in his system were taking a goddam time about working. He swung his truck close to the yowling black and reaching down from his cabin gave him a shove. 'Haul ass!' he screamed again. Christ! The mother-fucker seemed to be crying. Christ!

Then the driver had leapt and taken Tommy down with him onto the coral. They were both skin-ripped and bloody. 'Oh you stupid son of a bitch!' the G.I. said, smearing away at his own bleeding skin.

Tommy let his blood drip down his fingers, down from his knees and watched the last truck plunge into the Channel.

There was nothing anyone could do about it. The dangerous gutters along the coast were nagged by tides. The equipment could never be pulled out.

Nothing was left behind but abandoned Quonset huts, fifty miles of new road the weather would claw at and memories of insanely wasted wealth.

For a long time the island felt empty.

Père Leyroud who had sat it through at the mission of St Pierre, saying Mass as if there weren't even the echo of a war, confessing troops, baptising their half-caste babies and making hospital rounds, offered Tommy Narota a caretaker's job for the mission school and garden. Tommy lived in a small hut at the back of the priests' house. He had three shirts, an old army jacket, two forage caps and a rifle he had found abandoned in one of the huts on the way to Bomber Three site seven miles from Mataso town. He had as well a great pile of mildewed copies of *Time* magazine. He concealed the rifle from Père Leyroud in a disused oil drum that he buried under a mound of leaves and garden clippings beneath the *tali* trees. Sometimes at night, he'd take the rifle out and sleep with it rammed against his naked skin. At weekends he took it to the old drying shed to swagger or flashed it before other young men who hung about the town's back streets. For cigarettes, they could hold it.

Père Leyroud found him interesting. He odd-jobbed, unhurried and cheerful as he scythed grass, swept out classrooms and mended snapped wires along the *burao* fences, all with a slow but positive calm, unlike the other islanders who had worked for him. 'I knew your father well,' he said one day to Tommy Narota, paused with a broom in the afternoon quiet of the school.

Tommy smiled and waited.

'He was a good man,' Leyroud said. 'Perhaps,' he added tactlessly, 'not by Church standards. But all in all.'

'I don't remember too much,' Tommy lied.

'Where,' Père Leyroud asked, settling his round little body onto a desk, 'are all those brothers and sisters, eh?'

'Go *finis*,' Tommy said, still grinning. '*Olgeta go longtai'm finis.*'

'Don't use Seaspeak, Tommy,' Leyroud said gently. 'Use French. Or English. You're a bright chap.'

Too bright, he was lamenting, understanding Tommy's irony.

And too bright for custom, for colonial rites.

He encouraged Tommy to read but apart from devotional works he had only a small supply of *romans policiers* and some travel books in English. Tommy preferred to pore over the mildewed copies of *Time*.

One morning after early Mass, Leyroud looked in vain for his yardboy. He wanted him to drive to the wharves to collect a crate of equipment for the newly opened science block. The door of Tommy's hut hung open. The nails where his spare shirts, two caps and army jacket had hung were empty. The mattress was rolled up neatly on the camp stretcher and a note in careful mission hand lay on the box he had used as a table.

Dear Father, the note read, this day I go to drive truks for a planter at Bay of the Two Saints. This is man work, I think. Sweeping is nothing thing. Thank you for much.

The dozers had moved him with a kind of poetry, the heavy long relentless sweep of the blade, the swing of the arm, the high cabin seat, *yeremanu* high, hands sweat-greasy on the steering wheel, sheltering under the cabin roof as rain or sun slashed, the plucking at gears. And control. Control. He was clearing great acres of *dark bush* for Duchard who wanted to graze cattle on the foothills. The Adventist mission had asked him to level a sportsfield. The *gavman* men took him on to help with road making. At weekends he borrowed the dozer and made a private track through custom territory to an inland place he had decided to settle for himself. If he ever settled. The tensions between earth and air, the consciousness of the glade, dealt lovingly with leaf and water. It was his private kingdom and he called the place Vimape. But when the jobs ran out with the *gavman* and the missions and the planters, once more he was hanging about along the waterfront cadging work on inter-island trading boats.

He was quick, a natural sailor, tuned in to sea-rhythms.

The next time he was in Mataso town Mista Bipi sent for him looking curiously at this brown fella whose prowess was talked about as far as Trinitas.

'You *hapkas*, eh?' Mista Bipa knew he was. Tommy swallowed his resentment.

'Malcolm Orwin was my father,' he said. Remembering Père Leyroud's words. He wouldn't use Seaspeak when *wai'tes* did. 'He was the best sailor round these islands.'

Mista Bipi went a small red.

He dropped the pidgin. 'You could be as good as him. If you wanted to.'

Narota smiled gently, as much over his little victory.

'Of course.'

He skippered a copra boat running between the islands, taking on cargo for the loading docks at Port Lena. Sometimes when he was off the tiny island of Buala he felt an urge to see the old place where he had grown up with his flashy white dad guzzling at the *lap-lap*, swilling grog and roaring out songs none of the bushmen understood. The old plantation and garden were still there running back from the beach and the huts papa had built. But a Frenchman had long since taken over and Tommy Narota stood on the coral fringe looking back along the colonnades of coconut palms, remembering his mama organising a feast for this or that and the messes of yam and manioc served up on banana leaves and the good bits of the coconut crab he fought his brothers for; and someone, somewhere, he couldn't remember now, making wistful sounds on a bamboo flute. The notes had been like tears. Perhaps it was his papa. That flute. And the fireflies through the dark and the chatter of palm fronds, the nagging suck-slam of reef waters.

Tommy cried. His tears were the flute's tears. He let out sounds because there was no one to hear, wanting oh wanting, now he had passed the years when the blood rages to leave family, to return. There was nothing to return to. The ruins of the main house, half a mile from the concrete buildings of the new planter, flapped their rotting woven panels in the wind off the sea. The stakes of the pig fences he had helped build were fallen over and the new *misis* had planted smothering vine whose noisy flowers shouted down all his memories.

Tommy sailed away though his tears and the watery ripples of the flute and on his next lay-off in Kristi took the first of his wives. Although he had thrown white, a darker tug decided him. For the *hapkas* there was nothing. He flung himself into custom and as the years floated in and out the floating islands and he took other wives to his house in Vimape, he felt in the black marrow of his bones that here was home. Others joined his community and the village lived with their gardens and the sound of the river in the gorge, taro lush, the *nabanga* trees clouding the great *nakamal* or men's house. Children clustered, grew. His wives aged and Tommy Narota plumped out with the spirit comfort of Vimape, bearded, benign, a *yeremanu* in his own village.

Oué, he would call with satisfaction, cross-legged and wiping grease and a baked mush of stringy chicken from his mouth. This is the life, *laka*! This is fine, fine.

Remembering.

His absorption in the new life he had cut out of the jungle had the violence of love. In his kava dreams he saw Kristi as a kingdom. He saw the *aeland* wiped clean of colonial settlers, unless they, too, were prepared to swing on the lianas of custom. Then, oh then, the whole *aeland* would assert the pride of its myths.

Take a look at these snapshots.

Louklouk olgeta piksa ia.

This one is clear. Walter Trembath, British Assistant Resident Commissioner, all six feet of him, beside his tiny smoothly fair wife, leaning back across the spanking white rail, leaning back over blue scrolls of reef water, leaning back. There is something about the angle of their bodies that proves their invulnerability to threat. Leaning throws their heads and their smiles high, curved over the residency launch, Eurydice. Their very British, always slightly amused faces, are screwed up in the sun as they stare across the habour to the French Commissioner's villa. Both he and it are concealed by trees but judging from the up-curve on those very British mouths you'd think he was totally exposed in all his porky folly.

Louklouk olgeta klos ia.

Trembath is wearing his man-of-the-people gear: shorts, a scarlet T-shirt and flip-flops. These are the clothes he likes best in the staggering heat of Trinitas. His wife wears a sleeveless sunfrock of undogmatic beige. Of course, these aren't Assistant Resident Commissioner Trembath's sing-sing rags. Here. Here's another piksa, olsem ofisol, Trembath with ostrich-plumed pith helmet, concrete stiff whites, my God, a dress sword, taking the salute from a contingent of sweat-gleaming ni-Trinitas in khaki shorts and shirts while a terrible bugle belts out a military tune.

And there's another, cut from the weekly news sheet of Port Lena: Trembath relaxing over a set of bongo drums. He's wearing a lap lap and his long good-humoured face has been caught by the flash in an inane grin. He is playing bongos at La Petite Différence, the only night-club in Lena. He plays, not every weekend, but most, at the invitation of the Trinitas jazz band and he escapes criticism from the Anglo residents who, in this heat, this latitude, are proud that all Englishmen are mad.

He's a charmer, the women say at cocktail parties. Knows his stuff, the men say. Does a damn good job, all things considered.

'A fool of a man,' says Agent Boutin, says Planter Duchard.

And here's another. Two more in fact. Who's this old man sitting outside a palm-thatch hut, a book open on his knees, a wide-brimmed panama concealing the eyes but letting us catch a glimpse of a magnificent nose and beard? He's ignoring the camera. He's a loner. He's an old island hand. It's Dick Lorimer from the Bay of the Two Saints, caught in a social moment but trying to ignore it. If you look hard, peer inside that open doorway, you'll just manage to make out a stove, three pieces of crockery and a pile of books. Young Trumble took that one when the old man was off guard. There are lots of things the camera missed but the placidity is there, the fortitude, a long-learnt tolerance. If you wait, you'll discover what he's reading.

And this. Oh this is Doctor Trumble talking with Planter Salway outside the Copra Trading Stores. They are both squinting into midday and certainly Salway is handsomer even though he's twenty years or more older than the doctor, with his mass of grey tumbled hair, his wild moustache and the mad blue of eyes hidden for the moment by ruddy folds of flesh. Trumble is smaller, leaner, with the mild stoop of a research assistant. He's laughing now at something Kenasi Salway must have said and just to one side of them, coming out of Bipi, is Gavi's maman looking girlish under parcels. So she should. She's mid-thirties and lithe, her dark hair pulled back under a cream scarf, and if there's the suggestion of a pout it's a trick of the camera. Or something else. Salway's grandson is half-concealed by Doctor Trumble. Old Mr Salway doesn't look much like his grandson except for a gravity about the lips, the compression of dreams. The cord linking maman and Gavi Salway is less tenous. The bones have it. The skin says it.

Don't pant at revelation! Don't tighten that stomach knot into a cramp! Put the picture away, manki. Here's another.

Why! It's Père Leyroud presiding over a confirmation class of islanders and colons and – where are you Gav? You've merged into your true –

Put it away. Away. Here's another of long-gone dad at a picnic party just after marriage, papa with his good looking blond head, the grin erupting, the lens so overcome by sunniness, maman is blurred and with that out-of-focus quality could be any one of the planters' wives, any one at all, prim groomed misis.

And these. Yourself. Gavi at six months, two years, four, seven, ten, thirteen, stubble and armpit hair, coffee skin off-set by cricket whites, a set of smashing teeth and dreams at the corners of eyes that read an older history. I see you, Gavi. I see you. You're poised to dive from the plantation jetty on Emba, laughing at a fish-net drag, learning to shin up a coconut palm, nearly indistinguishable, with the poor film, the bad focus, from the plantation boys, from Bonjui Taureka, from Solomon, from Jubilee. Don't look. You noken louk louk.

But this one. This one here. It's not a snapshot but a clipping from Le Monde Pacifique, a fortnightly broadsheet Michel Plombe runs out in his printery off the Boulevard d'Urville. Everyone knows who this is. An older man, hapkas, humble moustaches dripping into patriarchal beard, a fly-away impishness on the whimsical round face which not even the gappy grin makes anything but sad. He's wearing an army beret and a T-shirt with a logo. The letters are just decipherable – Talasa Pati – as he half turns to an eager crowd. Look at all those heads! There's a headline just above the mango trees behind this smiler: 'Tommy Narota demands self-government'.

And there's more. There's more. Two clippings from the Island Times, another three from Jeune Kristi, a subversive monthly, and one from an Australian Sydney paper: Tommy Narota at Flag Raising Ceremony ('Tommy Narota declares himself king of Kristi'); Tommy Narota at Talasa Pati Headquarters ('Election rigged,' says Kristi's breakaway chief); Tommy Narota being driven in an army jeep along the Boulevard d'Urville ('Native Rebel Sitting Pretty: Dark bush man poses threat to British Government').

He's plumply benign. He's a dark-skinned Feste. He's made for comedy. Here's a photo of his alleged fourteen wives and at least thirty-seven children. He has a tusk round his neck. This photo is the most dignified of all. The bare breasts see to that. At least eight of the women and four of the children are kneeling, legs tucked under as they squat, grass skirts wispy, on their heels. Wife nambawan is wearing the shapeless dress hippies made popular ten years before and the missionaries fifty years before that. All of them are arranged for this picture outside the open doorway of a custom house. It could be a tourist brochure. And there's another, not nearly as dignified, of Tommy

Narota with thirty of his rebel forces and three of his interim government ministers. The troops are terrifying in shorts and thongs with bows and arrows at the ready. Narota wears army issue trousers and shirt, an enormous digital watch, his chiefly tusk, and has just begun to wave. In the backgroumd, the security building has its push-out shutters raised and Narota's eyebrows are pushed up as high under that cockily askew engineer's beret above the Santa cheek pouches and the eye twinklings. Emi seki. He one cheeky fella!

The last picture is of Mataso town.

It has to be the town for if you wanted – and always you want – to display aeland Kristi, where to start?

The island is a green boxing glove, a baseballer's mitt. It has an insolent thumb. Do you commence with the north and its two-sainted bay? In the jagged western ranges, their saw-teeth greened from root to tip with jungle? The bays of the east coast with blasting-white of the beaches? Any angle – post-card stuff: palms, shores, more palms, blue lemonade seas. All under sluggish heat.

Go for the town with its one wide main street of official buildings, Chinese stores, hotel, cinema, banks, market, mango trees and flamboyants stretching along a sharky Channel to wharves with copra boats, inter-island motor-vessels, stray yachts, all soft-sucking chatter by the docks, hugged in by brochure blue.

Scrubby. Dusty. Untidy.

Listen! It's different if you live there.

This is Mataso town blong Kristi, ramshackle and forgotten on the narrow sea-plain where waters rush up and sky rushes down between town and the tiny island of Emba and its partner claw that dangles to the west. In that other world this one will never know, strangers move through their urban neon to pore longingly over atlases (with what expectations?) to discover an island like this.

The irony of it.

They breathe, those searchers, the shallow air of dreams, walking the frail crust of longing, while the reality absorbs the pummelling of sun or rain, not rain whose gentle persistence might feed the spirits of lovers or readers drowsing over unturned pages, but shocking fists of it, that – and drenching light, as the whole of this benign fiction they seek floats its dangerous velvet reality always beyond reach.

Gavi closed the family album as if he were trying to close off a confusion in his mind.

Hello, little *aeland*, he said. I love you.

For Gavi Salway it had all seemed to begin that day, the day of the cricket match between St Pierre and the British school. Six weeks ago? Nine? Make it a term. He was certainly younger by what felt like a decade.

He was lying on the grass behind the oval along with the rest of the team and even under the mango trees, dense as they were, at the end of the mission paddock, the heat was almost improper.

The game had that silly staged look school matches have. Keeping their colonial ends up, straight back in a straight sun, no matter how punishing. There was a row of chairs drawn into the shade along the fence where old Corders was sitting with that slob wife of his, leaning across her and talking in his awful French to Père Leyroud.

The Malatao team, a baggy lot, had come out by bus with Hedmasta Woodful who was now sagging under the marquee, his hand gripping a lime and rum. Everyone was simply keeping the props going, the match being one of those stays needed in a stinking climate where there was no weather, only hot and hotter with rampaging wets in the monsoon months, quick sunsets and sudden daylights as the world cracked open like an egg and everywhere this spinach green, this straining blue.

Père Leyroud had begun the ritual early that morning, welcoming the official guests, District Agent Cordingley and his wife, Belle, and French Agent Boutin and Madame Boutin and Hedmasta Woodful. There was a sprinkling of mamans and papas. He had greeted the visiting team with manly encouragement and had felt sorry for his own. For Leyroud, the whole business had the hairshirt flavour of a public day of obligation.

Gavi was feeling sorry for his own team, too, with its ragtag eleven and the sports shit pumped out by Mista Pulvers who had taken over the team training from one of the curates, when he came to reorganise the science department of the school. 'What a wank!'

Rogo Trumble was complaining, head on arms in the cropped grass as they rested during the long lunch break.

Elbow-propped, Gavi stared with half-closed eyes at the mission grounds that sprawled beside the Channel Road. The rusting iron roofs, the wooden shutters, the chapel with its French provincial turret, coloured glass lozenges and its triple doors were more familiar to him than his home. And now there were assorted parents mopping, fanning, picking at sandwiches and gulping Malo cocktails. His grandfather had come over from Emba with maman and both of them washed up in deck chairs were talking to Hedmasta Woodful and the Trumbles. Lee Fong who ran the Ciné Mangrove and Madame Guichet (trembling on retirement) hovered between marquee and drinks bar, Madame Guichet already tottery on her pins. It was her last official match. Gavi could not know she was drinking to the blankness of the next year. Planter Duchard was arguing with Mista Bipi and the manager of La Banque de l'Indochine.

'What a wank,' Rogo Trumble repeated, angry, even while Gavi wrestled with a sense of history and nostalgia. The mission had been there for sixty years and Père Leyroud, growing steadily gentler, vaguer and pudgier, for forty of those. Once it had been a school for the children of *colons* and diplomatic servants; but times had changed and there was now only a handful of Europeans, most of them leaving by fourteen for boarding-schools in Noumea or the mainland.

Little place. Little school. Rags of tradition. 'In this heat,' Rogo Trumble complained, rolling over on the grass. 'The empire in this heat.'

It wasn't the match that obsessed Gavi Salway. There had been some runs made against scratchy bowling and as fifth man he had made ten before a strapping island boy from the British school, Joseph Keti, took his middle stump. Much much cheering. Dutiful clapping from parents putting down drinks for the shortest of moments while the whole scene, as Rogo grumbled to Gavi back in the marquee, had all the nonsense of village green rites except it was taking place in latitude 15° south on a field overlooking a water full of thresher sharks and barracuda.

17

It had been, Gavi realised worrying at the memory, after a social studies lesson.

Mista Pulvers who doubled as *storian man baout kantri baout gavman* had just given the two senior forms forty minutes on colonial rule in the Pacific. Pulvers was a young idealist and told it the hard way. He had wound up the lesson by pointing out the essential difference in British and French rule. 'You will notice, boys,' he said, 'that in any British pidgin grammer there is no word for "please". Only in the French. I think that just about says it all.'

The boys had roared, especially the ni-Kristi.

On the field outside at 4 the class split neatly into two, European and islander, four and six a side with two smiling Vietnamese as onlookers.

Fidel Vuma held stores of ancestor spleen. His great-grandfather had been a house-boy for a flogging planter; his grandmother had been raped by Americans. His tongue spun tightly and savagely, flicking accurate shame-spots with bravura.

The French Agent's son was white with fury. '*Gammon!*' he kept yelling. 'Bloody *gammon!*'

'Don't talk Seaspeak to me!' Vuma said coolly. He pushed his face threateningly close. 'Don't give me that *masta* talk! Say crap. Say bullshit. Say *fatras*, French boy. But don't ever talk down with that *tok blong pikinini wai'te falla*. Okay?'

Raoul Boutin flung a weak punch and found his nose bleeding richly on the grass.

Pulvers came out of the building balancing a coffee cup and began sauntering across. He hadn't meant to start this but he felt an interested excitement at seeing Boutin getting delayed vengeance. He sipped his coffee and took his time.

When he reached the group the boys were moving apart and all he had to do was lay a dampened handkerchief on Boutin's nose and a few damp consolers on his pride. The grounds emptied as the day pupils rode off on their bikes and boarders began queuing up at the refectory door for their *tartines*.

Vuma followed Gavi down to the jetty where he tied up the plantation runabout.

'Hey!' he called after Gavi's striding legs. 'Hey, Salway!'

Gavi stood with his back to the Channel, blinking against sun-slant, the dark shape of the other boy blurred, threatening.

'Listen!' Vuma came up breathing hard. 'Listen, Salway. You understand. Why were you so weak, man? Why don't you stand up, eh? You're one of us. Almost. I see it. The others see it too. Long time, now. But we never say.'

'What?' Gavi asked. 'What don't you say?'

Vuma stared at him, his eyes insolent, a smile starting somewhere on the full lips.

'Tell me. What don't you say?'

'You mean you don't know?'

'No. I don't. I don't know what you're talking about.'

'Oh man!' Vuma looked almost sad. '*Hapkas* is nothing. We don't want to hurt your feelings.'

Gavi's whole body rocked. He had to turn away and began unhitching the rope. His stomach felt a boot in it. He bent his shock towards the water.

'That's a lie,' he said finally. 'You don't know what you're saying.'

The whole Channel was spinning.

'No lie,' Vuma said. 'Don't be like that. Listen, man. Listen to me.' He caught Gavi by the shoulder and tried to force him round. 'Hey, listen a minute.'

Vuma's handsome face was smiling, the curly surfaces of shining skin, vigorous and intense.

'Things are changing. I'm sorry it had to be Boutin I punched. The French are the only ones who give a damn. But there it is. I couldn't stop myself. Things are really changing.'

'What do you mean?'

'Oh come on. Don't act innocent. You know what's going on. But the big one – pretty soon, man.'

Young Salway didn't want to think politics, didn't want to talk politics. He could only think of himself swirling in Vuma's statement. He didn't want to think of that either. He wanted . . . wanted . . .

'You mean independence?'

'God no! Not that! That's good. But not enough.'

Gavi could barely think. He wanted to be sick. The other boy gripped his arm hard, refusing to let him go.

'I mean ours,' Gavi said, 'Kristi's.'

'Oh yah! Right! That's more like. Now you right right right like Pulvers he right.' Vuma was mocking the pidgin he used. His hand moved down Gavi's arm, thumb and fingers printing themselves on the flesh.

'You with us or against, man?'

'With you, of course'.

It was easier that way. He hadn't even thought about it. Sweat was bulging in fat drops along his forehead. His head throbbed. Was he for? Was he against? His tongue, in its easy affirmation, seemed to be betraying Kenasi, pipe-sucking in his battered chair on the verandah, so old now, he sometimes forgot the drink at his elbow, staring away with his bleached eyes beyond the hibiscus and coconut palms he had planted so long ago on the sea-edge of his garden. Yet grandfather had been one of the decent ones. Hadn't he? Hadn't he? Vuma's rancour drowned him in bile.

'Look,' Vuma was saying, letting his fingers drop, 'you're in a lousy spot. I know. I see that. You're a two-part really. Aren't you? Fucking two-part. Now one bit of you, say, is just as good as that one bit British. God, man, see what the *wai'tes* have done to you. You've got no natural place, *laka*? Not black. Not white. Listen. I'm not blaming you. It's what they all did. Took our land, used our women, threw them out when they'd had enough. Here you are. You proof, man!'

Gavi fought for time against giddiness, against the concussion of the words. He swung the painter, back and forth, back and forth.

'What do you mean, two-part?'

'Oh come on! Jesus! Why do I have to say all this? You ever look in the mirror? You watch you maman, eh?'

Gavi shivered behind his school shirt.

'You never ask you nice white granpappy?'

'Look,' Gavi said, 'I've got to go. I'm running late.'

Vuma pulled him close again, by the shirt this time, not roughly but with a dreadful gentle persistence. It was more frightening.

'Your maman,' he said, ' I bet she came from Emba. You should find out who her *grand-mère* was. Her *tumbuna mama*. You're close to things. Closer than you think.'

Gavi could only stare as Vuma mocked and nagged.

The other boy laughed watching the closed stunned face.

'Okey okey. You think about it. This *aeland* going to get a big shake-up soon, oh *smôl smôl tai'm*.'

It was a threat.

'*Smôl tai'm*.'

Gavi shoved the boat out, stumbled in, lowered the outboard and started it after the second angry jerk.

He didn't want to look back. But he did.

Vuma was still watching him. As Gavi looked Vuma gave an ironic wave.

The wave still washed across his mind like the flapping of a dirty rag.

He looked now at Rogo swabbing off sweat with a towelling hat. His whole world was overturned. Trumble was spinning somewhere on the off-side unaware that he wasn't even part of the day. Unaware.

Under the marquee Père Layroud found he was lifting his cassock and flapping it like a woman's skirt, a buffer state between the government agents. He had spent the first thirty years of his life looking for reasons, for spiritual allusion, connection and explanation. Now, dried out by tropic missions, he had almost forgotten the small village outside Toronto where he had grown up, his seminary days, the early years of supply as all the fusing summers on Lenakel and Wala pickled him in sun. Problems of the field, the spiritual ascents at first unscalable, crumbled into well-trodden hillslopes, flattened, became hollows of habit. Sometimes he feared God was hiding behind the altar and the tabernacle gaped empty. Sometimes, too, he feared he might more easily speak pidgin than the tongue of Racine and Molière. His English often had more practice than his French. At the end of most days, collapsed beneath the ceiling fan fluctuating with the generator, he made ritual of his first glass of wine by toasting vaguely remembered friends in three tongues. On desperate evenings when God refused answers from the dusty tabernacle of the chapel, he would add riders in dialects from Omba and Tanna and a rare Melanesian tongue of hills people he had learnt on supply at Tsureviu.

He barely listened now to the agents chopping each other's languages to gross lumps. His eyes were on the senior students taking round drink trays. The island girls were so shy, giggling at their shyness, mouths wide on their beautiful white teeth, hands flapping pink-palmed to hide their laughter. Leyroud felt for them in this island where women rated far below double circle tuskers and he turned his gaze on the boys noticeably more assured, even aggressive, he decided, as they came over towards District Agent Cordingley, a melting Bunter chap in tropic whites. A little distance away he could see Doctor Trumble and his jittery wife, Letty, being mildly savaged by Fidel Vuma, the son of a custom chief from Emba. Fidel did not smile. He toted his drinks tray with a stubborn lack of grace, holding it out carelessly, his own head half-turned so that he did not have to look. He hated playing house-boy to the visitors.

Leyroud leaned back farther in his chair and caught the science master's eye, and nodded his orders. Pulvers went out into the bright heat and crossed over the paddock to young Salway and Trumble, leaning down so that his voice was audible only to them.

'Okay, chaps. One of you fellows take over from Vuma, will you?' He looked hard at Gavi Salway. 'Vuma's feeling the burden of domestic politics. Someone's going to notice. The black man's burden, that is.'

Rogo Trumble sat up, all look-alive, his bright eyes glued to Pulvers' careful face.

'Well, aren't we, sir?'

Pulvers smiled with deadly sweetness. 'You'll never make it into the diplomatic service, will you? You need a third from Cambridge, then they slice off half your chin and post you to the islands. Now get going. One of you.'

The boys looked across at the lunching guests. Rogo blushed as he regarded his mother who – well – never quite fitted. Everyone knew Letty was a reader, stuffy, and not much of a drinker. This worried other wives. It didn't 'go' in Mataso town. And she was a monstrous and untidy smoker. Of course they were all monstrous smokers but with Letty it was as if she ate them, this nervy ash-trail and spoor of burns snailing through house after house. Once she had started a small fire in a waste basket at the Cordingleys and now, yes, now she was dropping her glass, her glasses as she peered after the glass, her cigarettes, her lighter, her . . . and Fidel Vuma was laughing for the first time that morning, outrageously loud, rocking about with his drink tray and watching while both Trumbles fumbled.

'Okay, Gav, get going.' Pulvers was swinging away and Gavi, despite a swoony feeling from the heat and the fact that he wanted to laugh as well, hauled himself up and went over to the marquee and said, 'All right, Fidel. I'll give you a break.' Through all that wild native laughter, girls giggling behind hands and white diplomatic faces stuffed with disciplined restraint and good breeding.

Vuma swung the drinks tray round sharply so that its corner caught the younger boy between the ribs and as Gavi gasped, Vuma dropped the tray and glasses deliberately on the grass between them.

'Okey, man,' he said. 'You go house-boy now, eh?

His back was to the guests. No one saw clearly what had happened and Père Leyroud made a mental marginal note about young Salway's awkwardness; he hoped they didn't field him in slips after lunch.

Gavi swore, then bit his lip. Kenasi had always warned him against argument, especially argument and temper. 'We're the intruders,' he conceded. Surprisingly. 'You must remember that. We are. Be careful what you say.'

'The other kids' parents never think like you.'

'They might well try. And I'm not other kids' parents. I'm your grandfather. And my crusty views are tried and tested. All right?'

'But so are theirs, aren't they? Duchards have been up at Thresher Bay for fifty years.'

'Don't argue, boy,' Grandpappy had said. 'I hate an arguing boy. I said tried and tested. His are only tried. Not proven.'

But yours don't even work, Gavi had thought scornfully but didn't say. He loved Kenasi too much. Kenasi acted papa as well, not remembering his own who had been a falling fire-wheel in Vietnam, going out in comet blaze. Kenasi had the permanence of a *rambaramp*, an ancestor statue, carved in his redly tanned flesh, his face netted in kindly lines whose firmness understood tolerance and whose voice was slow but always steady. When Gavi was smaller he had told his grandfather he thought him to be like a *rambaramp*.

'They leave them to decay,' Kenasi said. 'I don't like that idea much. It's a monument to a nothing man.' 'Oh you *know*!' the boy had said. And his grandfather had understood the compliment, paid askew, but paid, and he became over the years the roof that sheltered the boy, the door, the very latch that would open.

So he bit his lip and served drinks for the rest of the lunch break and when he took the empty glasses finally to the bar where Père Thibault was in charge, he found himself confronted by Vuma who did a blocking jock leg-straddle, his rich voice menacing, as he hissed softly, 'Nearly wore my *nambas* man. My penis-wrapper. How do you think the nice *pipol* would have liked that?'

'They all know what a dick's like,' Gavi said, 'exaggerated or not.'

'Oh man! That exaggeration! There's a lot of those *wai'te* ladies wouldn't have seen a dick like that for long long time.'

How punch before a watching crowd of parents, priests, nuns?

He shoved past Vuma, thrusting out the tray to Thibault, a pallid young curate still holding memories of northern ice crystals in his eyes. He was testy with his work, screwing back the caps of whisky bottles, banging empty soft-drink cans into bins while he hated the heat the heat the heat.

'Closing bar,' he said. 'Closing. Anyway, we want them sober, do we not, for the second half. Mr Cordingley seems to expect the miracle of Canaan.' He mopped at himself with a tissue, looking beyond Gavi at the steaming field. 'You'd better hurry. I can see Mr Pulvers making a start out there with the team.'

So the afternoon ground on and the poetic crack of wood on leather was a bad joke under the biting sun. Hedmasta Woodful's team swaggered away from the pitch with their winner grins and 'That's how it goes, Gav,' Rogo Trumble half-consoled Gavi. Trumble was inclined to rub it in a bit. He did fancy cutting motions with his bat. 'That bugger, Vuma,' he said. 'Did you see? Bowling straight at my head in the last over. He must be crazy.'

They walked back together to the mango shade, for the last of the ritual, the speeches, the cup handling, the thank-yous.

'This part's a fag,' Gavi said.

'Because you lost?'

'No. Because – oh I don't know. Listen. Come over here and I'll tell you what Vuma said.'

But Mr Pulvers, his narrow pleasant face tortured by climate and struggling for heartiness, came up behind thumping a pal's hand on a shoulder of each, and steered them firmly towards the gathering teams.

'Line up, chaps,' he ordered. ('*Chaps!*' Rogo whispered.) 'We've got to do the full bit. The parents like it. Père Leyroud likes it. Mr Woodful likes it. So – on the double, eh? On – the – double!'

The sun was sliding its flat orange disc over Serua Point when the last of the visitors had driven away along the Channel Road and Gavi, walking back behind Kenasi and maman to the jetty, thought again of Vuma's remark and instead of being shocked, outraged, any of those things, began to laugh. To laugh and laugh.

Maman stopped near the landing and turned inquiringly, eyebrows, lips, hair, all curly with question.

'Tell me then'.

The boy tried to get his mouth straight but managed only gulps of words between giggles.

He went red at the thought of telling her.

Somehow the whole moment with Vuma was comic to aching point. Perhaps the other things Vuma had said were right as well.

Planter Salway had come to the islands in the early 1930s working as a store clerk in Lena. He'd been a purser before that for one of the shipping lines that ran between Sydney and the American west coast. But he made only one-and-a-half trips. On the way home, his mind scrambled by sun and water, the sly mystery of atolls, he had pleaded with the captain to cancel his contract; and the captain who was an understanding man and had felt the contagion of palm tree and reef in his own day, agreed. He was sorry to lose such an earnest, such an honest young man who had not even begun to chart his own sensibilities, but there were perilous things happening in the western world as it staggered out of the Depression and he sympathised with anyone who might have to go back to the soup kitchens of Sydney.

Salway left the ship in Suva, found a job with Bipi, was moved to Port Lena, sickened by double-entry ledgers and the claustrophobic atmosphere of island store-keeping and jumped at the chance to manage a copra plantation on the north of Trinitas. The persuasive landscape drew him farther. On a trip to Kristi he found the plantation in Emba. It was filled with ghosts. He could sense them. In Mataso town he was told of the man who had worked it, a butter-soft Frenchman given mostly to champagne parties and the cultivation of orchids, whose bonhomie ended at the door of the boy house. There were stories of dreadful beatings whose vicious harmonics still rang through the clattering shutters. Its empty rooms were scoured by unendingly nagging sea-wind off the Channel. That could dilute the wails, Salway hoped. Purge the uneasiness of the limestone coral walls flickering in leaf light.

It was too humid for desolation.

He bought the place and began working it alone. Two years later he brought back a wife he'd met on leave in Sydney, a tall lemon-haired girl he married within the week. Her splendid laughter and striding vigour expelled the shadows from the place. She sang a lot and whistled like a boy and in the granulated evening dark loved him with a kind of desperate candour. Salway had never been so happy.

'We're putting other ghosts here,' he would whisper.

Shutters stopped grinding their teeth. Rooms ached to be used. Within two more years he had persuaded a team of islanders back to work for him and the boy house grew accustomed to the sound of mouth organs and singing and the deepness of sleep.

Salway remembering, remembering, sitting late on his verandah in moth-light, watching his wife slide out on the tide of her own blood when their son was born. Ayé, Callie. I grieve for you. Oh how I grieved. The plantation girls grieving for me, grieving for the blood-smeared child squawking and kicking as your body drained, heart-stoppingly, watching, unable to weep for the shock of it and the boy howling in the next room and the soft voices of the house-girls unable to check the monstrousness of that disaster.

So quick to tell. So long in the happening.

And the boy grew through his grief, grew through the Puritan rage that convulsed him for three years, in spite of everything, grew. And then one of the house-girls, too much for him, too much, the grief diminished, another rage taking over, and the house-girl, Seruwaia, seen like a dispensation of mercy, seen, under the rain-tree curved against its trunk, pressed up against the allamanda vine by the water-tank, segments of her swinging dress glimpsed between hibiscus as she moved along the coral pathways, seen. That girl, shy and soft, dark and soft, and the trees bearing and the sky plump with rain in the monsoon months, going down with the child, his second, on the first night of the big rains. All the waters bursting.

He closed his eyes and could still, but faintly, recall her cries from the small hut at the back of the plantation house, her cries slicing the ropes of rain away and himself, silly bugger, unable to bear it, white as a coot, ploughing off through the night, his hurricane lamp swinging.

A girl-child this time, creamy skinned and exploding into the world at the moment of the Pacific war. Plantations emptied as owners fled to the mainland and within the month Salway found

Seruwaia and her baby gone. In Mataso town he was told she had run off with a French trader who was making for Noumea. The nipping feelers of his guilt were forgotten in the turmoil. He arranged for his son to be cared for in Sydney and offered himself as store-runner for troops in a made-over copra boat. He was a charmed man. Guns cracked round him like golden palms, shells splattered him with blue sea. Even when a torpedo ripped the hull of his boat like rag he managed to swim ashore. Later, later, he became a coast-watcher, months of that in the slippery hills of Kristi camped down in some bush-pole shelter with his radio, watching skies so alive with stars and the poetry of stars, he could almost have missed planes that drowned in shivering light.

So quick to tell. So long in the happening.

The war ended. His boy grew away from him in the blubbering terms of boarding-school, grew back towards him in the plummy holidays – a barrage of years in which he asked himself over and over should he leave, should he stay, hearing of better chances but still keel-hauled by the floating islands. Once, someone told him, he couldn't remember where or who, that Seruwaia had married Trader Fouterre and he thought briefly and feverishly of the beige moth that was his daughter and then put the memory aside as others before him had done. These things, he told himself, remembering now, belong to an imperfect tense. He had plugged ahead with a resolute clouding of memory, thinking of himself as a one-child man whose whole being was concerned solely with that sprig. The days merged so fast. It seemed to be no time at all before Robert returned to Emba with a wife, a pretty French girl he had met in Noumea.

The horrible circles of completed fate.

Everything was so brief. The marriage ended when Robbie, stupidly patriotic in airforce blue became a falling fire-wheel over the rice-paddies of Vietnam.

The perfect tense ended. The imperfect puddling on with his grandson's questions that, these last few days, had walloped memory and guilt.

Oh Gavi, I grieve for you.

What was left of those years, those lives? Paper ghosts. A wedding photo for *La France Australe*, the newsprint revealing Lucie Ela's ancestry less kindly than nature did; some snapshots of Seruwaia caught in sunny moments on flower-crazed paths around the plantation. Salway had cut out the photo, the little paragraph and tucked both away in some long-forgotten drawer along with the fading summer semblances of Lucie Ela's maman. To be rediscovered in that mouldering drawer by another.

Here he was sifting old sins in the dark. And the boy. The boy always on the wavering perimeters of discovery.

Vuma's insinuations became the mite beneath the skin. Gavi spent furtive hours nosing through old photograph albums, examining maman across meal tables, tossing questions about maman's family. 'Tell me about the Fouterres,' he would suggest cunningly, catching her in unguarded moments in the kitchen, and she would push his questions carelessly aside as she worked, saying she didn't remember much. What could an eight-year-old know of the car accident that had orphaned her? She knew more about the dangers of the road from Waieme to Pam. The sisters, she told him, busy with salad, *les bonnes sœurs*. Mother *and* father.

Both Kenasi and maman had been absent that day, shopping in Mataso town. Gavi had mooned through the empty rooms, poking his way at last into the office where Kenasi kept a desk for plantation accounts. It had never occurred to him before to probe those half dozen drawers, for here was the effigy that meant only the boring ritual of adults, the 'run away, I'm busy, boy'. No mystery. Uninterest. Yet now.

The walls shifted with the green shadows of banana leaves. The room smelled permanently of Kenasi's tobacco and work clothes. The long blond face of his dead papa grinned at him from the desk top, and kept grinning as the boy began pulling and opening and lifting and probing. There'd been the press clipping, that first of all, along with the time-smudged snapshots, and a pathetically small packet of papa's possessions returned by a thoughtfully sensitive government to the mourning relatives.

Gavi put the bundle back carefully and took the snapshots into his room propping them along his dressing-table beside the photo of his father, examining his mirror-image against the qualities of the printed faces. *Oué*. His heart quickened. There was this stranger woman in her flopping Mother Hubbard laughing among the croton bushes, her hair, her skin, all shining in sunlight. His mother smiling up at papa. His own face, with no lineal registration of the up-turned world on his own smooth mug. Only this pounding beneath skin as he worked at the clues. He shoved up a snap of himself standing on the tennis court banging a racket against his knees. His face peered back from the women's. He could see it. See it. Oh a double glimpse of Vuma's truth.

He shuffled these facts, these guessed at facts, around for days before attack.

The old man, his grandfather, caught in twilight on the verandah and his own voice feverishly pestering. He had the pictures, the clipping, in his hands.

'Well,' the boy asked pushing the photo of the woman in the garden forward, holding it so that it rested against the newspaper clipping and snapshot of the wedding, 'who is she?'

'Your mother. Your mother and Rob, of course.'

The old man was playing for time, fatuously. *Oué*.

'Not that,' Gav replied, furious. 'Not that one. The other.'

Kenasi looked at Gavi for a moment and then began fumbling with his tobacco pouch, tapping the bowl of his pipe. Fiddling.

'How old are you boy?' he asked finally.

'Thirteen.'

'Old enough to be sensible, I hope. Almost a man.'

'If,' the boy said cunningly, 'I were an islander, I would be a man.'

'So you would,' Kenasi agreed. 'So you would.'

He relit his pipe and drew on it, lingeringly, not looking, not daring to look at the persistence of the face in front of him.

At last he said, 'She is your mother's mother. The *grand-mère* you have never seen. She was Fouterre's wife.'

The boy thought about this.

'Then what was she doing over here on Emba? Look, there's a corner of the verandah.'

'It was taken here,' Kenasi replied, managing not to lie.

'She doesn't look very French, does she?' Oh he was so unyielding.

'I suppose not.'

'But she's terribly like maman, isn't she? And me.'

He stared hard at his grandfather, almost blotted out by dusk.

'Come on. Tell me. Who was she, really?'

He turned the snapshot over and shoved the writing on the back rudely under the old man's nose. Seruwaia, 1940, it said. The old man was confronted by his younger handwriting.

'Just some' – and how he despised himself for the rejection – 'island girl. Not a full blood. We didn't know too much about her.'

Gavi found he was towering over his grandfather shrunken back now into his chair, just an old man sucking on his comforter with age spots blotching his cheeks and his hands. The boy felt increasingly powerful. His demands were like blows.

Kenasi shifted his body, took his pipe out of his mouth and felt all the clubbing shock of the past. So long ago, *pastai'm bifor*. Oh *bifor*!

And what did it matter?

'It matters to me,' the boy said angrily.

'She was a girl here,' the old man said at last. Oh Seruwaia. 'So long ago now, young feller. There's nothing to be gained.'

He found himself smiling. Against reason – for the memory of lack of it.

'Isn't there?' The boy flashed about and seemed to grow even taller in the dark. 'That house-girl,' he said. 'My grandmother. Tell me.'

The old man heard the groan as if it came from someone else. It was his own throat unclotting. He began to feel anger himself.

'You want to know. Want to know! Well, take it then. She was my comfort, do you hear. My comfort. She helped raise your father when Callie died. He would have been lost without her. I would have been lost. For a year, for two years, perhaps, I was lost until Seruwaia. There. You have it. And then I was lost another way. In her. You understand what I'm saying? In her.'

'And you wouldn't marry her,' the boy said with contempt. 'You loved her and you wouldn't marry her. She was just *puspus* to you.' He was deliberately obscene. 'That's all.'

'Marriage,' his grandfather said. 'You don't understand. Things were different then.'

'Oh I understand,' the boy said bitterly. 'I hate you.'

'You're wasting a lot of energy doing that,' his grandfather said wearily. The dinner gong sounded through the house like glass shattering. 'I thought you were more mature than that.'

He leaned forward from his chair as if pillowing a sudden pain.

31

His shirt gaped over belly bulge. He was a-sop with sweat. But Gavi had a hand on his arm, was pressing him back for the final revelation, his eyes sharp and shining in the light that sprang out from the dining-room.

'Then maman . . .' He hesitated. He couldn't bear it, couldn't cope with these unwanted outgrowths. 'Then maman is your child.'

The old man sensed sky crack.

'Don't deny it,' the boy was pursuing relentlessly.

'I'm not denying anything,' the old man said. 'You chased at this. You've worried at it. Oh how you've worried it. You wanted it. All right then, boy. Lucie is my daughter. Yes. It's worse than you imagined, isn't it? And Rob my son. Half and half. You might as well face it, seeing you've pushed so far.' He could hear Lucie calling them to supper and he caught Gavi's arm in his turn. 'But I warn you, your maman does not know.' He pulled himself out of his chair and once again stood over the boy. His turn now. 'And mustn't know. Do you understand? Must not know. It's no good talking about it now. It won't solve anything. Why upset her? And it would. What good would it do you or her? It's happened. It is.'

He began to walk away down the noisy dark of the verandah under palm scrape.

He could hear Gavi saying 'Oh Christ, Kenasi!' and Lucie's voice raised more loudly and her footsteps coming to chase theirs.

The old man was beyond the giving of comfort. 'And who was Seruwaia?' he said, pausing and turning to look at the crumbled figure of his grandson in the dark. 'She was Tommy Narota's sister.'

Since Vuma, since the photographs, since Kenasi's admissions, Gavi Salway had been trying to decode the ciphers of genetic shock. Even kinship had fraudulence. He was maman's nephew. Papa would have been an uncle. Should he say Tante Lucie? When he wasn't examining the tangled geometry of family, he was obsessed with skin, ransacking his features for betrayal. He hated the shame he felt.

He avoided Rogo Trumble. He brooded in corners of home and school. Was he imagining Vuma's victor smile?

Later that week he took the runabout over towards Serua Point on the pretence of fishing but mostly he dozed his wretchedness in the gently rocking boat a few yards out from the Channel Road, anchored in mangroves, his line dangling. It could have been baited with betrayal.

At first he was unaware of the motor-vessel that swung round the western tip of Emba. Then he tried shutting his ears to the insistent whump of the engines but they closed in on him like thunder and he sat up to see the boat ploughing a tangent towards the landing ramp. He read its name, *Polyphème*, and saw men moving about on deck.

The engine throb was duplicated in dissonance as somewhere along the Channel Road a truck racketed above the beach-way. He could sense the truck swing into the side turn that would bring it down to the ramp, then heard the skid as it braked, the idling chatter of the motor and the cutting out. The *Polyphème* nosed in to the jetty.

Back on the road a truck door slammed.

Hand-paddling the runabout till it strained at the end of the anchor-line Gavi looked back along the shore in time to see Lemmy Bonser of Kristi Motors come high-stepping confidently down the coral track to the landing. Aslant, his shadow leapt black in the late afternoon.

Gavi waved.

The wave fluttered into nothing.

Two deck-hands on the motor-vessel were moving crates close to the rail while Bonser, busy helping with stay-ropes, did not look up.

There was a laugh, some quick joke in French, and then the three of them began hoisting and stacking cases on the jetty. After a few moments Bonser went back to the truck and backed it down the track, scraping through scrub until the tray-end was almost at the ramp.

'Hey! Mr Bonser!' Gavi's shout cut clearly over the water. His boat tugged impetuously at its anchor, swinging out farther from the mangroves; and looking along the beach the boy was aware of consternation as the three men turned and located him. Through oaths, he thought. But Bonser waved back in a too pally manner, his taffy hair blown all over his face, tossing some question about how the fish were biting, words flung like gull wings. Yet already the boy had hauled in the anchor and was rowing the dinghy along the shallow margin towards the jetty. Even as he rowed the fifty yards or so, the last case was being dumped on the pile.

The men's faces became flat as he slung the painter round a mooring post and asked if they needed a hand. Bonser spoke softly to the two men, turning back as the boy clambered up the steps. His grin was over-wide like a character defect. 'Okay Gav,' he said. 'You're just what I need. You can help me get this stuff on the truck.'

The men from the launch went sullen, one of them arguing with Bonser in French. Who seemed to swell, the big bruiser in his stained khaki shorts, shirt opened to the waist displaying a brick-red chest with a flag of orange hair. Everything else was muscle. He was grinning too much.

Bonser ended the protest with one sharp and splendid gesture of the hand, fingers slapped down on the palm like a lid. In the syrupy light there seemed nothing but that and Bonser's great white teeth. The deck-hands, bluffed, took their surliness back on board and in a few minutes the *Polyphème* had slipped its moorings, backed water and swung out into the current.

A matey hand clamped down on Gavi's shoulder, ham-like, heavy.

Although the boy disliked Bonser, his current turmoil demanded explicable assurances, and he was aware of rebellion against his grandfather's contempt for the fellow as he smiled up at the looming face. Oh he's a fair enough mechanic, he could hear Kenasi admit grudgingly. Knows his boats. I'll grant him that. But there's something . . . something. Perhaps it was because he strode Mataso's streets in the stink of his sweat and seed as if he had created them. All the islanders knew him; but then he used their women. The boys he employed found him tough but fair, especially when he lent them an old car to hoon off up the coast road to their home villages near Thresher Bay. What's a woman? the boys asked each other. This way! That way! It wasn't as if he fucked pigs.

Gavi hoped he could feel Kenasi's disapproval across the Channel air and he suffered the hand as he watched the *Polyphème* shrinking across the snail-grey water, rounding the southern tip of Emba. He said, warm, boyish, 'They're crazy going that way. Why didn't they go up Channel? The rip's really bad this end.'

The big man looked down at him. His chunky face was temporarily decorated with a mixture of friendliness and grubby fury.

'Well,' he said. 'Well.' He raised comic eyebrows. 'There's a reason for that. Come on, feller, and help me get these bloody things into the truck.'

The weight of them! It took both to hoist each long box up onto the tray. Gavi felt his knees buckle with every swing. What was inside he asked.

'Just machine parts,' Bonser said carelessly. 'Just an order I've been sweating on, mate. Look, you grab this end and I'll go backwards, okay? It'll be easier that way.'

When the last of the crates was stacked Bonser tucked a tarpaulin round them, folding the flaps tightly beneath the front cases and wedging the canvas down the sides. As he rubbed his relieved hands he could have been rubbing thoughts together but he only said, 'Well, that's that, then. Thanks a lot.' His hesitation – the boy was sure there was hesitation – might have wanted to add something else but suddenly he swung into the cabin of the truck and had the engine rapping before the boy could do more than raise one goodbye hand.

There was this feeling of discomfiture afterwards. Persisting. As if the outboard were pussy-footing its way in the dark, cutting through glue to a rocker horizon.

He decided not to tell anyone about it.

But the meeting was to mean more.

Two afternoons later, Gavi rode his bike in from St Pierre to place an order for maman at the Comptoirs Kristi and to collect the mail. As he passed Kristi Motors, he saw Bonser standing in the doorway talking to Planter Duchard and he braked to a stop in a skid of memories: old Duchard whipping Kenasi all over the panting tennis court on Emba. All over. Ball-boying for two red and gasping old geezers, their knobbly veined legs staggering over hot asphalt under the twang of rackets, the women in their flapping hats as they doled out iced tea and rum punch on a verandah full of leaves. Oh Kenasi, he gulped inwardly, I grieve for me. Smiling his hellos now into Bonser's sharp eyes. Into Duchard's. Could they see it in him? This *hapkas* strain?

Yet they acted out all the glosses of delight.

Bonser was pallier than ever and Duchard bursting with smiles and enquiries about the family and promises to come over to Emba soon. Gavi rode off to confetti of *à bientôts* and *see you, mate* and a last yelled invitation from Bonser to drop by on the way back.

The Boulevard d' Urville stretched a mile alongside the Channel and in this late afternoon, the shadows oblique, sweaty pores of mid-day closing, had its shabbiness softened. It was busier than usual and there were blacker faces and fiercer talking among the islanders lounging outside the Comptoirs. There were more *man bush* than he ever remembered. Like me, he thought bitterly. Like me. Or half of me. Pedalling his resentment. Can they see it? Really see me?

The trouble with islands, he thought, echoing his grandfather's criticism. But he'd always liked that. The knowing. The being known. He enjoyed feeling he was in the tide of things, the scratch of island politics. Rogo Trumble's older brother, Dan, had been at boarding-school in Sydney for the last year and when he had come home for Christmas was leaking with world-weary complaints. 'It's the size,' he said (he meant Sydney), 'that I hate most. You don't get a say in anything. And I don't mean just school. Not just that. Outside. There are just too many people. Go into town on a weekday afternoon and you can't move and no one knows you and no one gives a damn and you'd have no hope in hell of knowing what really goes on in government.'

Ben Trumble was destined for Law, his eye already career-cocked and most times he talked like an old man. His school had given up trying to make him play football.

'Stupid sods,' he said to Rogo and Gavi.

'You mean the footballers?'

'Them too. No, I mean the polit boys. The country could go down like a water-slide – it *is* going down like a water-slide. And the public doesn't notice and the elected members don't care as long as they've got their freebies and their perks. That's what I like about here. You can't help being aware. You've got to notice. It's part of you.'

'Oh shut up, Ben!' Rogo had flung a friendly punch at his older brother who rolled exaggeratedly over and over on the Paddock grass and cried, 'My God, it's good to be home!'

Gavi had listended to this with hawkish interest.

'But is it home?' He gave Kenasi's views and Ben sat up and looked approvingly at him. Gavi had thought it was approving then. Was it quizzical, he wondered now. Did Ben Trumble know? But, 'Go away, moron,' Ben had ordered Rogo kindly. 'Go *haus-boy* and fetch us a lime juice. Listen,' he went on turning to Gavi, 'I see it this way.'

And they'd argued and agreed and disagreed and Gavi felt as if the words rather than the pubic hair which was just commencing made him a man.

So, as a man, he dropped by Bonser's on his way back and Bonser could have guessed at a discovered and secret maturity because he said and how about a cup of cha old chap and took him into his house among the frangipani trees and wondered if he wouldn't prefer a beer, winking to indicate his own preference, and served some and sat opposite the boy, observing him with great interest.

When Bonser asked, unexpectedly, 'What do you think of Tommy Narota?' Gavi found his hands tightening round his beer mug. He saw Seruwaia smiling into a plantation morning where

Bonser might or might not be simply talking politics as Ben had done.

'I think he's a pretty nice chap.'

'Oh come on. Everyone knows that. Sure, he's a nice guy. Let me top you up, Gav. Right? What I mean is, what do you think of him politically? What do you think about what he's trying to do for Kristi?'

The boy's mind jazzed with suspicions. He wanted, oh he wanted, to give an intelligent answer, one unformulated by his fears of uncovery. He didn't want to start off saying 'Kenasi says'; he wanted to . . .

I am *hapkas*, the boy thought. Like Narota, who is my blood. I can't even think like Kenasi. Shouldn't. Kenasi wouldn't have the feelings I have. Couldn't. Maman, perhaps. But then maman doesn't know. Would the feelings be instinctive, he wondered. Despite his grandfather's prescriptions, he knew he would tell her one day. Knew.

The responsibility of that secret piece of knowledge, the realisation of his own quartered blood, strengthened him.

'It's the right thing,' he decided aloud, and confidently. 'The island is its own place. We're too far from Lena for the government there to care.' He could hear Ben Trumble saying those very words. 'It's the distance. You can't control people or know what they want or what they need if you're hundreds of miles away across water. Anyway we're – they're – *man* Kristi. Not Trinitas. I think we ought to be independent.'

'Well,' Bonser said, his eyes widening, 'well well well well well.' He grinned. 'I always thought you were a man of parts, Gav.' (Was that a crack?) 'This island's got some terrible dick-heads. Christ, don't quote me, but what about that turd Cordingley, eh? What about him?'

He launched into Cordingley stories. He had the boy laughing. Bonser could peer through the streaky windscreen of his own intentions and see only this rocking kid, howling with mirth across the table from him. He braked before he got carried away into Trumble myth. He spoke affectionately of old Duchard and what Duchard had done for the island.

'You know,' he said confidentially, 'if the Lemoa bunch has its way they'll boot the lot of us out. You see, Gav, Narota wants the sort of things for us that they've got down at the capital. He wants them here. That's the point. Narota's got vision. He isn't just thinking of himself. He's thinking of the future for *man* Kristi. Think about it.'

Gavi nodded. He finished his beer. In the hot back room he felt pleasantly giddy. He hadn't laughed like that for days.

'And,' Bonser went on, warming to it, to something, 'all that stuff about foreign investment wrecking the place is a load of old horse-shit. God knows there's enough foreign investment down at Lena. Investment means buildings and buildings mean jobs and jobs are what *man* Kristi wants, right? Independence for us will mean our right to settle our own problems without having to go two hundred miles to get an answer. Right?'

'Right,' Gavi agreed.

'Of course you're right,' Bonser said cunningly. 'Of course. You see, Gav, the trouble with the Nabiru government is they want all the land to go straight back to custom owners. Okay. Okay. I can see that. I sympathise. But this is the point, mate, and I say this in confidence, mind, not all of it for God's sake. Most. But not *all*. What happens to blokes like Duchard, say, and your granddad and old Madame Guichet who've worked on the island for years? What happens to them, eh?'

He could sense the boy's uncertainty, anticipated protest and swept on before the kid could get a word in.

'A lot of sour-shits say they were just in it for themselves, for what they could get out of it. That's not true, old cocko, not true at all. And you know it's not.'

Gavi found himself nodding. He wasn't sure. He remembered Pulvers and he wasn't sure.

'Hell,' Bonser argued, 'why would anyone stay holed up here for a lifetime if they didn't think they were helping the islanders, giving them some of the things other people have had for centuries. They're better fed now than they've ever been. Better health care. I tell you, Gav, if we move out it will all grind to a halt. Yes. Grind to a bloody halt.'

He ground to his own.

The boy felt he was expected to say something. He was smothered in the other man's words. 'I think,' he began hesitantly.

Bonser looked up at him, eyebrows raised to net whatever Gavi tossed. He waggled them comically, questioningly, and the boy relaxed and laughed.

'You're right,' he agreed, forgetting leaking thatch, fast food, the cheap trade store clothing. 'Père Leyroud's talked a lot about the early days. Do you know Mr Pulvers? Well, he's told us of the times when planters first moved over here and all the islanders got was a third-rate justice dished out by third-rate magistrates. That's what he says.'

'Narota,' Bonser said slowly, 'will change all that.'

Bonser let him think about it. He filled the boy's glass again and spoke, his voice lowered collaboratively.

'I'll square with you. You're intelligent. The sort of fellow we need. Frankly, Gav, I'm right behind Narota. Right behind him. So's Duchard. But that's confidential. So are 80 per cent of us. Lots of people you know but I mustn't mention names. And we all want to see Narota do something for Kristi. God,' he added with feeling, 'I love this place.'

'So do I.' Gavi was unexpectedly excited by it all. The beer was boiling up an enthusiasm, even for his *hapkas* state, in this old kitchen with its wooden louvres, the walls papered with dying sun and leaf. 'It's the only place.'

'We're going to secede.' Bonser said quietly into the shining eyes. 'We're going to secede, boy, and nothing is going to stop us. No European-sponsored government is going to tell people twelve thousand miles away how to think. Will you be in it?'

'Of course!' Gavi didn't even have to think. He was swept along. It was like the Channel current. 'Of course I will!'

'To me,' Bonser said, 'Narota's a bit of a saint. He's set himself up and that takes guts. But he's doing it for Kristi. Always remember that. Everyone loves him except the bloody Nabiru Pati and they're run by a pack of self-centred Lena-based bureaucrats. Narota's for Kristi. You can take it from me.'

Then the boy said what Bonser had wanted him to say.

'Let me help!' It was a plea. He found it hard to remember that less than an hour ago he'd been getting the mail and placing an order for groceries. 'Let me help!'

'Okay,' Bonser said. 'If you think you're up to it.'

He examined the young face in front of him carefully and assessed its eagerness. He had to go slowly about this but he felt he had judged the precise moment. 'Okay. This is what we do.'

How do you count the years on these islands?

There are no seasons, making it easy for the one two three four of it.

Perhaps you could say two: the wet and the dry; the lousy, the lousier.

But for someone born in unending summer – more than that: equatorial lava uneased even by the Trades – born into the lap of hurricanes, where the green juice of jungle cascades in torrent gushers and the earth that has built up over the submarine coral swings out of the sea into fold after fold of giant pleats, there are no years. Flame trees and scarlet creeper repeat sun-warnings. Birds rattle through vines as they rattled through pre-history, skimming the *nakamals* of hill villages, skimming Quiros's tatty camp at the Bay of the Two Saints, the new Jerusalem, skimming the sweating bodies of the sandalwood gatherers blackbirders missionaries. The islands hold stickily close to humid secrets where *man ples* remains paramount. Planters have come and gone, *rabis pipol*. The islands know. At last, at last, all will be driven out, *long wé, long wé*. There is this abrupt coming and the slower departing; but it will happen.

And Lemmy Bonser doesn't know it yet.

Still, he was born there. It's like an ectogenic gestation, this breeding of an outsider in a place whose *mana* rejects.

Bonser's great-grandpapa had come to the islands on the *Daphne* and had slipped cable in Port Lena where, against all reason, he had persuaded a planter's daughter to marry him. Between sundowners as it were. A month later he sailed away with the monster captain of the *Carl* which was trucking flesh to Australia. When he went back to Lena, pockets a-jangle, he found he had a son; and regret – was it? – for those barbarous moments in the hold of the *Carl* decided him. He took up land in an island to the north, a vast area of coast plain and beach in return for a bolt of cloth and three axes and started his plantation.

It was easier than anyone can imagine, this translation to agrarian wealth.

The viciousness in the genes seeped through two generations, dribbling down the chukka chuk of the blood and emerging refined as greed or duplicity or callousness. *Tenkyou tumas, gran'père!*

He conceded: I am a rough-as-guts bugger, an island club man, shagging around the *meris* by the time I'm sixteen, one hell of a diver, thresher shark wrestler in the heavy blues beyond Pig Harbour, taking the copra load off father and letting the place run down, father who keeps croaking 'You're an Australian, son. Pure bloody Australian. Never forget that' though I do despite the six terms at some chicken-shit boarding-school in Brisbane, before they kicked me out for keeping condoms in my locker and the old man took me in, right-hand bloody man, all right, not much of a planter when it came down to it but handy in any sort of boat. Set me up thank you kindly, before the plantation gave its last gasp, in a building works. Best hulls in the Pacific and not too bad with the old motors either. 'You've got it or you haven't,' the old man would say, 'and Lemmy's got it.' Magic-touch Bonser. I could scare shit out of a diesel just by looking at it. And after work, well, a touch up of the old drink glands, a nosh *chez* Chloe, bloody crazy name that, a screamer show at the Ciné Mangrove with the rain like *naleng* drums on the tin roof and after, well after, always plenty of *puspus*. Even after Angie, the wife, good sort, all of that, stacked blonde, the full clean-skin bit, but you know how it is after a year or so. They've got something those brownskins, whatever. Maybe it's because they think I've got everything. Sometimes it hits me they're only pretending, the sly bitches, giggling away behind their great white teeth or their hands, those bloody pink palms, eh? How about those palms? And Angie, well, she's a great sort like I said looks the other way, sensible. There's plenty of money around, legal or not, and she certainly gets her cut even if I sell her short in other departments.

That's how it is. Mi Lem Bonser *blong* Kristi. *Man solwata.* That's me.

There were others who felt the same way, *colons* who'd picked the islands over like bones, never really wanting to be back in the dusty towns on the flat plains of Europe. They talked about it sometimes, late at night under sea-sound; went back, sometimes – *mon dieu,* Paris – but always returned to the sucking green and throb of sun-blue, lamenting theatre and cafés and *le seizième* and the girls in the Quartier. Just to be there, they'd sigh in high December over their gins, their rums. But their hearts weren't in it. Their tongues slid over dream words as easily as waters slid through the Channel. The heat, the wet had become components of their minds as well as their skins. They made money and they lost money and still they stayed. It was the tug of the Pacific that clutched them, the *idea* of it, the leisurely drawl, the casualness, the supremacy of ruling their own three, four, five thousand acres of colonnaded palms with the cattle dawdling beneath. *Man ples.* But not theirs. When the kingdom rocked, when islanders sassed, sulked, loafed, ran away, there had been beatings. And that powered them too.

Lemmy remembered his daddy telling him how grandpappy had built a road around the old place with marker-posts at every beating along its ten-mile length. Perhaps the old man had been glad enough to sell out when the time came. Resentment saturated every acre.

Bonser's customers in the main were *colons*. He felt at home with them, barking away in his putrid French. He believed they understood the necessary brutality of colonialism better than the British: the brutality and the sophistication. He maintenanced the yachts and motor boats, fixed up the dying car engines of anyone at all and serviced the big diesel motors on the fishing trawlers at the Ambusa Fishing Co-operative.

When Tommy Narota was taken up by the Duchards out at Ebuli, their friendship based more on heavy share buying in the Salamander Corporation land deals, Bonser decided it might be useful if he too helped Narota get a little fishing boat. He put it together with parts his daddy had scrounged from Americans before they had shoved the world into the sea.

That, Lemmy Bonser often told himself, was a cracker move; and he shot whistle sounds through his teeth. Could he recall, in the ancestry of his blood, the dark master of the *Carl* whistling 'Marching through Georgia' as he gunned the black men down?

He whistled now as he backed his truck out onto the Boulevard and headed towards Vimape. Outside Mataso the ground rose in swoops, lodging on plateaux to get its breath back as it climbed from coast plain to foothills.

The boy sat beside him in the cabin and now that the persuasion had spread its contagion Bonser hardly bothered to glance across or even make conversation. All he wanted was to get the stuff out of the back of the truck and beyond his responsibility. He didn't really need this kid to help him but Mercet had suggested he find recruits, especially in the British section. And recruits, Bonser thought sourly, he would get. If the whole thing came off, there'd be something in it for him. If it went the other way, then he didn't want to be involved. A friendly country drive should they happen to be noticed; otherwise he prayed he wouldn't be seen. No names no pack-drill was one of his favourite expressions.

This shouldn't take long, he was thinking. Pity he couldn't have got the stuff up there the day it was unloaded but Angie had been sniffing around. He was lucky she had decided to go down to Lena for a couple of days. No. This was fine. Just right. A few words with Narota and Leblanc and back in time to get the kid unloaded and packed off home. When they entered the bush road the light turned green and he could sense his passenger eager and fearful and curious.

The little bugger was determined to talk.

The boy's voice, cracking with adolescence, broke across the steady grumble of the engine. 'Hey, what's in the crates?' Bonser thought he said that. He leant a repeat-ear towards the boy's shoulder. The question came again.

Bonser swung his head briefly to stare at the snub profile then looked back at the road.

'What do you mean?'

'What's in the crates?'

'I told you. Engine parts.'

'But up at Vimape? I mean, what would they . . . '

Christ! Bonser closed his ears to the wittering. Hadn't the kid realised after all? Was all that yap and admission wasted? He could still hear himself bleating that political hogwash. He'd never worked so hard at anything. Hell! Maybe he ought to keep up the pretence that they were engine parts. Jesus! No one but a ding would believe he was taking stuff like that into the scrub. He must be kidding. He'd seen the crates. Handled them. Was he trying to trick *him*, the

45

old Bonser, by playing innocent? His fury surprised him. Well, let him try. He'd give him innocence! He'd dump that kid into the whole shebang right up to his eyeballs.

'You know bloody well what they are.'

'Guns?'

'Guns.'

So he half-knew. So he wasn't sure. Old Kenasi Salway would kill him if he knew what he was doing with the kid, implicating him, setting him up. Tough titty!

That brief word had silenced the boy, detonating like the weapons themselves. When it had merely hovered, an abstraction within the limits of his speculation, it had seemed unremarkable, a word on the page of an adventure story, a paper monosyllable that was a hackneyed prerequisite linking right and wrong.

This was real. He was appalled and sickeningly excited at the same time.

Involuntarily he bent forward slightly, clutching his stomach which had contracted and felt as if it were disappearing. An ache throbbed in the pit of it and he found his mouth brimming with saliva.

Bonser's skin was attuned to the slightest of fright-stirs. Christ, he thought. More jockeying, is that what he needs?

He said with an effort, 'You're fighting for your country now, Gav.'

'Right!' the boy managed. Automatically.

Bonser gulped back spleen that wanted to rampage with wild oaths. He drove faster, wondering if he should risk the next remark. He plunged in.

'And you've got more reason than I have, haven't you mate?'

Gavi's stomach plunged crazily. Bonser sensed the plunge.

'What do you mean?'

Bonser licked his lips.

'Well, you're *hapkas*, aren't you?'

The boy's white half flinched.

His first impulse was to deny and deny and he was back in the sleepless toss of the nights after he'd first discovered and the rage, the unreasoning rage, he'd felt with maman and Kenasi and his sulky silences and a certain private sobbing humiliating talk he'd had with Père Leyroud. Who had known all along.

'Pride in your humanity,' the old man had said to him, riddled with hokum in the shadowy candle-smelling chapel. The flames had looked like burnt honey. 'That's what counts. It doesn't matter whether you're pink or yellow or grey or brown. We're all mongrels. That's the only thing to remember. You become what you become through what you are.' He lied with all the decades of a confessor behind him. 'You must be proud of self.' The boy had been silent, his eyes glued to the flickering candles and the black centre at the base of each golden tongue. 'God wants it,' the priest had persevered, wondering after a lifetime in these parts if He really did. 'God made race. To reject any portion of what He made, is to reject Him.' Leyroud believed it but he knew the world didn't. He was surprised to hear the old arguments emerging so glibly.

But they were new to the boy. He thought about that.

And he thought about that.

He looked now at Bonser's great bull neck, the heavy paws on the steering wheel, the blaze of drinker's skin.

'Yes,' he admitted. He wasn't going to ask if it showed. 'Yes. I am.'

Bonser couldn't have cared less. He'd lost the thread of what he was going to say. He let it go. 'What we're doing tonight mustn't be talked about. You understand? Not even Angie knows. Well, not all of it. She guesses maybe. You can keep your mouth shut, can't you? For now, anyway. About your part in it. As for me, Gav – ' he thought carefully about his next words – 'I don't want to take any credit.'

They were on the outskirts of Vimape. They had crossed the bridge over the northern tributary of the Tasiriki and were coming down the long stretch of road to the village. The headlights cut into the jungle walls and Bonser blinked them three times as he eased the truck to a stop at a tiny sentry post.

Jacqui Leblanc stepped out of the pill-box shelter, swaggering his grin up to the window of the cabin. He was in full battle rig and his tilted beret sported an anonymous colour flash. He was lean and small and dangerous. Two ni-Kristi carrying *nalnals* appeared at his side, sliding silently out of the dark.

'*Okei!*' Leblanc snapped his fingers at the gate-guard. '*Ouvre ça!*' The man stood helplessly. '*You ovenem fanis!*' Leblanc's voice was shrill. He came back to the window and shoved his face close to Bonser's. 'I'll ride up with you, okei?' Then he vaulted, puma-light, onto the truck tray and squatted with his shoulders flat against the cabin, shoving one impatient arm round the side in Bonser's direction and clicking fingers. *Allez allez.*

Gavi's eyes widened like the beam of the truck lights until they became the whole lit clearing, round and hollow as a coconut shell, thatched huts and *nakamal* trapped under the curve of enormous trees as if the derivation of *man ples* sprouted from the earth itself and had grown into buildings along with the cloak of leaves. Beyond them the river shouted in the gorge.

There were the lights of cooking fires, gabble behind those fires. A banyan draped cloud over the *nasara*, the meeting-ground, an ancient tree of such massive growth that the aerial roots hung like organ pipes from the canopy fifty feet up where the first dense foliage began and the canopy itself soared for another forty feet, staining black against black and casting shadow that spread like felt. The darkness was so intense the path that led away to the small school, the yam houses and the hut of the *yeremanu* glimmered like a tenuous rag strip. Everywhere a soft ripeness, the silence of papaw and taro and dragon plum.

'Okei!' Leblanc said, leaning round the side. He was unmoved by the irony of bringing together succulence and steel. '*Ici. Par ici.*'

They sweated. In the hot dark they sweated as they heaved crate after crate onto the narrow benches under the *nabanga* tree, stacking them in rows. 'How about getting some of your men to do this?' Bonser snarled. The curious eyes of the rebel soldiers standing about humiliated him.

'Don't trust,' Leblanc said tersely. He smacked each packing-case lovingly as it was stacked. He was one of those terrible freaks of nature, a man who had never understood what had given him existence. His real world and his dream world were the one place of running men and sudden shots, of snipers and machine-gun bursts to which the torn flesh, the spilled guts, the screams, were untidy riders. His geometry of living was a single theorem exploring the perfection of the eye's sighting along a barrel, a bullet's trajectory and the scarlet rose of the target.

It was a simple theorem. He needed no other.

Bonser dumped the last crate bad temperedly.

The three of them stood and looked. Two admired. Bonser and Leblanc moved away from the boy but he could still hear them talking of other supplies, of times, of dates. Reality had cracked him apart, a ruined boy who tried not to listen. He kept watching the cooking fires and the smoke's peachy blur as it sifted into the trees and hearing the night-rhyme of water in the river.

Two of the soldiers began calling Leblanc and one of the rebel guards came over and spoke softly, pointing down the ragged white path towards the *nakamal*. Narota, flanked by advisers, was hobbling across the *nasara*.

Leblanc snapped into salute. Only Gavi caught the wink he gave Bonser.

Looking now. Looking now. Different now. The boy had seen Tommy Narota often but only briefly: on market days or standing in front of Talasa Pati headquarters or driving his jeep along d'Urville. Now his eyes glued fascinated to this old man limping between attendants and he was struck at once by his homeliness, how like Leyroud he was. It was the smallest thought. And the largest. He bit his lip, wondering which way blasphemy lay in aligning their chubbiness of spirit, priest and *yeremanu*. He gave them a moment of twinship.

And the blood that raced between them, between Narota and his *hapkas* self.

The priestliness of him! The moment wouldn't leave.

What was it?

Even Bonser, stilled by some untranslatable ambience.

Narota was standing a few feet from them smiling in turn at all three.

He forgot to return Leblanc's slaute and the forgetting, unconsciously, became a snub of supreme dignity.

His eyes, alert and kindly, paused on Bonser but lingered on the boy. He knew Bonser. He judged him a *nating* man. He leaned forward a little as he watched the boy.

One *hapkas* recognising another, Gavi thought, hoped; strangely wanted the fullest recognition. Something in him longed to race forward, to hurl himself on the warmth of this smiling stranger-relative but he fought the impulse away, knowing it the wrong moment. But he knew the moment would discover itself to him.

One *hapkas* recognising another?

It was more than that.

Bonser shifted uncomfortably, shuffling about on the grass like any *manki*.

Narota smiled, more deeply, more fully, and held out both hands in greeting.

'For Kristi,' he said.

Bonser nodded, grunting something chewed but the boy, unable now to stop himself, charmed by this Leyroud soul-brother, stepped forward eagerly and cried back, 'Oh yes! For Kristi!'

Narota fixed his eyes directly on him and the boy wondered what was behind the special smile given to him and not the others; and then the *yeremanu* turned away in his crumpled battle jacket and limped steadily and with dignity down the path through the gardens into the greater distance, into the heavy dark of another culture.

Mataso town is full of restlessness.

This is a gaspingly blue morning in what would be winter in other latitudes and District Agent Cordingley, his mouth still savouring some residue of breakfast bacon, drives from his hillside residence in the Paddock. He catches glimpses of the quick blue of the Channel as he drives down the mild green curves of road to his office near the wharves where he finds custom leaves, the fronds of the *namwele*, placed on his doorway.

This warning brought his mottled key-turning paw to a stop.

Below his shock-opened mouth, he felt his chins quiver.

There was no one in sight. No sign of his office cleaner, a rolling-eyed *man* Emba, full of custom terrors.

There was nothing but these cycas fronds, green and still fresh, the sun biting the roadway and the indifferent closed shutters of the building.

He backed away, his arm coming stiffly to his side held tensely by his thigh as if it might involuntarily touch.

The heat surge, the black dizziness and the cold. He had to mop away at his face as the salt sweat stung his eyes. Twenty yards away the French Agent's building sat among trees and he went at a half run along the lawn strip to find shutters and doors opened to the morning and the 8 o'clock boy flicking with an insolent duster.

The duster held its comment mid-air as the boy examined Cordingley with unspeaking interest.

Cordingley was forced to look away first.

'God!' he said under his breath and stumbled back across the lawn and up the slope to his car. Belle was right, had a nose for trouble, you might say, a touch of Hopi despite that righteous American presence of conformist two-note Amen-ers.

He was still hung over from yesterday's cocktail party, last night's row. These days the trouble was that the parties, the rows, fused and he got the sequences muddled. There is only one party, Belle would croak ironically, only one steaming freaking party, my dear, and you're right bang in the middle of it.

But was yesterday a party, that panic consultation at Boutin's after Narota's morning broadcast once more declaring Kristi's independence? 'He cries – how do you say it? – wolf,' liar Boutin had declared, administering more whisky anaesthetic. Belle, Cordingley remembered, had argued fiercely with Boutin. She kept insisting she had the feel of the town.

And then 'You drank too much,' she had commented as they drove back through a tropic night made for domestic rage.

Drunkenly he had ignored her, innocent buck teeth biting into his receding lower lip in a way that gave his face a wondering, marvelling look of cartoon gullibility. They were just passing the *relais* that had been opened two months and was still guestless.

Belle repeated her remark.

'Why didn't you tell me there, then, in front of everyone?' Cordingley said. 'That's your style, isn't it? Why wait till we leave?'

'You might be a fool, my dear, but I don't generally tell you that in company.'

His voice was like dried-out velvet. 'What tact, Belle. The true diplomat's wife, aren't we? Your great gab-mouth of a Yankee daddy would be amazed at the turnabout. Everything in private.'

'Well,' Belle had said, consideringly, and trailing her vowel, 'there isn't much else, is there? In private I mean.'

Cordingley had worked away at the gear stick. 'Don't start that! Christ, don't start that!'

Belle's voice had persisted and persisted. 'Sitting there, gulping whisky after whisky being as undiplomatic as hell in front of that creep Boutin and his little throwaway *nambawan* wife. She took in every damn gaffe you made.'

'You do your job, my dear, whatever that is, and let me get on with mine.'

'If only you would.'

Belle Cordingley's large blonde good looks were like some stage set being gradually dismantled. Impatience and bitterness trickled between breasts and thighs as she replayed in seconds twenty years of marriage: a reckless summer in Washington where she would have done anything, *anything*; the nasty little posting in East Africa, the move to the Seychelles, four years of that and his goddam French never improved (what *was* there with the English?); still third secretary in Jakarta (they were beginning to imagine he loved hot places); a lost island in the Solomons – then this. Her fantasy of playing residency wife, delivering snubs and love like well-timed volleys, had long collapsed in a series of rented timber bungalows whose floor space was in exact ratio to salary along with government supply furniture. She'd fought against that one and a series of monster packing-cases would trail them in container ships across the Indian Ocean and the Pacific, always arriving almost too late, just as it was time for the next move.

'Listen,' she had said and suddenly felt marvellously calm. 'Those stupid bits of bitchery about that teacher at Woodful's. God,' she said, 'I thought it was women who were supposed to be gossips. Didn't you know Boutin's laying her? His face was a marvel of supercool! But then so was hers. Madame's I mean. *Nambawan.*'

Interestedly she observed her husband's teeth savaging lip.

'And,' she pursued, enjoying herself, 'you certainly spilled the beans about the R.C.'s attitude to the Nabiru Party. I mean you handed it to Boutin on a plate.'

Cordingley's loose cheeks shook with rage.

'Nothing he wouldn't know. Nothing. Dear.' His face felt congested, all wattles and puff. He thought he might have to stop the car and wait till his anger subsided, his heart shrank.

'But' – Belle's creamy American voice flowed relentlessly – 'it wasn't simply last night. Take that cricket match last month and your little speech when you congratulated the winning team. I mean I don't think a win of two runs – three, was it? – by the British school over the French quite deserves a comparison with Waterloo.'

That – was – it!

Cordingley jammed down on the brakes so hard, the car swung drunken on the coral surface of the road and spun into the dark shadow of the *burao* fence. Belle adjusted her shawl.

Cordingley had sat for a moment breathing noisily while Belle tinkered delicately with tissues.

'Are you finished?' he managed after a few minutes.

His heart was too fast and he sneaked two testing fingers to the jumper-pulse in his left wrist as the night air all about him closed and parted. 'Are you quite quite finished? Because if you are . . .'

And then Belle had jerked out long-sufferingly, 'Oh God, Cordie! Oh God! Let's get going. Please. These hellish *ofisol* gigs.'

She felt better now. He knew it. And sorry. He knew that too. She would have burst if she hadn't spoken out. It was part of their marriage style.

'How do you fancy an omelette when we get back, with some of that cress Letty Trumble gave me?' Belle was a splendid cook.

Cordingley had felt like weeping. He could see nothing that would ever break the pattern.

'You're a bitch, Belle,' he said, moving one shaken hand to the ignition. The moon had risen and was rushing at him like a bomb. 'A total unmitigated bitch.'

Now he kept seeing the *namwele* leaves. He wished he had listened to Belle.

'Of course you know, don't you,' he was to say to her later that morning, 'you realise what those damn leaves mean, eh? It's bloody *juju*. *Puripuri*, my dear. Not that I worry about a bit of the old *juju*, not after Kenya, but it's a warning you understand, Belle, a palpable warning. If anyone other than the person who put the leaves there removes them, things get very nasty indeed. You see, Belle, I can't get into my office.'

Belle hooted with fat-sounding laughter.

Cordingley reddened.

'Look, dammit, it doesn't matter whether I believe the nonsense. The important thing is that *they* believe it. They most definitely believe it, and I'm no fool, Belle, not in these matters. No fool at all. I don't believe in asking for trouble. The Talasa Party doesn't give warnings for nothing, not now, not the way things are.'

'We've been through all this,' Belle said. 'Last November. You panicked then, my God. In January. Those kids from the *Jeune Kristi* movement out at Port Ebuli. You wouldn't listen to me. Now I suggest we ride it.'

'You don't seem to understand,' her husband said pettishly. 'This is personal.'

He acted out variations of disaster, swilling coffee, quacking ceaselessly into the phone, his diluted assumptions making only his fear apparent. When he finally got through to Lena, Trembath's voice over the fluctuating wire was cool, British and unsympathetic. The beautifully rounded vowels advised him to stay put for the moment, sit it out, old chap, unless of course . . . *if* he felt it were necessary – long pause for Cordingley's self-assessment – *if*, then perhaps he ought, well, he must be the judge. And the line went rudely dead.

Humiliated, Cordingley took a brandy out to the verandah and drank glumly, watching the town road south of the Paddock.

'It's too damn quiet,' he kept telling himself.

Nothing stirred along the wharf road nor on the east bend where traffic normally passed on the way to the copra research station. Nothing moved near the *bureau de poste*.

At 12 he saw Boutin's car pull away from the French office and became a fast blue dot along the Boulevard. He wandered over to Trumble's place after lunch but Trumble was busy doing rounds in the small hospital annexe, his wife gone visiting. Reduced to thumb-cracking, to fiddling with a despatch box he had brought up last week from the office and meant to return, to twiddling the radio short-wave knob only to be blasted sideways by that Narota stooge, Mango Wilson, jamming the transmission with freelance disc-jockeying from a radio station somewhere up in the hills near Vimape.

The day swelled and darkened, moved them through drinks, dinner, petty argument and brought them together before the supper-time radio to hear the soft voice of Tommy Narota repeating yesterday's warnings and adding that a provisional government had already been formed.

'Now what? Now what?' Cordingley began spluttering. He hauled himself from his easy chair, seized the phone and began dialling Port Lena.

'For Christ's sake!' Belle protested, trying to wrestle the phone from her crazy husband. He smacked her arm sharply and she began screaming at him. 'Don't ring. It won't do any good, for God's sake! There's not a damn thing they can do. Why don't you hang in here and wait and see what happens before you go off half-cocked. You're making a fool of yourself.'

His face twisted into violent lines. 'You think I'm waiting for that?

You think I should calmly sit here waiting for the blood-bath? You're mad, woman. Quite mad.'

'Oh my God!' Belle cried. 'Oh my God!' Her disgust was beyond words. Her contempt beat him down. Into whimpers.

Belle both hated and wanted to protect this craven blubberer of a husband.

They slept badly, the fans puddling the gluey air. Just after 6, Belle went out to the kitchen to make herself coffee when the muted woomph of an explosion back in the hills brought Cordingley out of his mussed bed to stand his fright beside her at the back windows. There were rifle cracks closer to hand, deadly punctuation in the morning's grey, and even as they cringed, united for once, behind their shutters, the first swarm of rebel soldiers, over a hundred of them, came slipping through the lightening dark, trooping up hill from the Channel Road and crossing the great grass expanse of the Paddock, waving iron bars, clubs, and sticks. A small distance away rifles barked again; there was the tearing sound of glass, the thud of beaten wood.

In the middle of this the coffee boiled over, seeping down the front of the stove to the seeping acridity of tear-gas that now penetrated the dawn air.

Shouts grew round their walls like creeper. Stones blasted off the iron of their roof.

'Oh God,' Cordingley hissed. 'That was police headquarters. Now it's us. Quick. Shove a few things in a bag, will you and we'll try to get out the front.'

She didn't argue. There was a doomsday crash as the living room doors were shattered, the crack of rocks showering against the kitchen walls and footsteps racing along the verandahs.

A native in loincloth and battle jacket had already pushed his way down their hall.

The Cordingleys, trying to stuff a lifetime's trivia into overnight bags, could only pretend his gun wasn't there.

They were all frozen in ugly attitudes. Outside on the morning grass the rebels rampaged through the native houses and the squeals of scuttling women and children fleeing, the yells of angered men, flooded into the house, settled in cane loungers, sifted behind curtains, papered the diplomatic white walls with madness.

But the man with the gun didn't intend to hurt. He only wanted them to go. He kept motioning them out towards the front of the house with his rifle barrel. At one stage, when Cordingley backed against an occasional table, sprawled and landed his lack of dignity against the drinks cabinet, the native burst out laughing. Cordingley would have preferred being shot. He shoved his wife unlovingly ahead onto the verandah past a dozen drunken islanders waving bows and arrows, out into the rip and cough of the tear-gas.

Was this the moment for words? The dazzling last-ditch stand? The empire builder's moment of glory? Going out in a splash of plucky headlines?

It was as if his tongue had been severed.

The car was where he had parked it the previous day at the bottom of the driveway steps. He felt as if the twenty yards between him and it were a slow bog in which his trembling legs made no forward progress. Belle was actually dragging him.

Windows! Fumbling and winding his desperation, shutting out yells as well, yells and machine-gun bursts of ironic cackles as he shook the car into a lurching reverse, swung and thrust it, jerking off down the track ahead of now running men while rocks and jeers skidded off black duco.

The car left the track in a spastic leaping run to cross the Paddock, past the flag-pole where rebels were already attacking the flag, buffeting and bouncing them across turf to the back road that would take them out past the plantations at illegal speeds, across the plateau, beyond hospital, sportsground, down down towards d'Urville and Mataso town.

'The others,' Belle kept nagging. 'The others. You should have stopped for them.'

There were the startled faces of Jim and Letty Trumble peering after them from the rebel-ringed porch of their house, the opened mouth (what words were blown away by the wind of their terrified car?) of Len Kendrick, the British police sergeant, gasping against gas, of Moses Taureka, Paddock odd-jobber, watching his boss skedaddling in the *ofisol* car.

Behind them now, that melée of loincloths and feathers, of erupting mouths, battle shirts, guns, *nalnals* and the confused welter of surly flesh. The faces kept flattening themselves on the insect-smeared screen.

Her guilt pressed. Cordingley decided to ignore her. He was

following instructions to get out. He kept telling himself this. That he had anticipated the official directive by half a day was neither here nor there. It was every man for himself.

His wife's voice kept asking about his plans. She begged for slowness. Terror had made her husband's accelerator foot reckless.

'What,' she kept crying at his deaf profile, 'are you going to do?' They couldn't simply keep on driving. The world had become filled with ragged men and cudgels.

He refused an answer as they sped his fright between the peaceful cloisters of palms. And her voice. It went on and on, trying to score out those startled faces at the Paddock.

Finally he told her pompously, 'It is arranged,' and swung the car in great whacks along the hill road.

'But what? What is arranged?'

'There will be a boat,' he hoped.

His teeth bit sharply, despite all his wishes to keep up appearances, to go out with the flag flying – well, half-mast, dammit – into his trembling lower lip. It was all too bloody bad, he kept thinking, and had a terrible vision of the time he wet his mattress in prep school and the chill 2 a.m. dark as he dragged and exchanged the soaking horror for that of another boy's whose empty bed lay at the far end of the dormitory. That monstrous give-away shuffling sound as he lugged his saturated bedding across bare boards, the heaving swapover, the dank but hoped-for dryness when Nuson Minor returned from his spottiness in sick bay. He blinked himself back into tropic plantings, giving his noddle a little shake as he drove. Belle slumped into silence beside him, sweating already in her linen dress, too many rings cracking on clenched fingers.

At the junction with Rue Quiros he slowed down, for there was still the township to pass through, the house cluster round the British school in Malatao, the rebel headquarters and the bridge at Tasiriki.

The sun rose and yelled at them through the windscreen.

Already Belle imagined she could hear the discord of a slob fate ring about them as the car swung downhill towards the houses, down steadily now past the school, down, slower, slower, down towards d'Urville and rebel headquarters where islanders thronged thickly under the trees staring then screeching at this early morning car. There were two men in a uniform of sorts balancing rifles as they straddled the northern entrance to the bridge.

'You'll have to stop,' Belle whispered. 'You must stop.' Even as she urged her eyes read the unsureness of the rebel guard despite the aggressiveness of their stance.

Cordingley did not answer. The car filled with the fug of his own sweat and fear. His clothes were pasted to his body. There were men racing beside the car now, hands beating on the glass of his driving window, the crack of stick and rock stormed round him; but he drove steadily forward, shoving the car between yelps and howls, and as they swung round the curve onto the bridge, he accelerated, staring glassily ahead through the smudged windscreen as if the soldiers and their rifles did not exist. Below the bridge the Tasiriki raced fast and green towards the Channel. The Magasin Lantane on the far side swung fleetingly towards him a moment of boarded windows and shutters.

One of the guards sprang, swinging his rifle, too close for this narrow bridge and Cordingley, gunning the car, raced between the guards, clipping the first man as both tried to spring aside. The next minute there was the crack of a rifle and a bullet splattered the rear window. In his driving mirror he could see a crazed spaghetti spread and obscure.

There wasn't time to bother with his yawping wife. Belle seemed to be moaning over glass fragments in her hair, slivers of it on her lap, rather than the bullet that had sped between them both to plunge into the dash board. In any case, Cordingley decided, without knowing what his predicate might be. In any case. In any case what? He was conscious of his fool of a wife cranking down her window and shoving her head out to see if that bloody nig had been hurt until another rifle shot decided her and there was only his foot banged down, the skittering of tyres as they roared through the scattered houses near St Pierre along the coast road, past Boutin's snug under flamboyants, out, out, craven as buggery so who cares, who cares, past the mission school, the little groups of black fist-wavers still plodding in to Mataso town, out on the Channel Road to Serua.

His speed made him miss the shy turn-off he was seeking.

Only the recovered voice of his wife reminded him.

'You fool,' she had been saying for some time, 'oh you goddam fool. If you'd killed that kid with the rifle . . .'

He didn't bother to answer.

He brought the big black car to a skidding pause, clashed it into reverse, trembling, oh trembling like the time he'd dragged the mattress his other big moment, trembling as he backed this hulking sod of a thing along the grass strip to Larsen's turn-off, trembling and smacking it into gear, bouncing south from the highway and shoving his way between scrub to the plantation sandwiched between road and sea.

They were not expected. The air reeked of unwelcome.

Bingi Larsen scowled as the car lumbered out of the *burao* copses to collapse on their front lawn strip. His wife, woken by racketing, appeared dragging on a house-coat, her hair hanging in lank tapes, her face unwilling to believe in the Cordingleys' presence.

Larsen cut gobbled explanations short.

'First,' he said, and tactfully manoeuvred the official car out of sight behind the smoke house. His wife steered their limpness and bags onto the verandah.

'And second,' Larsen added on his return, 'there's really no need to run. You *are* running, I take it?'

Cordingley plunged his nose into the Larsens' breakfast coffee.

'I mean,' Larsen went on, 'this whole thing isn't going to amount to anything, old chap. Not a thing. Why, only yesterday some of the boys from Vimape came door-knocking – they did it all round town, in fact – telling us very politely that there was going to be a revolution and that Tommy Narota's government would be taking over. Now you couldn't ask nicer than that, could you? They suggested, again very politely, that we stay indoors until everything was over. They really didn't want anyone hurt.'

'No one came near us,' Cordingley protested. He was too ashamed to tell them about the *namwele* leaves.

'Well of course they wouldn't,' Larsen said. He was a beanpole of a man with a long amused face and rimless glasses. An unlikely planter, they said. He was suspected of reading. 'You represent the power. They were just being nice to us simple folk who want to get on with living.' He couldn't help smiling.

Cordingley detected laughter. 'Whose side are you on, man?'

He hated the sound of his own truculence but he'd had a bad fright. 'Christ, they were shooting at us! The Paddock's a shambles. Tear-gas. The lot.'

Larsen's wife held the coffee pot like an interrogation mark. 'This morning? Already?'

Cordingley began choking on his anxiety. He refused a second cup. He kept saying there wasn't time, no time at all, he hated asking favours but . . . But what? the raised eyebrows of the Larsens invited . . . could Bingi possibly run them down to Buala? They could fly out from there.

Shock. That was it. Shock. The whole drowsy garden between house and beach which had been moving in response to the swelling heat paused. Flower leaf branch, all static as if the morning had stopped and personal history had reached a stand-still.

Larsen turned away, took his time about answering, took so long, in fact, that Cordingley would not examine unspoken imputations. He was a-jump with nerves.

'If you're wise,' he said stupidly, 'you'll be thinking about getting out too.'

'Might have to after this,' Larsen said. He poured himself another coffee. 'All this aiding and abetting of undesirable foreigners!' He let out a roar of laughter.

The women looked away from each other.

'Only a joke, Cordingley,' Larsen went on, sipping his coffee with infuriating slowness. 'Only a joke. Frankly I've got a lot of sympathy for Narota's crowd. They're non-violent – no. No. Don't interrupt. They are, in *principle*, non-violent. What you had this morning was just a spot of fire crackers. They only want to see some progress for the island. You can't really say Britain's done much, now can you, except a lot of colonial flag-waving, cocktailing and a whack of exploitation. Charlotte and I aren't moving, you know, not unless they force us. Too much money at stake here. Far too much.'

He drank some more coffee and looked at Cordingley from under shaggy eyebrows.

'No regular salary like you chaps and a cosy pension at the end.'

He set his coffee mug down and began moving away from the table. 'Well, I feel a bit dubious about this, frankly. Implicating myself.' He asked, without looking anywhere in particular, 'Didn't anyone else up at the Paddock want to come? What about Doc Trumble and his wife? And young Rogo? They sitting it out?'

Belle watched her husband's face with a rush of spite as the pudgy features worked away at possible replies.

'We all have to make our own decisions in these matters,' Cordingley offered finally. 'Come along, Belle.' He began walking along the verandah and out onto the coral path that led to the beach. The others were automatically trailing him. 'I've been in contact with Port Lena. I talked with the A.R.C. I've made my decision. I can't make it for anyone else.'

'Can't you?' Larsen looked at him curiously. 'Thought you were O.C. Paddock.'

If anyone had punched Cordingley, the sawdust would have shifted.

'Listen,' he said, 'I'm chartering your damn boat. It will cost a packet. Now let's get moving, shall we?'

'Oh I'm not charging.' Bingi Larsen smiled. 'Not in a case like this. Principles, old chap. Principles. You should have asked Bonser if you wanted to pay. He made a mint during the scare last year. Just thought you might have been concerned for the others.'

Scarlet-faced Cordingley strode ahead and stepped heavily into the dinghy at the jetty's end. It wallowed horribly. Belle followed with the bags and the two of them sat stolidly – it might have been a beach picnic – staring up at Larsen, casual on the jetty's end, his ear cocked to the persistence of phone-shrill from the house.

'Hold it,' Larsen ordered. He went leaping back along the jetty and up through the garden. The Cordingleys stared at blazing water. Minutes stretched like blue rubber.

When Larsen returned he still stood without making getaway movements, observing these twinned eggs nestled in his dinghy. His wife had followed him and had one hand lightly assuring itself on the hot skin of his arm.

'We might have to re-think this,' he said. 'That was Davis from Bipi. The town's a mess. I really don't think I ought to take you any place now. Charlotte and I will have to stick around.'

Cordingley almost wept. The sun wouldn't leave him alone. He'd forgotten his hat. He hadn't even the strength to bluster.

'It would take far too long to get you down to Buala,' Larsen was saying. 'I can't leave Charlotte here. I can run you to Serua.' He looked at the fat white eggs consideringly. 'They tell me they're organising boats to take people off from the point. But that's as far as I can go. You'll have to wait there with the others.'

'Jesus,' Cordingley whimpered.

'It's that or nothing.' Larsen picked up the painter and swung it loosely.

'All right,' Cordingley snapped. 'Oh all right. Just let's get on with it.'

He was doing fingertip tapping on the coaming, drumming away with his gut emptied, avoiding Belle's eyes as she squatted with her lap filled with that bulging bag, her brassy hair blown every way by the wind. The stupid bitch, he thought, when it was himself he hated. The stupid . . . stupid . . . Mumbling away. Eyes. Keep eyes on the water. Adjust to the rock as Larsen steps in. Try not to touch Belle. Christ. And as Larsen drags on the cord. Contempt all round him. Contempt.

This was it. The last look as the dinghy puttered out. The last look with Bingi's wife a shape to be waved at briefly as she stood on the shingly beach under the rasp of palm fronds. The last long haul down the Channel, the town receding, receding, what he could glimpse of it, the roofs on the Paddock hill just visible through trees and the flagless mast, eyes dropping from the surprised faces of Trumble and Moses Taureka and the gasping Kendrick, head turned away so he couldn't see, couldn't couldn't remember.

Just before 7 Hedmasta Woodful closed the back door of his teacher house and strolled across the lawned slope to the school buildings.

All through his sparse breakfast of black coffee and Palestrina he had been conscious of something amiss – the day wrinkling with anxiety, the heat scratching at his windows to get in. The 6 o'clock news had been interlarded with transmissions from Vimape and between boilings of rock music and steel guitars he had heard for at least the fifth time that *aeland* Kristi had seceded and that the government of the revolution was in control. Woodful had smiled sardonically, poured another coffee and turned the radio off. The delicate planes of silence on which his early mornings were created held the distant sound of shouts like bum reception on some brum receiver. At one stage there was a muffled explosion.

Ah yes, he said, already drained by humidity. Ah yes.

Yet when he came down by the front of the school none of the buses that brought islanders in from as far as Port Ebuli and Serua had arrived. The road's blankness held him poised in public service shock.

There were three ni-Kristi, boys from the junior class, wheeling their bicycles into the weather shed.

Their faces became blank discs to his questions.

'Fetch Migo,' he told one of them.

The yardman, half Spanish, half islander, was flaccid with confusion.

'Do you know what's going on?' Woodful asked. 'The buses are late. Has something gone wrong?' He refused to use Seaspeak.

The yardman kept inspecting his feet. He shook his head.

'Radio say *trabeul. Olgeta i mekim trabeul.*'

'What sort of trouble?'

'*Tekova.* No bus *tedei.* No bus. Radio say *tekova.*'

Hopeless. Woodful sighed. Perhaps it was genuine. He was tired of these fright-jumps, these moments of sudden political passion that decorated his years on the islands like painted beads. One simply – well, inexorably – pressed on.

He went over to the classrooms and began unlocking doors. Could there be more to this latest nonsense? Usually the staff had arrived by now. There was no staff. There was no sign of more children arriving. He found himself humming – refusing admission of fright – a theme from the Palestrina motet. He sat at a desk in Wally Coombe's room and watched the clock. At 7.10 Coombe arrived with two of the native teachers. Some dribbles of kids appeared and huddled in groups along the verandahs. His other European staff member, Bimbi Jackett, was absent, precluded, he imagined by warnings from Boutin. He felt a spasm of fury at the thought of fornicating one-upmanship and decided on an impromptu staff meeting while the Palestrina kept singing through his skull along with a headache that spread like a stain. There was, unexpectedly, a nervous throb at the corner of his jaw.

Formality was a refuge in the hugger-mugger of insanity.

Coldly he inquired of Miss Jackett.

Coombe blinked. Still young, still enthusiastic, his mere six months on Kristi found him still honeymooning with the exotic, plunging into custom and the beauties, as he argued, of Seaspeak, the infinite subtleties of pidgin. 'Have you tried translating Eliot's Quartets or Pound's Cantos?' Woodful had asked irritably. The nonsense yap of beginners always maddened him.

Mr Coombe blushed and said he thought she had gone to a beach party at Ebuli.

Not this morning, Woodful hoped, watching Coombe's form captain face.

'Last night,' Coombe replied.

Woodful frowned. The gossip of the place was another thing. Work, that was all that mattered. He turned to Lela Ombi, a mission-trained woman from Trinitas.

'Is the situation serious? Is there just another scare?'

Lela Ombi plaited her fingers in distress. She looked from Hedmasta Woodful to the children now clinging to the door-frame of the classroom and back again.

'This time,' she said, 'it is real.' She described the ragtag march from the hills, the gathering army of nearly eight hundred now, who were in Mataso Park, the mob she had seen milling round the Paddock as she cycled in, the smashed shop-fronts along d'Urville.

When she finished speaking the ticking of the wall-clock took over, slicing Woodful's indecision into worry fragments.

Finally, 'We will close the school,' he decided.

He looked round the classroom at the empty desks, basic aid-abroad issue, the pictures on the wall, the static globe, the hanging map of *aeland* Kristi with the red dot marking where he now sat. The Palestrina kept rocking. His neat pleasant features were having trouble composing themselves. 'I suggest' – oh he was always so bloody formal. He could hear the careful phrases coming vomitously from his mouth even at a moment like this – 'that you all return to your homes as quickly as possible. Miss Ombi, you can see that the children outside get away at once. There are only a few of them and they're all locals.' He hesistated, looking down at his clenching fingers. The others helped him examine them. 'You, too, Coombe. I'll wait around for a while and turn back any staff or students. Miss Jackett,' he couldn't help himself adding, 'must have been forewarned.'

Though his face remained phlegmatically colonial service, the provocations of the moment were startling his blood. Twelve years in Mataso town and he was still a stranger, nobbled by his own routines. Still a stranger though former pupils were now married and dandled gurgling brown babies at him on the steps of the *bureau de poste*, along the Boulevard outside Bipi and the Magasin Lantane. 'Hallo, Hedmasta,' they would sing, turning their great flashes of shy smiles sideways into the protection of a baby's flesh, a baby's cap of frizz. 'Hallo.' And he would respond to their chant, poking one grave finger into cheek or skull. 'Hallo, Lamana. Hallo, Rosella. Hallo, Abigail.' And they would drop back into Seaspeak, despite all those years, babbling away in that bastard tongue he'd tried so hard to extirpate.

'And what's her name?' he would ask fatuously, inspecting the chocolate wriggling bundle, to be greeted by screams of laughter. '*I pikinini man! Oué! I pikinini man!*' Hands to mouth, fingers splayed over amusement at the *bigfalla mistek*, but not blocking it, no...

'Good morning, Rosella,' he would say, smiling too. 'Good morning, Abigail. Good morning, Lamana.' Behind him came the chorus of *Babai, ayé, babai*. Goodbye. Goodbye.

Always a stranger, even with expatriates serving similar terms of service. With *colons* and ocker beach bums milking fortunes out of the country. Greeting or farewelling, he was still a stranger, settling new assistants in, seeing off the old, stuck with his cassette player, a stack of re-read paperbacks and some over-thumbed poetry collections. The long evenings. The long evenings. Aware of his small placement, the margins of self in an island full of the unknown. There was, truly, in all the years, the hot stinking sweating years he had been striding from house to classroom in his mad belief in service through a wife's death and a daughter's absence in a Sydney boarding-school, only the gentle and always slightly drunken wisdom of Madam Guichet that sustained him.

She was island jetsam, beached in Mataso town with her fine olive skin barely etched by more than six decades and the abandonment of a lugger master, her grey head ashake from too much morning bottle. Afternoons drowned her. 'I take it, you understand,' she would explain to Woodful in her broken English or more decorated French, 'to get me through the day. Père Leyroud calls it swimming to Paradise. He is a man who understands many things.' And she would smile, her broken teeth enchantingly white still in her tanned face. Père Leyroud had wept a little with her when she retired from St Pierre, when not even a double brandy got her through the morning. 'It is your capacity to love,' he had said, 'that we will miss most. Not your history. Not your grammar.' And that was what Woodful had discovered also during those forlorn evenings in the months that followed his wife's death. There was not so much bottle then. But there was welcome and talk if he wanted it and belief in the hopefulness of unfolded days. She would pat her dog against a background of Ravel and improve his French and lend him books and tapes. 'We abandoned ones,' she would say, but laughing. 'We must – what do you say? – gum together.' And he would pull his shirt away from his sticky body and gesture comically with the freed section and then they would both laugh.

Standing alone beneath the flag-pole on the overgreen slope outside the classrooms he wished she were there, knowing she would understand exactly what should be done, wearing her delicate commonsense like a skin. She would know. Despite, he told himself wryly, her Anglophobia, her rebel sympathies.

And what were his?

In all these rumblings he had tried to be dispassionate, in all the years of months that had preceded this morning. My little town, he admitted, with your white houses and your rusting Quonset huts buried under *burao* and the vine everyone calls 'American', with your trashy stores filled with junk and dust, with your market days down by the Magasin Lantane and the heaps of *kumala* from the gardens, the taro and the dragon plums and the *nakatambol* fruit, their bright yellow globes heaped in the woven baskets and the fish. All under the flame trees of summer with the stench of copra waiting at the docks for the *Sagesse* or the *Colombe* or the tramp steamers taking off for the south and west. Little town, I concede your victory. You never were mine, despite the dozen years and the hallos of Lamana and Abigail and Rosella. Despite.

Dispassionate?

Not that. Especially not that. Not after the visits you had made to Vimape, staying for *lap-lap* beside the rushing water of the Tasiriki; not after the talks under the banyan a hundred paces from the thatched utopia where Narota prodded away at his identity. And what did he think of Tommy Narota?

He avoided the answer. His public service mind dreaded the answer – for he saw nothing but gentleness and smiles. Smiles mainly. Smiles despite the anger of British agents and planters. Gentleness despite the rheumatism that nagged. In those black months ten years gone now when Augustine Guichet had sustained him, he had found comfort too in the green walls of Vimape, with the smiles and the courtesy and the passing of the kava cup.

No. Not dispassionate. But morally strait-jacketed by the job and a lifetime of service.

Back in his house, he was ashamed to find himself locking all doors and windows. Before he went inside he took one last look from his verandah and could just make out a great trail of people heading along the waterfront towards Mataso Park and coming down from the back hills Cordingley's long black car swinging away from the township to the bridge.

He paused, one hand on the glass door. The car did not hesitate but plunged straight onto the bridge curve.

Babai, Cordingley, he heard himself say sourly. *Ayé*.

He began phoning. He dialled Trumble's number. It rang and rang. He tried Kendrick's home. The phone complained for a long time before it was picked up and he had only just begun to speak when the line went dead. The receiver dangled uselessly in his hand yet he replaced it gently, gently as a custom leaf.

He heated up more coffee and took it back to his living-room, switched on the radio and sat back in a hail of static and the-news-of-the-world heartiness of Mango Wilson.

So he was unaware when the first of the rebels came at a half-trot, half-march across the grounds of the school, beating on walls and verandah rails with sticks in a rising tattoo like December rains.

The drumming closed in on him. The battering threatened, crashing louder and louder until half a dozen of the men, clubs rising and pounding in rhythm, came through his small back garden, ripping shrubs apart, and stalked his verandah, whacking the iron railings, banging and banging and banging in accompaniment to throaty whoops.

The words had not shaped themselves yet.

Woodful sat huddled on his divan, coffee cup half-way to his lips, his back to the sunny glass of porch doors, staring into and not seeing his frozen cup, his hand locked to the rim of it, stomach sick and tight as a drum skin while he awaited the crack of glass, the blackening smash on the head.

Words took shape. '*Wai'te basat*,' they screamed 'White bastard! Get out! This is our country. Get out!'

Unmoving under the voices as they rose in a kind of frenzy.

No thoughts.

Ashamed he crouched lower, the back of the divan between him and the black faces he knew must be pressed against the glass.

No thoughts. And many thoughts. Muddled visions of hair and purple skin and powerful limbs, the shining arms swinging the iron bars and the sticks, and the horrible unending shindy as *man bush* bashed the railings into submission while he sat, cowardly and motionless, still as a tree-fern god, as the carved head of a slit drum.

They thought him gone. He hoped they thought him gone.

A small notion burrowed its way through his immobility: he had worked for them. Only for them. It would mean nothing, his fuddle-brain told him.

The rock crashing through the glass door sailed over his head and landed at his feet. His shaking hand spilled coffee.

Yet still he could not confront them. Now he stared beyond his cup at the rock and behind him the shout chorus gave way to single spaced mockings and then laughter. He could only watch the lump of coral on the matting until the lump wedged itself in his mind holding all his terror and shame within it.

Even after the shouting and the drumming died away, he still sat, unable to move. When he finally straightened his head there was only the nausea of self and silence.

Trembling he drank what was left in the cup. It was bitter and cold.

The schoolyard, his ragged garden, the road behind the house, all held mere colour slides of those moments as air steadied and the cries, the chants, filtered across the rim of the hill.

It was then, too, he realised the radio had died.

He tried the phone again, uselessly.

He went back to the radio and found himself slapping it.

He began to edge the needle across the bands, catching a hum, forcing it, forcing it up until at last, faint but deliberate on the Mataso town wave-length, he trapped the broadcaster from Vimape. The message came in gobbets and splutters and settled into its warnings of triumph and disaster....*this is a message*...Wilson fading as he had faded from his job with the survey department, surfacing with the fisheries... *rebel forces of the Talasa Pati have taken* ... pulled out from there, unseen for weeks then mysteriously re-appearing on trucks, on jeeps, busy round Talasa Pati headquarters, swaggering with something that was now explained... *officially declared its independence within the island group*. The voice repeated the message in bastard French, in Seaspeak.

Woodful hung unwilling and pained, over the set until a corrosive rock number finished and Wilson's voice again crawled across the wave-length:

We repeat those messages. The British Paddock has now been taken and the yeremanu, *Tommy Narota, is now president-in-chief of the northern island of Kristi and surrounding waters. People are advised for the moment to remain in...banks and stores...*

Woodful punched the radio off.

The very flatness of that voice seemed to energise him.

The lout accent (yes, he was a bloody-minded snob!), the treacherous opportunism of one he knew, oh he knew, to have laughed at Narota, revived something in him. Oh Christ, he kept saying, nudging his shrunken pip of courage. Oh Christ!

He unlocked the back door and forced himself out to his car.

It was better to look neither left nor right. That way, nerve might return.

There were dents all along the bonnet and a deep wound in the duco of the boot. They seemed less than his own wrecked self-esteem.

His lips compressed against all inner urgings to stay, Woodful drove slowly down the hill where he had seen Cordingley's car pass earlier, along the Boulevard, nudging his way cautiously between rebel marchers who took stray whacks at the car, past doorway pockets of rebel army and native police of the Talasa Pati swaggering along the sidewalks, old army berets riding like pancakes on the electric humps of hair.

One of the soldiers stopped him, but only for a moment – in the township he was well known, *hedmasta solwata* – and shoved the car along past the Ciné Mangrove, the Taiwanese restaurant, the Dancing Bears, out along the Channel road towards the British Paddock.

The gates were closed and under the mango trees near the entrance a cluster of rebels stood waiting to block intruders. He got out of his car and stood uncertainly in the prying light. He could see bunches of men moving along the line of houses. The smell of tear-gas still hung about the Paddock, the incense of riot over smashed windows and gaping shutters and a mournful line of washing at the back of Moses Taureka's place. The guards at the gate inspected Woodful, grinnned and began talking rapidly among themselves.

Within that suspended moment a racket of raised voices from the doctor's house rang over the Paddock lawns and Woodful looked up to see Letty Trumble, pale with affront, marching down her verandah steps and come striding angrily towards the gate. She swung a shopping-bag defiantly like a talisman for normalcy and she stepped out with erect head and back nourished by fearsome British outrage, her eyes masked by sun-goggles.

A guard stepped forward, his gun at the ready, but Letty Trumble swept past, one arm up, and pushed the rifle aside.

Just like that.

'I must do my shopping,' she said coldly to the guard.

She saw Woodful. 'I must do my shopping.' Her voice was high on the repeat. 'They must allow me to do my shopping.'

Hedmasta Woodful was still stunned by the glinting vision of arm and gun.

He heard himself asking doltish questions.

She ignored them.

'Could you drive me to town?'

Woodful was conscious of a lot of chatter and movement among the guards. Letty Trumble had chipped at male dignity.

'Listen,' he said softly. 'Listen. The best thing for you to do would be to pack a couple of bags and leave now.' Her mouth, he noticed, had a strangely fixed look as if it were pulled back in a permanent social smile, her cocktail smile, and the hand clasping the shopping-bag was spasmodically shaking. Poor bitch, he thought. Oh you always were a silly bitch, almost as silly as Belle Cordingley with your tiny snobbisms and colonial pretensions. But now you're a poor bitch.

She kept insisting, as if his first questions had only just reached her, 'We are all right. We are quite all right.' Later, much later, he discovered she was lying.

Woodful spoke to the men at the gate. They stood aside sullenly to let her through.

'This is a nasty business,' he said to her. Fatuously. 'By the way, I think the D.A. has left. I saw his car earlier heading out of town.'

'Oh yes.' Her voice was half an octave higher than normal. Each cheek bone was blotched with red. 'Oh yes, the Cordingleys have gone. Almost before. Oh yes. One mustn't be critical, but almost before it happened.'

'But didn't he speak to Jim? Didn't he offer to take you?' Woodful marvelled that there was not a quiver on the mouth. 'Hasn't he organised anything?'

'He passed us,' she said bitterly. 'We were out on the verandah and he passed us.' She turned her gleaming bronzed lenses on him and slid into the passenger seat. Her smile was even wider. 'Jim preferred to sit it out. Chose.'

She stared ahead through moving landscape. 'This lousy place,' she said softly and viciously.

Later that morning Woodful drove back to the Paddock to see if he could be of any help and found the buildings a chaos of broken glass, ripped railings, shutters and doors drooping from their hinges. There was no one left on the Paddock except the rebels.

They had admitted him grudgingly. They disliked answering his questions. Where were the Trumbles? Talasa Pati, someone said. And Kendrick? *Wanples*, they said. The same.

Rebels were still wandering about the ruined buildings, drunk now, and steadily smashing to pieces furniture they had dragged from the houses, flailing in a listless way, as if the afternoon heat were too much for them. Some lounged in armchairs hauled into the shade of the flamboyants, taking an occasional pull at a bottle pilfered from Cordingley's magnificently stocked bar. They were genial, these drinkers, and even waved to the *hedmasta* as he walked past. Others, studiously obsessed, were tearing up books, page by page, page by page, giggling as they watched the black and white confetti flutter away in the Channel wind. In front of Jim Trumble's house, in Letty Trumble's planter chairs, two natives sprawled watching a heap of the doctor's medical reference books smoulder lazily, as the white *puripuri* of diagrams and colour plates, the legends of diagnosis and prognosis yellowed, blackened and burst into soggy flame.

The wreckage at Cordingley's house was especially vigorous and outside Kendrick's a large black youth was grinding something into the path. Woodful recognised him.

'Hello Solomon,' he said. He moved closer to inspect.

The black boy looked up, scowled and went on with his footwork.

On the ground was a child's white plastic doll, broken into a dozen pieces by the sedulous boot which was now working it deliberately and with great attentiveness into the coral drive.

It was more an attempt at obliteration.

Woodful was shocked by the concentration on the boy's face, the mashing action that pasted the flattened bits of leg, arm, head and belly into the gravel, the screwing motion of the heel and over all these movements a fog, a fog of rejection and contempt there in the hot sun under sky-glare in splintered Pacific light. Nothing hidden. Only Solomon's eyes rising occasionally to meet his with a challenge that directed his own eyes to the movements of the relentless foot.

He wanted to shout at him, *olsem hedmasta*, command him to stop, tell him that he'd got the message, that the symbol was overwhelming them both and could only reduce them to nothing and for a second a clotted but choked-back sound squeezed from far down his throat but only echoed fearfully in his head.

After another moment the boy looked up at Woodful and hooked into the teacher's eyes as if they were fish to be played, inspecting, silent. Somewhere behind them came wild high giggles. The outrageous smashing went on one house away.

Woodful bit off words.

Walking back to the car he was conscious that still they ignored him as if he had no body, no presence. This, he thought bitterly. After twelve years.

Now he noticed another small fire burning on the porch of the dispensary tucked away to the side of Trumble's house. Above a stinking pile of office carbons, mouldering bandages, pill cartons, tubes of ointment, injection ampoules and patient record cards, the smoke lifted in soft grey roses. Hedmasta Woodful began an agitated trot across the grass to the stoking native who, glancing up at Woodful's undignified cries and recognising the once resented power figure, perceived with indifference now this bumbling *wai'te* reeking of fear, gammoning fierceness.

'Stop!' the frightened *wai'te* kept crying out. 'Stop! Don't do that, Pascal. Pascal, that's stupid.'

The voice coming at Pascal was cutting into the last two syllables an emphasis that had served well enough three years before. That's *stu – pid*! But *hedmasta* magic was gone as voice rather than body confronted a husky adolescent hunkered above a ritual fire of tokens.

Hopelessly Woodful let his protesting arms drop. Even as he stood watching Pascal a sudden chill underscored the panic in his bowels informing him in this moment of lost *hedmasta* authority that to the squatting boy his face had become almost featureless. Only the whiteness mattered.

'Go!' Pascal shouted. 'Go go go!'

'Please,' Woodful attempted, 'you don't understand. Please.'

'Don't explain *nating*,' Pascal ordered brutally. 'Don't want to hear no explanations. *Tri* years you talk talk talk. Now it's my turn. You just go.'

Woodful took his humiliation back past the wrecked houses, the drunken men, past the heaps of shattered crockery and glass. The guards at the gate laughed aloud this time and the hurtful mirth broke on his over-straight back as he passed them.

'You learn us too much, Hedmasta,' he heard one of them say. 'And not enough.'

When he tugged open the car door there were suddenly more men about him but as if the laughter had dissolved anger their shiny faces were unexpectedly crumpled with real amusement for after all, most of them knew him, knew his kindnesses, his unending wish to help. The processes of revolution require the observation of clichés and these had been conducted with ceremonial gravity.

Inaf. It was as if they had said it. Enough.

Woodful forced a smile, acknowledging the absurdity of the whole bloody business, as absurd as his continuing presence these last dozen years; and when he smiled the threat in his guts slid back, his heart stopped thumping and he became aware of the bite of the sun.

Opening up the boot of the car he indicated two gunny sacks.

'It's food,' he said. 'I wanted to help.' And he could hear and loathed the pomposity that crept back into his voice. Staggering among word thickets. 'To see if anyone was hurt.' His glasses shone like fire discs as he looked from black smile to black smile.

'No one hurt,' they assured him. 'Not people. Only things.'

They kept smiling at him.

He asked if they could use some of the food. If there were anyone left at the Paddock, any women, any children.

'Gone bush,' he was told. 'All gone, *long wé, long wé*, go go go.'

Not as far as that, he knew. Cringing round the edges, probably, as he had cringed, or fled to the school. Heaving one gunny sack out he gave it to the nearest soldier, a twenty-year-old with khaki shirt flapping over torn bush shorts, his hair stuck with a *lokalok* flower.

He detected shame, then, on the faces close to him and all the men kept their heads carefully turned from the havoc at their backs, the oily smoke of the dispensary fire, the fluttering pages of the books that kept blowing and settling, nevertheless, like black and white butterflies. In the Channel wind injured shutters flapped worn-out dreams. The bits of broken doll had long become part of the coral.

This is the real nonsense of history, Woodful thought. The idiot comic gravity.

'Thank you,' one of the soldiers said, dropping the Seaspeak and handing Woodful his rifle to mind. He hoisted the food sack over his shoulder and headed up the hill towards Taureka's little house.

Saddled with this gun! No one found it strange, enemy handing weapon to enemy. Woodful looked at it resting on both hands, heavy, deadly, and had to smile with the irony of it. He regarded all the watching faces and they too smiled.

'Here,' he said, handing the rifle carefully to the nearest soldier. 'Not for me, *tankyou tou mas!*'

They collapsed with laughter then, doubling up, slapping each other at this crazy *wai'te* who had always feigned deafness – *hedmasta i stap yau pas* – to the bastard sounds of pidgin, the lot of them standing easy, relaxed in the munching heat, while Woodful, hurdled by all the teacherly jokes he had made over the years felt the prongs of his four decades jab at his foolishness. Was it bad theatre or good, this idiot paradox, the current-riffled Seaspeak, the smoke glaze across the tree line losing itself in the palms – too many of them – that soldierly insistence of palms, rank upon rank like Jason's iron men, striding along and back from the lumpy waters of the Channel?

Or the naive pretences of Pati headquarters to which he now drove for advice, rational advice he hoped, in a day that up-ended even its own revolution as if it were some knockabout burlesque in which all the actors made up their own lines and movements.

His orderly mind, accustomed to sifting reasons behind unmarked attendance registers, half-empty classrooms, the logistics of school sports days or concerts or bazaars, demanded four-square direction on his next moves – the prompting behind the dust-filled curtain, the hissed direction to some clumsy bumbler stage-front, the dramatic entry stage left.

The Boulevard was quieter when he drove back. Had everything stopped for lunch in this *opéra bouffe?* Houses, stores, public buildings, all turned closed faces to the morning's opener. Sun shone on an empty stage.

Talasa headquarters were in a low-slung building huddled behind banana thatch. A rebel flag drooped above the doorway and beyond that the corridor and rooms seemed asleep. Then a guard appeared and sauntered over to Woodful's car, looking down at him, eyes large and amused and holding no threat at all. He gave a winner's smile.

'Good afternoon, Hedmasta.' His smile widened. (Were there shouts and lout hoots from the stalls?) Woodful remembered him as form captain three years before. 'We have been expecting you.'

The grin exploded into mirth. He'd had four years of Hedmasta Woodful raging against Seaspeak. '*You go insaid long ofis,*' he managed. He could hardly get the words out for hilarity. '*Smôl tai'm. Youmi tok tok bisnis.*'

Woodful's years of struggle, like the riot day itself, were dissolving in slow and expected reversals.

Chloe of the Dancing Bears was conscious, oh too aware, that her face was disappearing.

Not, she knew, like some of the colonial faces that had the appearance of crumpled brown paper smoothed out hastily for re-use.

No. It was as if, my God, the features, made of some lardy substance, were melting away, a little bit more each time she looked in a mirror, something she rarely did these days on the wrong side of fifty. Eyes, nose, eyebrows, mouth, chin – all, all were changing, the contours altering by agonising millimetres. There was no bone, no patrician bone, to sustain that fleeting – well, not prettiness but great flower-opened-eye who-me? innocence of the flingabout years when sheer blurred roundness of cheek-curve flowed pleasantly to small chin, slim neck. Now, the curves flattened out, there was a limpness, a sparseness of structure. The hollowing cheeks were only that; the small chin a token thrust at the bottom of a face whose eyes once bluely challenging, clenched too often against sun and island gossip, were becoming vestigial.

Every time the camera trapped her, Augustine Guichet behind the click-button of her Instamatic, she could see, strongly emergent, that slightly idiotic cross-eyed look she had had in her early teens, a look that later muted to a melting blue astigmatic vagueness that wasn't cross-eyed at all, that gave off that impression of vulnerability.

This town.

Well...this *town*!

The Dancing Bears was finished.

And so was she. No longer counting in years but decades. Four of those decades since she had sway-bummed down the Boulevard d'Urville, all her clothes rammed into a buckled carry-bag ready to leave, to follow mother and father and two brothers out of town in the first windy scare after Pearl Harbor. Father's plantation at Thresher Bay, so he insisted, like those of all the other east coast planters, would be the first place taken over once the Japanese troops landed, once their wasps of planes had strafed their houses tucked into palm nests like rich egg clusters.

Everyone was getting out – on mission launches, copra boats, government motor-vessels – whatever could be boarded was taken and the boats streamed out down the Channel heading for Port Lena and the evacuation ships leaving for Australia.

Mother kept telling her they weren't running away.

'British don't run, darling,' she said.

The night before they left, Chloe had kept leafing sentimentally through the big family photo album they had decided to leave behind as a talisman, leafing despite the early moths worrying the grain of twilight to thud against the lamp and rain wing-dust on snapshots of picknicking planters, the real thing in pith helmets and whites, moustaches bristling over hampers; on greying prints of her waving from the deck of the *Tulagi* as it carried her off to a mainland school; on solemn house-girls in Mother Hubbards, that dreadful ruching and ribbons fluttering from sleeves against the shiny black flesh, making them look....well, yes....*blacker*. All under the blinking eye of the lamp. 'It is,' her father added, drawing the black-out canvas, 'what is known as a tactical retreat. In any case, the government has advised this. Civilians will only be in the way if the worst happens. We help the forces best by leaving the field clear.'

Her two brothers leaned goggle-eyed against her as she turned the pages although they had seen these crummy photos a dozen times, and placed various pointing sticky fingers on smeared snapshots of Chloe in first Communion dress standing stiffly outside the mission church at Ebuli along with six cocoa-brown communicants in white voile and veils – and again, blacker, blacker – supplied by the nuns.

There was giggling and kicking and the squashing of moths.

Father cuffed the older boy into a howl.

'Is father going to enlist when we get back?' Chloe asked. 'Monsieur Duchard, the young one, is joining the Islands' Defence Unit.'

No one replied. Father must be getting terribly old, she had decided then, to be blocked by her innocent question, though now, confronted by the gasping flesh, she realised he would have been only in his middle years.

They were stuck in Port Lena for a week in an old pub on the waterfront with nothing much to do except stare out at the islands floating in the blue and green streaked harbour and watch the residency motor-boat beetling its way each day across to the wharves. Father did a lot of drinking on the hotel terrace over the water which didn't quite reach his whisky while mother spent irritable time fussing after the boys who would keep wandering their boredom along the scrubby waterfront. There would not be a boat, a residency official assured them and three other trapped planter families, for yet another week. After this one. The eyes of the Administrative Officer, Class B, roamed interestedly over Chloe.

She kept her own eyes down.

Then, during the next few days, a fleet of American ships appeared in Meso Bay, a battle formation of aircraft carriers and cruisers and destroyers and the gadflies of landing craft. The dreamy circle of blue water was threatened and crowds of natives clustering along the sand-strip gawked, stunned, as barges grated onto shingle. It was a western takeover and within days artillery units moved to strategic points around Port Lena, batteries were established, sentry posts sprang up at town crossroads, court house and waterfront shacks were appropriated and huge teams of marines commenced building an air-strip. Planters, drinking on the terrace of the Hotel Kokonas, made grumbling noises about their crops. The departure of the evacuees was delayed another two weeks.

No one inquired how the islanders felt about all this. It was assumed they didn't.

After this, Chloe's parents found it difficult to keep track of their daughter.

There were jeep rides to lagoons, drinks at the Bar des Pêcheurs and some long hand-claspings with several smooth-faced boys from upstate New York, Maine and Connecticut. The flotilla bearing fleeing Europeans from the northern islands had trickled its last ship in days ago and the hotel was a muddle of make-shift beds on side verandahs, in dining alcoves and even the office.

Two nights before the *Tulagi* was due to take them off Chloe yielded languidly to the ardent demands of a particularly pink naval lieutenant. By the time dawn had blazed over the world-rim and the lieutenant had sneaked back to his base, Chloe, rumpled and abraded by beach sand, had made a decision.

She announced it to her parents at breakfast between the crumbling French rolls and the coffee.

'I will not be going with you.'

It was such a simple statement she could not have imagined the inverse complexity of their anger. This was moderated in the presence of interested hotel guests who had been dying of boredom. Later, in her parents' room lashed by ravings about her age (she was not yet sixteen), her family obligations and in any case the sheer impossibility of bucking colonial administration, she sat creamily content, deaf with discovery. Her parents were forced to abuse her in whispers.

'I am staying,' she insisted once more on the last morning among the bloated suitcases and cabin trunks. She seemed to have grown overnight. Her mango blonde hair electrified them. 'I have a job to go to. A job here. The Americans need office staff. If you're worried about me,' she added, 'about *that*,' – her mother winced – ' then the nurses will arrange something.'

Other planters, bemused by her clear and carrying voice, were eyeing the family across the crowded dining-room.

Her father was choking in the middle of 'it is absolutely forbid –' when Chloe solved the problem by rising gracefully and leaving the dining-room, the hotel, and lugging her suitcase to the home of a French family in Lena, people who had always disliked him and were staying on. Flummoxed by the shrillings of the *Tulagi*, their squabbling sons and the absorbed attention of fellow evacuees, her parents found there was not time to enlist residency aid. It was then or never. They departed leaving disciplinary threats and the garbled promises of action from the hotelier.

Soon, it was too late for anything to be done.

The war accelerated. The pink lieutenant from upstate New York was killed in Guadalcanal.

Not really marooned, Chloe refused the advice of the Administrative Officer, Class B whom she allowed to become, for practical reasons a quick substitute for the American. Declining a wangled passage on a transport plane to the mainland she managed, instead, to island-hop by U.S. military aircraft onto which she was smuggled by a friend of the lieutenant.

Mataso was a changed town of canvas tents and row upon row of Quonset huts, cinemas, demountable hospitals, a huge PX store, a sophisticated telephone network and radio station, torpedo and patrol boat maintenance shops, air-strips, hangars, offices, tennis courts, sportsgrounds – and where there had been no roads, roads; and where there had been no bridges, bridges. The building binge stretched from the western end of the Channel in a dense fringe of New World chewing-gum know-how almost as far up the east coast as Thresher Bay.

But more. Oh much, Chloe, more!

It was temporary home and base for one hundred thousand servicemen who passed through on their way to the blood-run islands of the north.

Chloe returned briefly to the plantation to defy the exhausted ghosts of her parents and rouse its green honeycomb with a party that drained the last of father's abandoned liquor. The photograph album was lying where she had left it on that last night. Geckoes had fouled the open pages, but she shook the detritus carefully off and in a moment of irrational sentiment took the album back with her to Mataso town.

Chloe's sea-change took a year.

She had persuaded someone, anyone, to allow her to work in an army canteen.

If the officers who used her and then rejected her or who loved her and were killed or even simply moved to another area of war, leaned the weight of their passion too heavily on her smooth blunt features, she did not show it. Her stoicism was remarkable. And then her cynicism. Believing it a folly to mingle pleasure with business, she left the canteen and bought a small house on the seaward ledge of the Boulevard d'Urville just opposite the abandoned branch of La Banque de L'Indochine, and with smuggled food gifts from admirers in the big army base opened a small café on the dawn-side of Mataso town.

It soon became more than that.

As naturally as breathing.

Two Eurasian girls helped out both in the restaurant section and the poky bedrooms that looked over the water. The business became more than they could cope with. Chloe was aware of grossness. She had to draw rank distinctions and the little house became an officers-only club which Chloe (feeling the tug of the chain) in a moment of inspired metaphor, named the Dancing Bears.

Every day, every steaming heavy-aired day or night through the next two years she could watch the ships in the Channel or the bomber squadrons that took off from strips in the hills removing her ten-minute lovers, and feel like any classic whore touting for trade. She was always a realist. She was even entertaining an army colonel when his satisfaction coincided with the hitting of a mine by a transport ship coming down Channel to the town wharves. Everything was interruped.

Perhaps that was the moment her lack of bone commenced failing her.

She was eighteen. She was eight hundred.

She had not done it for money, she kept telling herself.

She had done it for food, for rent, for good times, for clothes, for the memory of mother and father whose pale British ambience had always depleted her.

Almost as suddenly as they had come, the troops pulled out, the hundreds of conscript islanders who had laundered uniforms, cleared bush camp sites, worked with coast-watchers and loosely organised patrol forces, watched their cargo gods and cargo vanish. The bone had gone out of the whole war operation too.

Chloe was left with a customerless bordello – well, almost bordello, almost customerless. There were the planters drifting back, the hugger-mugger army of visiting post-war experts: cartographers and botanists, anthropologists and ecologists, forestry advisers, geographers, photographers (one did not count Augustine Guichet, then young and between husbands, pounding masculine and feminine genders and the causes of the French Revolution into unwilling skulls at St Pierre), geologists, historians, linguists, health inspectors, education experts, housing consultants and colonial politicians. Some of them visited the Dancing Bears – there was little else to visit – and after they had achieved their abrupt and temporary pleasures, Chloe cooked for them, something she did even better. Her whole enterprise teetered between respectability and bawdry. On a holiday in Sydney she married a chef whom she took back to Mataso where he cooked, drank, shouted, bounced the last would-be carnal visitors, showed her three splendid ways of cooking reef fish and left.

After the town died when the flush of post-war enthusiasm for those strategically needed but nuisance outposts of empire faded, and after the decades melted, turning to water in summer after summer, she was simply Chloe Dancing Bears whom all Mataso town knew, whom some of the planters spoke to – usually the French who had a tolerance of what they called the genial sins – and who was cut dead by British wives fed on the long tentacles of legend. Before the final collapse of the flesh there was a second husband, a trawler operator until a Taiwanese boat rammed him off Emba. And there was a lover or two.

Could you call them that?

Chloe scratched a living from a little this, a little that, the café, an occasional land deal, the whoring gone now, *long wé, long wé*, abandoned entirely as a present to herself the year she turned thirty – not that there was much to abandon and not that it was whoring really, just a sad flutter with lonely men who stopped at the Mataso Hotel while they filled in their temporary duty service and their reports in triplicate. A kindness you could call it. And there was a pension of sorts some guilty aging American had arranged coming regular as clockwork until a year back, was it? two?

The mind was falling off the bone, as well.

She could suck at memory and it skidded like mango seed.

Augustine Guichet handled time with more aplomb.

'They do not understand, these newcomers,' she would say to Chloe sipping coffee on the little Channel verandah of the Dancing Bears, 'that they must allow the island to devour them. They try to eat it. That is their mistake.'

The two women knew they would never leave.

'I am almost fully digested,' Madame Guichet would say. 'I await the total absorption.'

So when on that heat-sullen morning of distant and fogged

explosion, of rifle fire and shouts and later the surge of rebels and sympathiser *colons* along the Boulevard, she heard a frantic beating on the seaward door, her heart paused momentarily with dreadful enquiry.

Was this to be the moment of supreme subsumption?

All her shutters were drawn. She had sat within the sea-light of her shell of a house, warned only yesterday by the most diffident of ni-Kristi – the soft knock on the door, the smiling black face, Pardon, *madame*, tomorrow we make protest march. Tomorrow there will be revolution. You should stay inside inside – aligning that moment with the endurance of an hour past when, between the yells and the random crack of rifles, her walls had shrunk from bashings and a din of obscenities: *wanem ples blong puspus? Oué! Wanem ples blong puspus?*

Not here, she thought. No place now for a fuck. Only a joke, she consoled herself. Oh the winding lengths of oral tradition! The thought stopped her fright even as the voices moved away leaving her to be only Chloe Dancing Bears, a dusty poke-hole for drip-dry trippers off the tour ships, brought to her little café by shreds of rumour, colour hunters sadder than herself.

But now this knocking. Its persistence fluttered. A voice filled in the diffidence of the beat.

'Anyone there? Please? Please? Is anyone there?'

Chloe drew back the bolt and opened the door to peer through the screen at Letty Trumble still clutching portions of shopping-bag, her hat clownish over a dust-striped face. One of her knees bled quietly through a dangling hem. There was an apologetic blink and her mouthing seemed to transmit words too early or too late for the muscles, like a bad dubbing.

Chloe found herself encompassed with memories.

Here was a mendicant who had waged border war on the Dancing Bears with velvet innuendo, snub, parochial blacklisting. How long since the Bears danced? Twenty years? Oh certainly that. Certainly long before Letty Trumble had set neat sandalled foot on Kristi. Was it merely the folklore analects of those lasciviously slow threshings while the sea rocked at the end of her garden that so agitated Dr Trumble's wife? That buckled the Dali shopping-bag? That befouled the dress and skewed the hat?

Chloe was arrested on this crest of payback for a decade of tacit insult. As if bone were once more asserting itself, she felt her face harden. Yet – accept, accept, she could hear Augustine Guichet advise, filled with tiddly wisdom. Submission is easier. The triumph is in that.

As the other woman's wretchedness seeped about her, as the insignificance of her enmity became the flaw in Chloe herself, she opened the door wide. She could take the movement no further. Chloe drew in her breath hard and then slowly let it out into the gasp of the morning.

'Quickly,' she urged, stepping back into her exhausted kitchen, conscious of the bedrooms, the pleasure domes, opening out their minuscule spaces from the narrow hallway behind. She felt she must resort to platitudes, spread like a volcano crust to soothe Letty Trumble's sobbed explanations with treacherous phrases.

'They're still savages, my dear' – (*my dear!*) – 'when it all comes down. My father' – (now who was he?) the words had come automatically – 'swore nothing would make any difference, not missions, not schools. And he knew. He knew the islands like his face in the mirror.' She didn't believe a word of it.

Her surprise stopped her.

That prim moustached assurance that must have gazed back at him from the shaving glass! His fleshy face and phanton twin both without depth. Not for thirty years had she mentioned him, perhaps even thought of him. For the duty letters she had written early on dear mother and father to somewhere in England had spaced themselves into cards at Christmas and birthdays and finally trickled into silence. On both sides. The plantation had been sold, she heard, and whether the blood-strangers of the mould-spotted album, parents and brothers in their roistering shorts, were alive or dead she did not know, seeing them permanently settled at a cantankerous forty and sub-teens, the sun bouncing off a jelly blue sea onto the verandah of the plantation house, father trapped in mid-shout as he roared at a house-boy, her mother purse-lipped behind a table set with 4 o'clock snorters and translated into an unblitzed Kensington houselet with her brothers forever in preparatory school.

This day, this sagging boneless day, she could have cried for the loss of all those sun-fired years surging up from her gut.

Locked in, in the little back room, they could only contemplate each other, across deserts.

'Try crying,' she suggested to Letty Trumble crumpled in a rattan chair. 'I mean with anger.'

Letty was too bleared with disaster.

'They attacked me,' she kept protesting. 'Me. And I've been so kind. And Jim. Always concerned. The groceries. Everywhere. I left them.'

Chloe allowed her to ramble. Her own eyes were glued to the trickle of blood that was making a lacy pattern down the front of Letty Trumble's legs.

'There was no where else I could come.'

Chloe kept staring at the rosy lace.

'I am truly glad,' she couldn't stop herself saying, 'to be of some use after all these years.'

Letty Trumble remained deaf. 'They were screaming at me, screaming, when I came round the back of Bipi. Daniel had lent me his bicycle. Yelling. Screaming filth. There was a stall for emergency supplies and the rest of the place was barred because of the looting down at Fong's. There was glass everywhere, more and more glass, and – '

'But what were they yelling?' Chloe was certain the insult would make them sisters.

The other woman's mouth twisted horribly as if there were an unclean taste. She challenged Chloe's eyes.

'They called me a whore. White whore. Dirty white whore. Give me a drink,' she demanded.

Chloe smoothed her satisfaction across her thinning scalp.

She had to turn her laughter away.

'There's only a little brandy. Will that do?'

But Letty was drowning in herself. 'They kept yelling that as they dragged on the bike, coming right up into my face and screeching. White whore. On and on. I spat at them. I couldn't help it. I spat. And then they started pushing and shoving and the bicycle was grabbed and banged up and down up and down against the awning posts and I tried to fight them for it. I kept hitting and hitting but they didn't hit back. Just kept laughing at me and I tripped and fell over and then one of the police came up, the rebel police, and he stopped them. Someone stopped them. I don't know. And then he told me to get indoors before he arrested me I was so stupid to be out after all the warnings.'

'Here.' Chloe set the brandy down in front of Letty Trumble and watched the nervous hands, too white, too veined, shake as they clutched the glass. 'They called me that too,' she said. 'It doesn't matter, you know. It's just a word. It doesn't mean much to them except a – a one-sound explosion of air.'

Letty Trumble could not look up at that moment. She gulped the drink in one burning slash at her own throat.

Chloe assessed her resentment at the linkage and savoured it. She would not utter defences, explain that whoring had been over and done with long before, rip down that lewd tapestry that a brief twelve years nearly three decades gone had swaddled her in.

'We're all whores,' she said, 'of a sort. Whatever you like. Living is whoring. Just living. It's taken me years to see that.'

Mrs Trumble, the brandy down, this melting elderly and logical woman before her, still felt as if she were seated on the feather-down edge of some voluptuous bed with the ghosts, the echoes of orgastic cries misting the mirrors, the pink quilts, the silk, the wanton spread-legged dolls lolling on chairs in a bordello of the mind; yet here she was, her feet on cracked linoleum under the grocery caddies labelled *thé, sucre, farine*, an appallingly humble gas-burner stove and a hallway at her back that led to four other rooms whose open doors, she knew, kept nothing to speculate on but dust, sunlight and old furniture.

She looked down at her torn skirt, her torn knees. The blood was staining the straps of her sandals.

Then she cried, gulpingly and long.

Chloe was practical if not warm, her warmth diminished by too many years of lack. She heated water, fetched disinfectant and strapped up the bony knees and hands while tears fell on her head. Inwardly she scoffed at her Magdalene. Between the gulps, she managed to discover more. What had happened to the doctor? The boy? They were hostages, Letty presumed. A jeep had driven them off to Talasa Pati headquarters, Dannie Ching at Bipi told her. He had seen the jeep going past, a hedge of rifles and arrows and the doctor sitting very straight, one arm about his son's shoulders. A quick film clip.

Letty didn't know what to do now.

'There is nothing to do,' Chloe said, 'but wait. It will be all over once they know in Lena. We only have to wait. With each other.'

She had to smile at it.

Letty Trumble was a guest at the Dancing Bears.

Confronted by sombre reasoning and a woman whose face retained mere flickerings of the prettiness that had been her legend, the meretricious glamour, the nonsense thinking all began to dissipate in the confidence of brandy, the bite of iodine, the firm grip of bandage. What Letty Trumble was beginning to see was another woman like herself, netted in this Pacific backwater and only licked at by memories of tides that now were all at the neap. Or low water. Even that.

She had her own guilty memories. The house, the bedrooms, the woman opposite, all started them like birds: some twilit beach party at Thresher Bay in the dark apses of the buttressed *nabangura* trees, she had once been crushed most willingly against the body of a sodden planter from Port Ebuli and wanted it; or swimming naked, Kendrick guiding her, in a sheltered pool at the Bay of the Two Saints; and then that time in Port Lena when she had gone down to shop – to escape really – for a few days and there had been that bushy American biologist with an interest in snails. She didn't think of that time if she could help it, his hot room at the Hotel Kokonas with the fans going and the bed rocking and the clear-eyed look she had to practise for Jim and the winking of a cheap-stoned signet ring the snail man had worn on his little finger that interrupted the clarity of her domestic eye.

Perhaps this woman with the face made ordinary by time, the myth removed as she sat flanked by strip plaster and disinfectant, was right: we are all whores. There is only that fragile differential. And the men as well. Whores. Or worse than that. Her nose was assailed suddenly by the dusty smell of brown flesh and the mouths opening and closing on their tongues, teeth; the shock of the pink.

'Do you mind,' she asked, 'if I stay?' The word 'please' occurred to her. She added it.

Chloe interpreted the hiatus and wanted to bawl out her

resentment. Oh the screechings she could vent in this box of drab memories she was trapped in beside the Channel. She could never leave. For where, anyway? It was a struggle to climb over the crest of each year on a scrap income that made her the most permanent of foreigners. She was sustained only by an out-of-place and obstinate dignity and Augustine Guichet's bottle cynicism.

Letty Trumble and Chloe Dancing Bears were looking cautiously into each other's eyes, blue into blue. Outside wind gnawed at a broken shutter and the dry clicks and rappings framed a moment so ordinary that Letty swayed with a surge of lascivious curiosity that rose like confessional bile.

'Tell me,' she begged, leaning forward across the table and surprising the other woman. 'As we are all whores, tell me.'

Chloe knew the surprise dance like fireflies down the dark of her spirit. She gripped the brandy bottle and refilled their glasses.

'If,' she insisted with impudent perception, 'you tell me.'

Emba swam in silence.

On riot morning as the heat swag dropped over the island, Gavi Salway rose in the sticky dawn and went out from his room and crossed the cracked tar tennis court, cut through the hibiscus hedge and reached the boy house.

It was empty.

He moved, calling softly, between the bunks of the long room, pretending there was nothing amiss and came out to the front of the buildings from where he could see two miles across the Channel to Mataso town. The water was wrinkled like canvas, was canvas colour, glimpsed between the trees along the waterfront. He ran across the lawn to the Channel bank, a potch of red from the breeze-falls of flamboyants.

It would be an hour before Kenasi heaved his frame from bed, an hour before maman began setting the coffee to simmer. He crept back across the lawn to his room at the northern end of the house, grabbed the airlines bag he used for school books, closed his moaning door and went out again, this time along the coral path between the crotons, past the cocoa drying sheds to the concrete walkway Kensasi had never quite finished and down the scrambling slope to the jetty.

The runabout was still there, smacking against the piles in sea-sweep. He wondered how the boys had got away – had they taken a boat from the next plantation along the bay? Then he forgot about them, stumbling on the uneven logs of the landing, hauling the dinghy in to the steps.

The roar of the motor shuddered along the foreshore. He could feel it ripping family dreams.

Stubbornly he steered across the current, not turning until he was a hundred yards out, the boat dipping and bouncing in tide run. The island still lay asleep. Nothing moved on the jetty, the beach-strip, on the path beside the cocoa sheds and the burnt-out smokehouse. No curiosity peered between fringing trees though he was conscious of eyes.

He swung the tiller, bringing the nose of the boat into line with the shallow landing spot near St Pierre, enlarging, shining whitely in the early sun. The boat cut through the canvas water as if it were silk, a slash of silver widening behind. The whole world was a pearl. Today it was being forced open.

After beaching the boat, the boy slung his book-bag across one shoulder and headed up to the Channel Road and the lawned slopes of the school. The gardens were empty except for the tubby figure of Leyroud walking between chapel and priest house. In the chapel turret the coloured glass lozenges flagged light over the poison fish trees, red, yellow, blue, and the doors stood open on a smell of dying candles and the stuffiness of hymns.

He began to run across the garden, trying to catch up with the priest before he went inside. There were distant and isolated sounds from the dormitory block at the far end of the grounds, but no sign of staff or students.

Leyroud turned to the thud of Gavi's feet. His hand held the knob of the priest house door questioningly.

'*Jour férié!*' he joked. 'There's no school today. You knew, didn't you?'

The boy was panting slightly. 'I knew. That's why I came.'

Leyroud raised his eyebrows in a mixture of censure and surprise.

'I mean,' the boy went on, '*we're* safe.'

Père Leyroud took the retort like a sting on the end of his tongue. The Christ had rested there ten minutes before and the taste of God held him silent.

His silence made the boy flounder. 'I mean,' Gavi was saying, 'we're on their side, aren't we?'

'What are you talking about?' Leyroud asked, forcing him.

'The revolution of course.' Gavi was impatient.

'It's too complex,' Père Leyroud said at last. He had just offered Mass for the peaceful progress of this day. 'Far too complex for a simple man like me.'

Heat was crawling under his soutane. He wanted his breakfast.

'But it's their country, isn't it? Not France's. Not Britain's. It's theirs. They were here first, weren't they? They didn't ask to be colonised.'

Gavi could hear the shameful simplicity of his words.

'They didn't ask for God, either,' Père Leyroud said. 'Not my sort of God. But I came. I offered it to them.'

'You mean you didn't have the right?'

Leyroud's hand gripped the door-handle a little more firmly and began to turn, to open, to push. 'Oh that's hard. That's hard, now.' His round face quivered above his comic white beard fringe. Forty lost years, he marvelled. The heat. The other islands. The heat. The trudging journeys in rain along beaches, shoving self-banishment in front of him, castaway for God. The stagger of jungle slopes. The unwelcoming villages. He had consoled himself over the years that he was merely giving and not taking. But he had taken – or tried to take. He had removed their gods and replaced with his own. He had tried to take their customs and their convictions and substitute others. Ram them gracelessly into the doubting faces. And always the heat. 'By my standards,' he said limply, 'my conscience, perhaps, I had the right. But by theirs? Well, who knows. You know,' he added, 'no one has ever put it quite like that to me before. Oh I have to myself. Yes. To myself.' His face broke into a smile. 'And I'm here chopping logic with you *petit polisson*. Would you – '

'Oh don't try to put me off,' Gavi protested, 'with a – a bit of a joke.'

'What would you like then?' Leyroud asked. 'I haven't had my breakfast yet. Would you like to go down to the dining-hall and tell Sœur Marie des Anges she's to add you to the boarders? Or would you care to join me?'

'Oh with you, of course. It was you I came to see.' The boy kicked, childishly, one sandalled foot into the turf and hitched his satchel higher. 'It's hardest of all for me.'

'What is? What's hardest?'

'Us. The family. Kenasi's British. Maman's French. Well, you know, Father, she isn't really that.' He reddened. 'Half and half. *Hapkas*. That means I'm native too.'

'Come along,' Père Leyroud said briskly. 'I need my coffee. Sœur Marie couldn't handle adolescent identity crises this morning. She has her hands full with Fidel Vuma who has been doing some quite

93

foolish things. *Bêtises. Quelles bêtises.* It is time we had a talk.'

How sharply, Leyroud thought, as he ushered the boy ahead into the shadowed parlour – the four chairs, the crucifix, the highly tinted Virgin gazing across the room at the Sacré Cœur as it bled to death – was he aware of alienation, remembering his first years in the field at this place and then that, forty, well nearly fifty years since his world at twenty-five had swung from Toronto sidewalks and the scent of coffee over snow to leaf-drench, the blaze of heat rash, the insistence of blue water. There was that: the background.

But there was more, oh far more, difficulty in it all: the understanding of a rigidly graded society, the *nimangki*; and more difficult still, the clash of custom rites – the diametrics of the slow, the musical, the expected rhythms of the Mass with its mild and ter-rible sacrifice and the Naleng dances, another sort of Mass, perhaps, when the men, their bodies slippery with coconut and *nangi* oil from sea almonds, their faces streaked in blues and reds from wood dyes and ash, the white the most terrifying daubing of all, stamped and chanted in their feathered head-dresses, flowers and fern fronds stuck in their dense hair, the hollow nut anklets jingling across the *nasara*, the tempo irresistibly speeding, rising by quarter tones, even in him, the consecrated Père Leyroud, as great hunks of woody sound were beaten from the slit drums. On. On. The feet faster, the whirl of bodies, arms, ceremonial flower trailers. And into this final fury (oh how place 'for this is my body' against this?) exploding into the sacrifice of the pigs, the blood and the squeals, their great circled tusks like hollowed Hosts. He remembered, too, how that analogy had clouted him in the greasy and sliding light of the cane-grass torches and his horror of blasphemy as the first pig was clubbed to death.

He understood now. He thought he understood.

The *yeremanu*, the big men, were no different in their ritual ceremonies from the college of cardinals. He felt he had his equations right at seventy-five, sweetened and dried out like copra itself by the never ending sweet and drying sun. The striving or yearning of all men towards the godhead boiled down to a set of time-strained parallels and the Satan figure of his own dark places was the stone *lesevsev* which blocked the way to the afterlife.

He looked at this boy sitting awkwardly on the rim of the kitchen

chair and knew him in his youthfulness aware only of differentia-
tion. Later, he would understand the sameness of things. How the
boy watched his gone-away eyes!

He put the coffee on to heat, set out cups and sugar and rubbed
domesticities off on his soutane.

'Another sort of Mass,' he joked, full of parallels.

'Father?'

'A joke. Just a joke. *Je blague!* You know that.'

'Look, Father,' the boy said, almost indignant, 'I'm sorry, but I
don't feel much like joking. Mr Bonser says Tommy Narota is right.
He says – '

'I think I know what he would say.' Slow sips at the too hot
coffee. 'Do you know Bonser well?'

'Of course I know him. He says – '

'Does your grandfather know you know?'

'Of course he knows. We all know each other here.'

'*Eh bien*, that's true enough,' Père Leyroud said. 'But how well?
That's another matter, *n'est-ce pas?*'

'I don't talk about him at home. What he says, that is.'

Père Leyroud smiled. 'I shouldn't imagine you would. Indeed, I
cannot imagine it. You know he has a bad name as a trouble-maker,
don't you? With the French planters, with the islanders and with –'
he hesitated '– their women? You know all that? You know, I
suppose, he's a gun-runner? You know he's hired a mercenary, a no-
hoper no-character from Algiers or the Sudan or whatever to train
the rebels at Vimape? You know that?'

His eyes bored into Gavi's over the rim of his cup.

'And you know, don't you, my son, that when the time comes,
when this is all over as it will be over and the little waves lap again
and the government down at Lena makes its reckoning, draws up its
accounts, say, then you know, don't you, that Bonser and *le
gendarme fou* and all the planters and townsfolk who have been
anti-government will get their marching orders. Oh they'll be out in
days. Hours. No matter how good they are or how bad. Even people
like Lorimer who's been known to be sympathetic, all those letters
he wrote to the *Jeune Kristi* paper and so on – out. Oh yes. It will be
just like that. Out.'

Gavi looked beyond this crazy soutane with the doom-nag to the mango trees in the yard. He'd swarmed all over them as a small boy, stolen the fruit. Père Leyroud had heard his first Confession and given him his first Communion and had watched him, for the last year since he had come down from the *école préparatoire* at Ste Cécile. He's old, Gavi thought contemptuously, older even than Kenasi. Older and more set in his beliefs. He doesn't want anything that could alter the way things are, white custom. Père Leyroud had caned him once, for cheating in an exam, not a big cheat, just copying an answer from the boy next to him which was wrong anyway. And not a big caning either. Six ironic taps that made his palm barely tingle.

'I am not caning you,' Père Leyroud had said, running one hand down the length of light bamboo, 'for what you have done. We all cheat, one way or another. All of us. I'm not the one to judge. But ' – and here he commenced tapping on Gavi's outstretched palm – ' I'm spelling out the word *vérité* for you: *v–é–r–i–t–é*. Truth.'

And Gavi had never forgotten.

'If I'd punished you in English,' Père Leyroud said when it was over, 'it would have been one stroke less. Do you mind?'

It was the humiliation of those non-strokes.

The boy said, 'My French needs improving, Father,' wanting to cry with the shame and the kindness of it.

'*You wan seki fala!*' Père Leyroud said with a laugh. 'Go in peace.'

Gavi looked back from the mango tree and set his coffee cup down heavily on the scrubbed table and asked, 'Please, Father, what really is the truth of all this? Kenasi tries to keep out of it. Maman believes in *man ples*. She says she believes most of the land should go back to custom owners. She believes this. Then what happens to us, to Kenasi? Kenasi asks her that and maman gets angry. Then he says "sit still a little. Sit still." He means for her to be patient. But she says that the government in Lena is wrong for us all the way up here. They don't care about us. They can't know. They're different, maman says. Different customs, different language.'

'Not very,' Leyroud said thoughtfully. 'More coffee, Gavi?' The boy shook his head, not really hearing. 'We're all too much the same, I've come to realise. At last.'

'Except for me,' the boy retorted bitterly. 'And maman. *You* must know about maman even if she does kid herself she's French. You must know.'

'I know. It makes no difference. No ultimate difference.'

'Don't you believe it!' the boy cried rudely.

'I insist,' the other replied gently. 'We're all the same.'

'Except for Bonser. You said that yourself.'

'Ah well, I was wrong then. Not even he.'

Gavi's eyes glittered with confessions. He wanted to shake this complacency. He said, 'I've helped him. I helped him take the guns to Vimape.' There. It was out.

Leyroud's gentle old experienced face seemed stuck on shock. After years of the confessional – shock.

'You've what?'

'I've helped. With the guns. I went up there on his truck one day last month.'

'And did you realise what he was doing? Did you?' The priest was grave, his smile lost somewhere. 'Guns kill. You know that. You do know that, don't you? I'm beginning to think, boy, you don't know too much at all. Holy Mother, Gavi, what got into you? What were you thinking of?'

The boy became angry and sullen at once.

'It's no good talking to you, is it? I thought you'd understand. I wanted to help. I wanted to help Narota. He's a good man. He wants to help Kristi.'

'He's a good man, right enough,' Leyroud agreed. 'Simple, perhaps. A bit misled. A prey for people more cunning than he will ever be. But he has been manipulated, manipulated as you have. Can't you see? How did this happen? Or don't you want to tell me that?'

Gavi shook his head.

'Well, then, does your grandfather know about this, eh?'

'No.'

'I think you should tell him.'

Leyroud inspected the half-man half-child face in front of him, a face at that indeterminate stage with the first smudging of down on the upper lip, the lank growing hairs about the cheeks as if the Ash Wednesday sign had run amok. And there was growth he hadn't been aware of before, a toughening in the shoulder and neck muscles.

'There will be,' he added, 'others who will. You can be sure in a place as small as this, that others will know. Know and talk. Officials will know by now. Gavi, you have been so stupid.'

Abruptly the boy shoved his chair back and stood up. His face darkened and his mouth gaped on words he knew would damage. Yet his throat caught on them and Leyroud came round the table, trying to take his arm. Gavi flung away.

'Don't say it,' Leyroud advised mildly. 'Don't say it. Not what you're going to say. I'm your friend, remember. I'm trying to help. You can't see this, but I am.'

'Words!' Gavi heard his ungraciousness hurtle out in the little kitchen. 'Words. All my life, words words words words words. There's a reason I did it. I don't want to tell you. But there's a reason more than all the words!'

Leyroud tugged his soutane straight, flapping the heat from under his skirts, touched the crucifix on his breast briefly and walked away towards the door. Automatically the boy followed him. As we all follow, Leyroud knew, something or other. *Samting. Olting.* He thought of Tommy Narota, a boy like this boy, when he first came over from Buala, a *hapkas* walkout from the Presbyterian mission. They had done nothing for him, those verticals of the Lord, except give him a smattering of English and an expectant interest in the parable of the loaves and fishes. They had certainly not given him conviction either in Christian principles or British colonialism, for after the Americans went and the cargo failed to come, Tommy had begun his own strange cult in the gardens of Vimape, a cult that drew its bits and pieces from half-absorbed Christian ideology and island myth.

Leyroud had always liked him, remembering the conscientious gardener and caretaker who had slept with his pile of digests in the workman's shed at the mission. 'We are,' he would joke with Tommy when they met in Mataso town, 'soul brothers.' Tommy would laugh, raising two brown hands in his own form of blessing that left Leyroud amused and humbled. 'You've brought something from Buala then.'

They had their private joke. 'Bible bible sing sing,' Narota would reply with a grin. 'No more.' And he would laugh and laugh.

Leyroud savoured, too, the tales that drifted after Narota like expanding clouds. There was the story from his fishing boat days, of his ramshackle craft packed with paying anglers from Lena splitting down the middle and Narota, diving overboard with a rope, had lashed the two halves together under the stink of holiday terror, and brought the crippled thing into port tied with a fancy bow and a lot of laughter. There was his quasi-apostleship for the Lord, the Royal Co-operative Ch' ch of Kristi, with its headquarters at Vimape, built with native labour and money from the Salamander Corporation. There was the beginning of a monthly broadsheet, *Jeune Kristi*, that cried for secession and a return to custom. Custom and tolerance, Leyroud recalled, and the guidance of dreams. No different from us, from me, he admitted to himself as he walked out of his priest house into the garden. No different. *Man solwata* believed and *man bush* followed and the charisma grew and opened wide like frangipani flower.

'It is Narota, isn't it,' Leyroud stated more than asked.

Gavi turned under the sun and word-whack, letting his satchel dangle as if the heat had affected it too. The waters of the Channel had discovered the sky's blue in full sun and the crumpled silver broke all along the current pulse.

'Yes,' he admitted. 'Oh yes. He's my *yeremanu*.'

'I see,' Père Leyroud said mildly. 'You've become a disciple.' He had hoped the boy might laugh and was surprised by the sudden rage.

'What's wrong with that?' Gavi was shouting. 'Don't make fun of me. Or him. What's wrong with his ideas? He's going to turn this place into something.'

'He's a puppet,' Leyroud said abruptly. '*Une marionette pour un gouvernement fantoche.* A charming puppet. But a puppet. And I do know him *well*. I've known him since he wasn't much older than you, *gars*. He used to work for me in this very garden. And he was always biddable. Forgive me. But he was. I've watched him led by the nose so often.'

'Because *you* couldn't lead him. You're angry because of that.'

'By a Christian nose, you mean? Oh I've learnt a lot more tolerance than that. I mean by the minions of the Salamander group, by the *colons*. Oh how those Yankee entrepreneurs sliced up the custom land round Ebuli. Didn't you know that? Narota knew. They'd promised him the world. They were fooling him. You'd have had Americans here as well as British and French. The whole island would have been hamburger if Lena hadn't stepped in.'

The boy refused to listen.

'That was nothing to do with him.'

'But it was. He didn't know how far the thing was going. They told him, those Yankee lawyers, that it would have been good for Kristi. Good! Oh the poor Kristians! They'd have lost their country forever. But they fed him money and the French fed him money. Mafia money, the story goes. Did you know all that?'

'Well,' Gavi said, and he couldn't keep the satisfaction from his voice, the yah-yah child in him, 'it's too late now. The whole thing's blown up.'

'In the way of things here.' Père Leyroud, too, looked out across the water glare, uncomfortable in his sweating cassock; and the patch of rash he had carried on his breast bone like a stigmatum ever since he had come to these parts began its devilish itch. He rubbed reflectively with his thumb knuckle.

At the far end of the grounds a couple of the boarders had come from the refectory and were chucking a soccer ball about. Along the road below the school grounds a straggle of islanders was walking in to Mataso town.

Leyroud's eyes moved from the players to the marchers and came to rest on Gavi.

'I don't have to tell you,' he said, 'but you should stay. You know you must stay.'

The boy's answer was to run, run across the lawns, down the slope and out on to the Channel Road, following the marchers. Leyroud's cries fluttered uselessly after him, in his old man's cracked voice. The itch began to dominate everything. He rubbed and rubbed at this irritation near his heart, watching the small, getting smaller running figure.

'He's lost,' Leyroud said to himself.

It would be, he knew, the first of many such losings.

R-day, says Bonser, locking the big doors of his workshed as a matter of form, though he knew, had been assured over and over by Mango Wilson, the radio freak who had been manning the rebel government transmissions, that Talasa Pati supporters' property was safe. Why, jesusgod, late last night even, right on the verge of it, that crazy bastard Leblanc had driven down from Vimape with a warning. The silly sod didn't seem to know that all the day before half the town had been door-knocked by scraggy black youth politely warning, 'There will be revolution in morning.' Christ! What a place! *There will be revolution in morning.* But Leblanc loved the excitement of it, one of nature's mercenaries, silly bugger, playing cloaks and daggers after midnight and hauling him off the nest. Wearing his damn military outfit, too, fat handgun stuck in his belt, army beret a-cock. Shit. I don't want to be involved, he'd told him. Not visibly. There's Angie to consider. I'm with you, mate, he had insisted, 100 bloody per cent but I am not visible. Repeat. *Not visible.* There were a hundred ways, he had told him, he could help without being seen to do it.

Stuff it, he thought, as he rammed the big bolt home.

He went over to his workbench and shoved a clutter of spark plugs to one side. The fluoro turned him blue. That shyster's only here for the big hit, for what he can make. And then he's off. His bacon isn't on the line. He's a blow in. The dust settles, he'll blow right out. Big noise from Algiers? Morocco? Port Said? Not like us. Not like Angie and me who sweat our lives out here.

Christ, he said, I even love the old place.

He began working on the generator motor that old Lorimer had brought down last month from the delta.

He was behind on everything lately what with frigging around with Narota and his crowd. And this generator was a challenge. Lorimer had written it off, poor old coot. He tickled the nipple of the grease gun delicately and deftly. The light blaze over the bench threw a great shadow obliquely back along the concrete floor. A tough, confident boyo, he hummed while he worked. On a shelf to his right the radio hiccupped its way to the end of a rock screamer and then Mango's voice dressed in phoney vowels came on with a news bulletin. God, Bonser said aloud, what's he think he is? BBC Battle of Britain stuff?

'. . . ish Paddock has now been taken.' The trombone voice echoed in the tin and concrete hollow of the shed. 'Hostages have been taken to Talasa Pati headquarters and later this afternoon, the island can expect a statement from the interim president, Mr Tommy Narota. At present all business houses are closed and residents are advised to remain indoors. The Nabiru government in Port Lena has announced a blockade. There will be no transport planes flying into Kristi. The telephone service has been cut. It is not known how long this state of affairs will continue but the government of Mr Willie Lemoa in Port Lena has indicated that its attitude is hardening and there will be no relaxation of the blockade until the rebel leaders surrender.'

'That's telling 'em!' Bonser smirked over the grease gun while Wilson repeated the message in French and Seaspeak.

He worked steadily at the bench, ignoring Wilson's switch to disc jockese hey hey hey man they can starve us man they can play no tok tok but man they can't beat us until the murky air in the workshed recoiled from the battering of electronic guitars and amplified drums. 'Can't give you anything but love' came the ironic scream and –

'Christ!' Bonser breathed. He reached across and flicked the radio off, put his grease gun away and wiped his hands off on a bit of waste.

Out on the Boulevard d'Urville he hung round lounging with hands dug into his shorts' pockets, watching the crowd gumming up towards the Magasin Lantane, a bunch of rebel soldiers coming in from Rue Dumont and a cluster of school-kids trailing them. Lemmy waved, a large square wave, and the kids giggled and waved back and one of the soldiers waggled his rifle comically. Bonser raised his hands above his head, then, in an 'I'm scared' gesture, bending his enormous knees and shaking them so that everyone went into fits. All down the length of the Boulevard there wasn't another European to be seen.

Well, one.

He strolled uptown, drawing closer to Mataso Park. *Man bush*, hundreds of them, were milling outside the closed shop-fronts, idly whacking at glass or parked cars, a lethargic sort of attack now the first gesture had been made. A few heaved rocks against the cyclone shutters but without much interest; and at the far end of the block, just before the Boulevard swung off to the wharves, he could see a mob of young boys, school-kids really, giving Misis Dokta Trumble a bit of hell.

He turned away at once. Silly cow, he thought. It wasn't as if she hadn't been warned. He saw her shopping-bag sail through the air and splatter on the road. There was a lot of shouting and the semaphore of thin white arms before she dipped from sight while he sauntered back past his workshop to the house fifty yards beyond, jaunty with guilt, straight into young Salway loping at a pant-trot along the road edge, shirt open and flapping.

The boy might have passed him in the heat daze, head down, eyes clipped to the feet jogging him on, running on perplexity and anger.

Bonser reached out and caught at one jerking shoulder.

'Where to?' There was a bantering note to Bonser's voice but if there were mockery, the boy missed it, standing gasping, blinking against sun, dragging a wiper-hand across salt-stinging eyes.

'You look bushed, mate,' Bonser said. 'Don't go on into town. There's a spot of trouble. Wait till things have cooled off, eh?'

The boy mumbled something, shook his head against the image of Bonser's amused and meaty face.

In their back sitting-room he gradually caught up with his breathing, absorbing air as well as concern from Bonser's wife, a tall strong woman whose whole body strained to mother something, perhaps the rifle that shared the lounger with her near the door or a triple scotch.

'It wasn't too bad downtown,' Bonser replied to his wife's arched eyebrows. He was busy at the refrigerator trapping beer. 'Not as bad as it might have been. They were giving Letty Trumble a bit of hurry-up but I thought it best not to interfere. She can usually hold her own against anything. Policy of stricly *laisser-faire*, eh?'

His wife regarded him coolly and said nothing. His mouth was creamed with beer scum. She didn't feel one way or the other about Letty Trumble but she did like to believe she had a hero husband. She lit a cigarette and ran one hand along the stock of the gun almost amorously.

'And there's no need for that thing either.' Her husband glared at the rifle, prickly with guilt again. 'Leblanc gave me his word we'd be okay. Anyway, there won't be any violence. Not physical violence. Narota's against the whole idea of it.' Poor sap, he added mentally and found his eyes flickering to the boy who was watching them both. Too sharply, he imagined. Too aware. 'And what about you, son?' He forced the jocularity out. 'No school? Come to see a bit of history in the making? They used to call it fieldwork in my day.'

The boy was sick with confusion. All the way in, the long terrible pad into Mataso town, he'd reheard Père Leyroud's words with every thud of his feet. He knew what he believed. Oh he knew that all right. But the guns. He couldn't take his eyes off the rifle. What if Leyroud was right? He thought of Kenasi and maman stuck over there on the island and felt his stomach lurch.

At Bonser's question, his hands began to shake. He put the glass down and hid his hands under the table edge.

Shark-eyed Bonser was aware.

'Okay. Out with it. Something's biting you.'

'It's Kenasi,' the boy said at last. 'Grandfather. Him.' He looked from one to the other. 'He's been against this thing from the start.'

'I wouldn't worry too much,' Lemmy Bonser said going back to the refrigerator for seconds. 'Nothing much will happen on Emba.'

The muscle knot in Gavi's throat seemed to have a life of its own, jerking away with the Bonsers watching. His face quivered. His mouth had become unsure. If only Bonser wouldn't gawk so hard, so close. The boy opened his mouth to speak then closed it. The eyes wouldn't look away.

'Père Leyroud said . . . ' he managed and fell silent.

They were silent with him.

Gavi pulled a little face and plunged.

'I've told Leyroud. I've told him about the guns.'

Bonser's eyes widened for a moment, an unbelieving speckled light.

He had to put his glass down. In the silence Gavi heard his own heart drum.

There was a spate of words, then, violent and shouted. Bonser's face was so deformed by fury, Gavi could not bear to look up, hearing only the shape whizz of anger as it beat all about him.

Angie Bonser tried to intervene and her husband swung on her his mouth still chopping at insult. But it braked him. She kept on, driven by the scared face of the kid. Bonser said to her slowly, a deadly quality to the lurch of his body. 'Shut up.' He said it again spacing his words. 'Just shut up.' His voice grew softer, sour with threat, as he turned back. 'You listen to me, do you hear? I thought, fool that I was, that you were a man ready for a man's job. You're nothing but a stupid whining kid with your brains in your bum. Look, you can dob yourself in all you like with your salvation bringers. But not me. *Not me.* Don't you understand anything? Old Papa Leyroud was right when he told you there'd be repercussions. He did tell you that, didn't he? He's not really French. Canadian French and that doesn't bloody count, mate. Anyway, he's safe in the arms of Jesus. Nothing's going to touch him. He's kept his consecrated nose clean like his pal up at Ebuli. Hasn't taken sides or been seen to take sides. Look, are you listening to me? Can you follow what I'm saying?'

'He told me,' the boy said sullenly. 'And anyway, you wouldn't know what he thought about it. Whether he took sides or not. You're not a Catholic.'

'Oh grow up, boy. I'm not a *hapkas* either,' he added nastily. 'Do you know how big this place is? Do you know we all know each other boringly inside out and back to front. Catholic! Catholic! What the hell's that got to do with it? You'd better start praying, boy, praying hard that this whole jam-tin rebellion comes off. Because if it doesn't, we're finished here and now.'

He bludgeoned on through the boy's protests.

'Finished. You too, lad. You too. You're not clean now. They'll heave you out along with maman and grandpa quick as a flash. *Hapkas* or not.'

'I don't care,' the boy said. 'I don't care.' His face was crushing tears back.

Angie Bonser swung her plump legs down from the lounger with a bounce, stubbed her cigarette like a killing and began to yell.

'Okay!' she shrilled. 'That's it! Leave it, will you Lemmy. Will you just leave it? Leave the kid alone. What's done is done. It's no good carrying on like this. You'll only make it worse, for God's sake. The day's only just begun. God knows what's going to happen.'

The radio in the next room was humming like hornets. The overhead fan stirred the racket into the slow air. From the front verandah came the sound of a fist pounding the lattice, a shout and then feet beating down the steps. Bonser was down the hall in three strides while the boy and Angie sat looking at and away from each other.

'You ought to go back home, Gav,' Angie Bonser said. 'They'll be worried. Did you tell them you were coming in?'

He couldn't answer. What was there to say? The island lay its shadow right across his mind. He felt clobbered by responsibilities he hadn't deserved and his lack of years came up, swaggering, and smacked him hard across the mouth.

Bonser had come back and was staring at the pair of them. His face was full of secrets.

'I should send you back,' he lied. He'd found a use for this moment, a way to turn it to account, like re-vamping a tired engine. For one horrible moment he saw Letty Trumble's striped shopping-bag hit the bitumen and he added this new deception to it. Could he? Maybe he should take the kid back but it meant driving all the way to St Pierre and he wanted to keep off the roads, remain invisible. The rebels were commandeering any stray trucks or cars they could find. There was always the chance some hill man who didn't know him might try to take over.

Angie went past him to the stove, the warmth of her body worrying him. Heat made thinking hard. See our three faces, he thought, flattened by disaster, no features on our mugs, scrubbed off by catastrophe. He went in to the next room and turned up the radio, fiddling about with the short-wave tuner until he found Port Lena. The air crackled into fragments of signature tune and then the ripe accent of Assistant Resident Commissioner Trembath braying and fading. Bonser raised a 'listen' hand. Only parts of phrases came to them. 'Oh Christ,' Bonser thought excitedly as he pieced bits together. 'This makes it easier. Easier.'

Back in the kitchen he demanded to know if they'd taken it in. 'They're moving the Brits out. Did you hear that? Shuttle service from Serua. Now, there's a turn-up!'

He took the coffee his wife handed him, gloating and sly.

He could squeeze redemption from this situation. The dark places in his bones told him. If things went wrong later what he planned now might divert retribution. He always had a bob each way.

'Well, you've stuffed up one situation,' he said to the boy. He held his coffee mug in both hands and drank piggily. 'Maybe you could unstuff another little matter.' Keeping his vocabulary light. Bonser avoided his wife's warning eyes, refused to acknowledge them. The boy said nothing.

'Can you drive?'

'Yes.' Gavi was tentative. 'Well, yes, I've been driving the plantation truck around for years. Why?'

'Then maybe you can do a little job for me.' He began explaining. 'And there's reasons of course.' He began giving them. Yet how could anyone explain the transection point at which the ideas that began as worthy abstracts eventually involved the bodies of those who had seized on them? That politics was a disgusting stew of opposites? – of insubstantiality and brute matter?

Bonser could deal only in the concrete.

His wife listened as if her face might burst open.

'You're putting Gav at risk,' she kept interrupting through his windiness and his snorts, having assessed him. She wanted to add 'for your own means' but hadn't the courage. 'Anyway,' she protested aloud, 'it's not legal. He hasn't a licence.'

Lemmy Bonser roared her down. 'At a time like this? Who gives a damn about farting little details like that? And what risk? Come on! What risk? He'll be in my truck. They'll let him through.'

'You said a minute ago they'll commandeer anything on wheels.'

'Not this way. Not now that radio announcement has come through. God, didn't you listen? Gav can go up the coast road as far as Ebuli then turn in to Mangarisu. God, you're always mewling about bloody acts of charity. The old boy's sick. Someone told me he'd had a touch of fever again. They'll have to get him out anyway.'

Expediency, Angie Bonser kept muttering, and told him he could do it himself until he swore at her, finally, forgetting the strangely silent kid. Why did she have to make things so difficult? He was in too deeply for his presence to be seen, for him, Lemmy Bonser *blong* Kristi, to be noted helping evacuate some old time island limpet like Lorimer with the union jack practically plastered across his sun-cancered dial. But *having* it done, now there was some sort of discreet insurance.

Gavi grasped at a few of the arguments. He didn't think about being used, could think only of Leyroud's warning and Kenasi and maman unprotected on the island and Lorimer, he'd always loved Lorimer, stuck up there in his lonely shack with the fever eating him. The consequences of anything he might do now were beyond unravelling. The adult world to which he had committed himself swung like a big dipper. He longed for the gentle rockabye of childhood. And in his heart he knew it was too late.

'Okay,' he said, feeling his pallor like a skin.

Bonser went hearty. 'Good man!' he said vigorously. He couldn't stand the sight of Angie's long accusing face battering him with 'child sacrificer', reviving images of Letty Trumble wheeling sideways. He took a large breath. They'd beat him up if he went bucketing through town with last-post Lorimer. Couldn't Angie see the logic of it? The rebels were too excitable, despite Narota's orders that there was to be no violence, and that fool Leblanc had them whipped up to trigger frenzy. That was the biggest problem: Leblanc working at them and working at them, not into any military orderliness but a sort of revolutionary exuberance that could discharge any way at all. It would take only the smallest exchange, the briefest flash of his unguarded temper, and he could soar into nothingness.

'You sure?' Bonser was squaring his supple conscience.

The boy nodded and Bonser steered him down the back stairs without another look at his wife and handed him the keys of his truck.

'Back her out,' he ordered, 'and take her along to the workshop. If you give me five minutes I'll have the generator crated and waiting for you round the side. Okay?'

And okay again.

The boy looked small in the cabin of the big truck.

Bonser was gone in a minute leaving him wrestle with the gears, churning up soggy lawn as he heaved the truck back and round and left it muttering while he opened up the side gates. In d'Urville the morning sun sliced his head in two.

When he reached the workshop Bonser was already waiting outside and the minute the truck slid up beside him, yelling for a hand with the generator. Between them they hoisted it over the tailboard. Bonser wanted to wish the kid good luck, assure him it was the proper payback for a loose tongue, swear he'd forget about his yap to Leyroud, whoever, tell him … He could see the kid's scuttled eyes and the face ashy below the tan, the mouth set in fear or excitement trying not to tremble, could see the clench of thirteen-year-old knuckles on the wheel and in the unexpected desolation that surrounded truck and boy, he wished suddenly that he hadn't asked this, hadn't put this burden on him.

There were no words. He slapped the truck, yobbo godspeed, and the boy gave the shortest of nods, put in the clutch and swung into a skidding turn on the side road before swinging back onto the Boulevard.

Bonser would have waved but the boy's face was frozen, eyes staring ahead, refusing to turn.

This last image imposed itself on Bonser's morning and hung its tiny shadow.

Whenever Assistant Resident Commissioner Trembath saw a black face, he instantly launched into pidgin, believing it to be one of those enduring symbols of colonial power. One *spoke* to them. Oh indeed one *spoke* but in a bastardised version of one's precious tongue, placing them, old chap, in the position of using baby-talk back. Frightfully funny, really. Of course they couldn't cope with anything more than baby-talk. Only the simplest thoughts going on. This linguistic interaction measured up their intellectual powers, didn't it? Was a kind of proof, well, proved it really, that those nigs were still way up in the trees.

What Trembath didn't realise was that the fractured words he used were part of a slave language developed out of desperation on the cane-fields of Australia, on the pearling ships, on the sandalwood runs – a language developed to give men from half a dozen different language belts a lingua franca. Boil it down, it was the islanders' parody but the parodees – the government officials, the traders and planters – too lazy or too dull to learn native dialects, seized on it as if it were their own vile joke.

He always addressed his driver in Seaspeak, even though the handsome ni-Trinitas, a product of mission school, spoke quite splendid English and much better French than the Commissioner. Trembath didn't even manage Seaspeak particularly well.

Now the long black official car was cruising smoothly down a back road of Port Lena, the little flag flying its insolent totem.

'You *tekim this rod long scoul*, Joseph,' Trembath ordered. '*Mi wantem stap ia.*'

'Here sir?' Joseph's voice was deep chocolate. 'This school here? I thought you wanted the secondary one. This is the primary school for the French sector. Would you like me to wait or call back?'

'You *wetim*, Joseph. *Haf klok*, *mebbe.*' Afterwards they would be going to the French residency.

He was dreading that. Colonel Mercet would look at him, his eyes tiny with irritation as Trembath, waving a diplomatic glass airily, would plunge in without any overt sign of embarrassment.

'M'sieu le Colonel, j'ai-er-lu recently que vous avez-um-décidé-er not to donner le-um-sewerage to-à-Paraka, n'est-ce pas?'

Oh he was so quick with his n'est-ce pas. Mercet, reacting as one does to a singer who merely cartoons the graph of a melody without quite reaching the actual notes, almost choked whenever he had to listen. 'Speak English, I implore,' he would say. 'Speak English. I will understand.'

After their first two years of parallel service they barely spoke. Cocktail parties at either residency were remarkable for the absence of members of the other governing force. The two men met only for official functions, keeping such a space between themselves that the consultative aspects of their supposedly joint administration developed into a kind of cold war.

Trembath went on amiably playing tennis and bongos, supervising the staff cricket matches, awarding cups at the British Secondary School in Port Lena and introducing the drama club's end of year Christmas cabaret. He could not help patronising the local educated islanders: 'University burao blong solwata, old dear,' he would say with a laugh to his First Secretary who would laugh obligingly back. His wife was splendid with all the other wives and his daughter temporarily with them from her minor English boarding-school was being squired by the second medical officer and laid (though Trembath didn't know this) by a charming part Tonkinese part Trinitas trading boat operator. Everyone was happy. Apart from this nonsense on Kristi. Happy. Happy tumas.

As for Colonel Mercet, non-communication with his British half suited him enormously. For four years, now, he had plotted an ill-laid course of Gallic takeover, encouraging a group of shonky developers from the States with roots originally sprouted in a fundamentalist religion. Born again, they declared, wisely, for profit. The Salamander Corporation, with the Colonel's connivance, planned to carve up great tracts of Kristi and turn it into a mini Florida.

Tommy Narota had been just what the Colonel needed: naive, manipulatable.

Ah, Narota, *mon ami*, Mercet murmured, finishing off a private letter to him, writing and sealing it himself. France needs you.

France had always played the colonial game with sharper instinct. True, there might have been more brutality from planters, a kind of sluttish jobbery, and true, there might have been more ruthlessness in the way they acquired their land. But they had a callous sophistication the British lacked. While Trembath entertained with native servants drink-waiting in hot black trousers and red cummerbunds or serving up, *mon dieu*, the roast lamb and the mint sauce at boiling Sunday luncheons, Mercet invited native chiefs as his guests – *en effet*, his guests – to late afternoon cocktail parties. And their wives. Their wives. What poise! What sophistication! In full ceremonial drag – feathers, paint, the lot – district chieftains had stood around his reception room clutching little glasses of French wine or dry Martinis and nodding, bemused, nodding and smiling fatly from their baffled shiny faces, when it all became too much. *Eh bien*, it *had* been ceremonial cloaks and feathers ten years ago when he had first come to Lena as assistant to the resident. But times had changed. Now the *yeremanu* wore safari suits and their wives, less modish, little numbers from the Comptoirs Trinitas. *Tout change*, he sighed. *Tout passe*.

Mercet slipped his private invidious note under his blotter and sat back, allowing himself, while he waited for Trembath, one of the six cigarillos he permitted himself each day. Yes. Times had changed. Islanders now took courses at colleges in Fiji, in New Guinea, in Australia. They spoke fluent and sometimes aggressive French or English or both. But – they were still his guests. *Mes convives*, he thought. *Mes amis*, he added, lying.

He pondered the gimcrack victory he was having over Trembath in forcing his presence and he thought, inevitably, of how he had first met Narota and how he had decided to use him. A staff picnic for *le quatorze juillet* at Cartouche Bay. All that wine-loosened *commérage* as they lounged about on sand, under palms. Some planters from Kristi had been invited, too, and Georges Duchard had lots of funny stories. Narota had already been a political prickle in Kristi a few years before with his new wave church, his yap about secession. The Kristi *colons* spoke of him in a positive and approving way. He had charisma, they told Mercet. Enormous charm. He had a great following. What was more (they laughed insinuatingly as they related this) he received instruction from dreams. *Comme Jeanne d'Arc!* cried the delighted Colonel. We must dream something up for him! How the simple ni-Kristi would love that. How he too loved it.

Eh bien, Mercet decided, stubbing his cigarillo out and wondering if it were too early for coffee, we might have failed on the land deals. Yet . . . It was that mass demonstration by all those damned public servants and do-gooders *mi-falla stanap long* Knox that wrecked that one. Plus the British golden boy, Willie Lemoa who was president elect of the interim government.

Repatriation of land was the new maggot in the British mind. It stunned Mercet they could be so concerned yet so ready to pull out after fify years of Seaspeak bullying.

Yes. Narota's Talasa Pati appealed to *colons* and ni-Kristi alike. Despite Narota's personal dreams of kingship on an island wrenched away from the group, despite his expressed desire to see most land returned to custom owners, he was prepared to tolerate the long-standing holdings of settlers there since the turn of the century. A simple man, thank God. A moderate. A half-half. If only the British would accelerate their departure, then the French, perhaps, could increase their authority. The trouble was it was like a *pas de deux* – they had to bow off stage together.

Mercet pressed his desk bell and ordered coffee. The young islander who brought it was a second cousin of Narota's, a slim beautiful boy with teeth obscenely white. He laughed a great deal. Mercet tolerated the laughter for his own reasons.

'*Là-bas!*' he said, pointing to a cleared space. And, '*merci*' he added carefully. He avoided Seaspeak, if only because Trembath was so addicted. He smiled in a kindly way at Seli Karae whom he had employed a few weeks after the election disaster of a year ago, just after Narota, in fact, proclaimed for the first time the Talasa federation's independent rule in Kristi. 'All British,' Narota had pronounced boldly and idiotically from Vimape, 'must leave within the year.' At least he was careful not to refer to the French. 'There will be no more clearing of *dark bush* for cattle. There will be no more fencing off custom land.'

To the hearty British guffaws that dismissed this ploy, Mercet had been forced to add agreement, acknowledging Trembath's shaggy logic that the structure of their joint constitution forbade the recognition of any form of secession. They could not *tok tok* as Trembath quaintly put it, *wantai'm long wan pati no mo. Merde alors.*

Mercet flew to Kristi, ostensibly for a cheer-up weekend with a planter friend at Thresher Bay. Privately he was giddy with intrigue and had Duchard drive him up to Vimape where, in the shade of the giant *nabanga* that nurtured much of the vision of the little commune, he assured Mr Narota (he was always careful in his mode of address) in front of nearly a thousand islanders who had come to support the Talasa flag that he, too, would back him in all matters. Advance. Sustain. Mercet marvelled at the fecund choice of verbs open to him.

Later he had visited Agent Boutin and discussed the problems of troops and organised revolt, conscious of being internationally daring, a maker of history. 'Now for possibilities,' he had said.

Boutin's list was very small.

'But he's not a military man,' Mercet had objected when Bonser's name came up.

Mercet would never have had Bonser in his living room.

That was the estimation test.

It was a lot of people's estimation test.

He loathed Australians and the islands seemed over-run with them. But he did admit there were qualities of toughness and ruthlessness that might be manipulated. Yet, 'every man is selfish,' he mused. 'Every businessman is especially selfish. It is a business-man I need. But my dear Boutin – the *strategies* of combat?'

'Granted.' Boutin had looked smug over his brandy. 'But then all Australians are so aggressive, are they not? They long for – what do they call it? – the punch-up. *Mais attends!* I know the man. I have the exact man for us.' He mentioned Leblanc and laughed. 'Like Smith, *n'est-ce pas?* A blow-in, as they say, working at the fishing company. He's been there about a year. Before that, a mercenary in the Congo. He worked again in Uganda. He knows the ropes. He would be perfect.'

Mercet had frowned. The answer had come too pat. He liked deliberation, the tossing about of premises before the orgasm of conclusion. It was part of the nature of the reasoning Frenchman. He made his deliberation and doubts known.

'Is he sympathetic, Boutin? That's a *sine qua non*. Is he sympathetic? And – and –' he raised a perfectly tailored hand to forestall argument '– given that, is he reliable?'

Boutin tugged his salesman moustache.

'I have already sounded him out. He is reliable. On the question of sympathy, does that matter so much? A mercenary is a mercenary,' he explained. 'He responds to money. I happen to know he needs money. He has bought himself a small fishing boat and is in debt to his eyeballs. He is exactly what we need.'

And after that? Ah! Meetings and non-quorums and postponements and demonstrations in Mataso town and Port Lena and uproar, absolute uproar when Willie Lemoa stated his intention of making English the *ofisol* language. There was loathing everywhere – of British for French and islanders for both. There were meetings in Paris to which district chieftains went. On Kristi, the Talasa Pati raised its liquorice all-sort flag and there was property damage and ripped emblems and burnings and British Agent Cordingley instructed the chief police officer to have tear-gas fired at the rioters and a native was killed. Someone aimed too low. The British were always bad shots, Mercet mused.

On and on it had gone through a broiling December with district agents from both sides disobeyed or ignored, plantations taken over and copra sold to illegal traders. *Quel gâchis!*

The outlines of political groups wavered and changed like sea-currents but the idea of total independence for the whole island group was gradually being accepted by die-hard colonialists in another hemisphere. These rites of passage! How, Mercet marvelled as he yielded and lit a second cigarillo, had a constitution ever been drawn up? Only God knew! That signing ceremony! *Yeremanu* in dacron! Trembath in ostrich plumes!

Thank God, he thought, that at the last Paris conference, his official compatriots spoke English, though maliciously he would have enjoyed the sight of Trembath floundering away in French at high level *tok tok*. Mercet had crossed his fingers over falsity and had promised immediate investigation of dubious foreigners, of shady investment deals and promised tax-haven activities. He could work quietly away, not compromising himself too much, and his country would be forever grateful. Like Narota, he had dreams of grandeur. The trick was to make the dreams fuse.

And now this latest trouble! Last year after the district election when Narota's rebels had temporarily scared the British out of Mataso town with waved clubs, arrows and charges of electoral fraud, Mercet had been terribly amused. Safely and officially in Paris. There could be no connection. Talasa Pati extremists and French *colons* with astute timing that was his timing as well, had opened their own office in Kristi and in Mataso Park before a crowd of hundreds had raised their own flag. *Namwele* leaves threatened British doorways. *Man bush* invaded town. The *yeremanu*, Tommy Narota, presided over all.

Now Narota's moves were more strenuous. British were fleeing in droves. Some buildings had been blown up. Stores and banks had closed. The time was ripe for something. Just how did he see Narota?

Your move, Tommy! My cigarillo is burning out. How do I see you, eh? Papa Yam, as they say. Papa Taro. Tubby. Lovable. Usable. A sublime mix of Polynesian and northern Europe with a dash of Kristi for practical purposes. A lifetime spent in Kristi waters. A gaggle of wives and children all streaked Kristi with only a shadow of your rip-roarer of a Devon daddy. You are brighter than Trembath, *mon ami*, although that is no compliment. And your idea of having passports printed for ni-Kristi was a masterstroke even if it did fall apart. How do I see you? You're no Papa Doc, *grâce à dieu*, just a genial old Papa Yam in your army dress with pig tusk decoration dragging you back into custom. How do I see you? Political tool? Smiler-host under the banyan tree with the ripping sound of the river slashing at the gorge below Vimape and unspeakable food I had to force myself to eat?

All those things. I want to believe that I am not merely using you. Am I?

And what can I do now, having to face this imbecile of a Trembath? Can he suspect we made the trucks available? The ammunition? The carelessly locked explosives? Could he know, could he possibly know, I gave the nod to Jacqui Leblanc? Truly, the thought of the Paddock in ruins at Kristi and the astigmatic

Cordingley sweating it out at Serua made his lips twitch.

'C'*est votre tour!*' the old chess-player said out loud, even as Secretary Brock poked his head round the door to announce the arrival of his excellency.

Mercet began shuffling papers about. He always preferred receiving with a work-cluttered table.

'My dear sir,' Mercet managed. 'What pleasure.' Briefly he touched Trembath's limp fingers. 'English, I insist. English.'

So they talked into the morning, the room becoming stuffier and stuffier with Mercet's horrible smoke, groping for agreement. A blockade, Trembath suggested boldly. Mercet was dubious. Cutting off radio and telephone communication? Well, perhaps. Mercet consoled himself that he could always charter a plane if he had to. He must display vestiges of outrage. His mind crossed its tubby legs.

'But no violence, I insist. We must negotiate. There is no room for violence in a matter so delicate.'

When Trembath decided on evacuating British residents from Kristi, Mercet could hardly conceal his delight at such a frightful tactical error. Yet this Trembath was so persistent with his talk of combat troops if the rioting continued. Mercet protested gently, 'Surely that is somewhat extreme?'

Trembath was firm. 'We must be united on this. There will have to be talks with the rebel government in the next few days. Otherwise ... Do you realise,' he demanded, 'it is only a month from Independence?'

'Oh indeed,' Mercet said. His spaniel face was genuinely regretful.

Then Trembath, with some worm of suspicion working at him, asked the vital question: 'Should you not be evacuating the French as well?'

'My dear sir,' Mercet replied, 'Frenchmen don't run.'

Cordingley could only goggle at his wife with a marvelling disgust.

They were not the first on the beach at Serua Point. A score of islanders were squatting fatalistically on the sand, simply gaping into a seascape that held less threat than the land at their backs. After an hour two British planters from the east coast turned up, an Australian missionary family and some lower white commercial orders from Mataso whom the Cordingleys had never invited to their cocktail parties. There they all were on the baking sand with the Channel beating along the beach, the heat drilling into them in the ripening light and no sense of picnic.

The expected boat had not come.

Bingi Larsen had put the Cordingleys ashore with his face turned stolidly north from District Agent Cordingley's ravings, insults, whimpers, pleas as they fell all about him. Belle wished for death as the rantings shrivelled her.

'When you've settled down, old man,' Larsen managed to insert finally, 'you might even say thanks. There's no way I could take you on in this thing. It's too bloody risky. Now for God's sake show a bit of that British cool you Pommy bastards keep talking about – or is that only for the troops? – and let me get her back, will you?'

At that Belle had burst into waves of uncontrolled laughter, her plump frame racked by many things. Cordingley glared at Larsen, ignored his wife and stumped off up the coral strip into a shade-patch from where he barked once at his wife and then sat and loathed.

Now they were sagged apart from each other, their bags as head-rests, pretending indifference to the eyes of the islanders, the critical inspections of Mista and Misis Bipi who had arrived only minutes ago and greeted the Cordingleys with 'God, you were quick off the mark! Thought you'd be needed to organise things back in town.'

Belle has said quickly, 'He's not a ship's captain, dears. He doesn't have to go down with the island.' And though they had laughed dutifully as they had always laughed dutifully over the whiskies and the Malo cocktails, Mista Bipi's muttered 'You could have fooled me' as he turned away was the supersonic insult always audible to colonial service ears.

So Cordingley sat and sulked and glanced occasionally at his partner to nourish his loathing.

She'd always been difficult, he reflected, from the moment he'd plucked her from that Washington typists' pool; always difficult at diplomatic parties where her tongue unleashed the most undiplomatic comments. At first he had thought her witty and erudite as he trod the chancy shores of love. She'd scattered intellectual confetti – the highly coloured name dab-spots of artists, writers, musicians – over tribes of cocktailing foreign corps whose wives were offended by the rainbow fallout. Belle and her damn bomb-shells. There'd been that time . . . he lolled heavily under the fringe of *burao* trees and dragged his handkerchief over his blazing face . . . that time she'd quoted that bit of Samuel Johnson (Christ! none of them had ever *heard* of Samuel Johnson, probably thought she was having a crack at Lyndon B.!) . . . something about dogs in their doggy world . . . and the Resident Commissioner droll behind rimless glasses because he was a bit of a books man too, hanging on her words, waiting for it, and she'd gone on about a pair of copulating terriers at a Washington embassy garden party, imagine my dears, dogs in their doggy world at a Nuremberg rally might have changed the course of history . . . and then without preamble straight into it, how those two damn animals did their doggy thing right under the flag-pole mind you, the flag, in front of two hundred startled guests, knocking trolleys of canapés, upsetting the drink tables, leaping and cavorting and . . . Belle made lots of amusing hand gestures . . . and the Resident Commissioner's wife and several other wives had walked off while the Resident Commissioner despite a practised diplomatic snigger had visibly flinched. Flinched . . . And then she'd sailed on to something else, breast-feeding practices among the islanders not even a pause . . . and he could see the under secretaries shaking with dreadful laughter.

She had no sense of timing. The groan he gave, couldn't help giving, lost itself in the growing crowd.

But it drew Belle. She got up and planted herself on the beach beside him and he was conscious of her sandalled feet digging slowly at the sand and letting it trickle between her toes. It was her gesture of repentance but Cordingley preferred to see it as childishness in a non-crisis world of palm and tropic water as if she imagined the nirvana had never been ruptured by guns and animal men with feathers and loin fringes, as if this were the glossy surface of some tourist brochure (X marks the spot where we sat, my God!) south seas idyll when instead there were now hundreds of islanders about them whose very silence threatened and scores more of them moving in through the trees from the road.

No one seemed to have any food, certainly not the Europeans whose numbers had now reached twenty. A lot of suckling was going on and this seemed to stimulate Mista Bipi into producing a hip flask. Cordingley watched enviously as Mista Bipi swigged from the bottle lip. There was nothing to do but wait while the sun crawled up the sky curve and the shadows of the *burao* trees shortened and forced them to edge back farther. All eyes were on the empty sea.

His dream took him back to that embassy party and the dramatics of his wife, younger, prettier, her hair swinging in the blunt bob that was too schoolgirlish, her round face with its innocent high colour totally giving lie to the outrageousness of her utterances. Only this time, the dream women were crowding her begging for more, their faces drawn into long bird-like looks of greed as Belle fluttered among dashing obscenities with the guilelessness of her face unmarked by the prurience of her stories and he began thrusting his way through the clustered women whose numbers multiplied, the group swelling and swelling as he nudged and pulled and elbowed trying to get at her, unable ever to reach that bright talking face at its centre, when the glass the R.C. was holding began to expand like a monstrous balloon, the brandy rising, rising with the expanding glass so huge it obscured the Commissioner himself, larger and larger and larger until the whole reception room was one enormous glass sphere that trembled and then shook with Belle's blustery laughter before it finally shattered.

The explosion woke him.

He dragged himself up and found that all the others beneath the trees were standing too, their heads turned to catch the dying sound. Down on the beach there were now about five hundred people squatting in their island groups, their faces passively reflecting the heavy boom which somehow trapped itself in the hills and repeated its threat in fading syllables.

Cordingley's mouth was too dry to speak. He found himself stumbling along the sandy ridge towards Mista and Misis Bipi and gobbling, but they turned their backs on him, their heads cocked listening for the next roar, perhaps, phonily alert, and he edged off humiliated, while the hills lost their voice and the sea chatter came back and the native quackings of surprise fell away into the mid-day heat.

Belle came weaving through the crowd towards him, her hat still crooked, her sandals swinging from one hand. When she had seen his face mottled with confusion and a kind of mindless panic, the brutality of the Bipis' snub still smarting, she felt, even as she knew she outraged his spurious dignity with hoicked-up skirt and bare feet, a tenderness for the stupid old swaggerer.

'Someone back there,' she said, gripping his arm, ignoring his withdrawal, 'has a transistor. I've just been listening to the latest broadcast.'

He pulled his arm away and wouldn't speak.

'Oh come on,' she urged. 'Don't you want to hear?'

'What?'

'The *Eudora* should be here in another hour. And there are a couple of copra boats coming out from town. It's just a question of waiting, Cordie.' The pet name irritated him instead of placating.

'What was that explosion?'

'No one seems to know. Mystification. That's the procedure. Create formless terrors.'

'You seem to know all about it,' he said resentfully.

She smiled. Trying. 'The Bipis appear to have dredged up a few sandwiches from somewhere. They're going to perform a biblical miracle.'

'I'd choke first,' he said. Oh she couldn't resist it, could she, the smart-ass crack.

Despite his loathing he let himself be led along the beach, the sand dragging at his shoes, filling them, so that his socked feet felt ribs of coral grit beneath. And the sweat. It pickled eyes, turning the tender rims redder, and worked down his neck and chest onto his stomach folds with the persistence of ants. Belle's back was sopping, a great vulgar splodge, and he could see her neck below the hair and that crazy hat glistening as if with oil. All the impurities, he judged unreasonably, will be sweated out of the bitch.

But Belle wasn't really that at all and even as she handed him a dried-up bun one of the missionaries had dug out from a gunny sack, her gesture made him feel unexpectedly as if he were the one who should be doing penance.

Another hour. Only the palms and the natives, now packed in their hundreds all along the narrow sand-strip, were surviving the pouring mid-noon heat. Someone farther along the ridge began strumming a guitar and there was soft-chorused singing around the plucked heart of the tune that played on his impatient blood. The words ran high in the native sing-song, floating shadowless above the beach-people, a song that had been popular round the islands for the last year:

> J'avais grand faim et j'ai mangé la banane
> J'avais grand soif et j'ai bu kokonas.

Over and over. The words sifted through the air like ironic flies, nuzzling and biting. More voices hit the refrain: kokonas kokonas kokonas, rich amused harmonies that assaulted the melting flesh of the huddled Europeans staring critically at a group of Chinese traders who kept up a constant nibbling at furtive food packets.

Another hour.

By now the singing had trailed into nothingness. A torpor had taken over the vast crowd pulled back into the roadside trees as the sun sloped into afternoon. The water of the Channel deepened its blue and the white lines streaking this shifting enamel became a scrawl of indifference that did not even spell out the memory of boat wakes.

When at last the Eudora, white superstructure sharp as razors in the sunlight, came down the 2 o'clock water from Mataso town, most were beyond caring. They were ready for mirage. Cordingley took off his steamed-up glasses and wiped them, polishing hard as the landing-barge bore along the current, flag a-twitch and deck-hands moving round ready to get the ramp down the moment the barge touched shingle.

At first there was unbelieving silence, then nothing but voices tangled in shouts and cheers. People began running along the beach trying to gauge the point of landfall, shoving each other, calling out and signalling the boat, while the *Eudora*, phlegmatically indifferent, moved steadily across the Channel until it was just off Serua Point, swinging to nose in to the beach.

Chaos. Instant. Wonderful.

Island groups carefully organised by missionaries and group leaders broke formation. There was a deal of sheep-dog scuttling and yapping from Missionary Lampton and the loose clusters closed, wavered, broke, closed, all under the roar of a loud hailer handled by the *Eudora's* master.

At first no one listened. No one bothered; but as the excitement and the shoving coagulated into a writhing knot at the water's edge, he could be heard shouting that only two hundred could be taken. The struggle for position went on. Whole Chinese families were forming wedges through the clustered islanders. Belshaw bellowed through the loud hailer again. He screamed for people to get into some sort of small island grouping so that they could be unloaded at their home islands more easily. No one listened. Or if they tried, the sea, the wind, the heat, eroded meaning.

Cordingley, using Belle's arm as a kind of tiller, began pushing her with the other European refugees through the ranks of black flesh towards the top of the ramp. Flesh parted for the *gavman* man. Then there was a massive grinding and scraping as the *Eudora* shoved its ramp up the beach. The world was chocolate and white. Missionary Lampton from Thresher Bay became unhinged. 'Back!' he screamed, his hands in a triangle of prayer. 'Back! Let the women through *first*!' His voice was a thin high-pitched stream of word wings as his lean fanatic body went under in the waves of his flock. '*Pipol Trinitas! Pipol Malua!*' The feathers were plucked from the syllables in a frenzied rush of money-bag rattling Asiatic merchants, who, swinging satchels vigorously like clubs, cut a clear-way for themselves straight through and on to the landing barge.

Belle laughed at the outrageousness of it.

Native women staggered sideways, children fell and bawled underfoot. Little baskets of fruits overturned and spilled dragon plums and bananas that began rolling down towards the barge where they were taken by the feet of the Kwee and Sing Fong families into a pulp slither, a greasy mash over which the natives following began to skid and slither.

Captain Belshaw leaned limp against the bridge rail as he watched the turmoil on the ramp. He had sent a sulky island boy to sort things out but he was next to useless. 'Jesus!' he prayed, watching the deck-hands miscount the surging mass. He shouted to them to haul the ramp up.

The loud hailer at his mouth developed an urgency of its own in its unrelenting yet ignored pleas for the crowd to wait. There would be another barge, it roared. Another. The *Eudora* would be back as soon as possible. A scuffle broke out on the deck between two of the Chinese and one of the deck-hands. The captain yelled repeats until his lungs cracked. It could take over a day to clear this lot.

On the beach, in the thick of it, Belle was pressed so close to her husband by the anxiety of the scared pack, the two of them might never have been enemies. 'What is it?' she kept asking. 'What is he saying?'

Cordingley grunted. His stomach had reversed again into swampy fears although he couldn't believe, refused to believe, that the rebels might march on their beach-head and mow them down in their scores.

He was surprised at the ease with which he submitted to this new disappointment. 'Come along,' he ordered. 'No good standing here. We'll make it on the next round.'

He was longing to get his shoes off and empty out the packing of coral sand but his feet were so swollen he might never be able to put his shoes on again. The thought of this made him moan, the deep tones of love almost, in a natural burst of pain, hobbling away up the little slope, head down, sweat dripping from the end of his nose. He was sun-blinded, one enormous prickly itch of shame and heat. His crotch was damp and trickles were running from the moist places inside his thighs to the tops of his long socks. He didn't even see the log that tripped and pitched him flat.

Belle bent over his fat sprawled body then straightened up to find a ring of grinning black faces. The grins aligned her loyalties immediately with him. She knew this for one of those brief moments of marriage within marriage when the force of a union expresses itself.

'Don't stand there!' she snapped. 'You help me. Please,' she added as no one moved. 'Please.'

A thin oozing line had opened across Cordingley's forehead. The blood ran down in a fringe. He sat up mopping and smearing.

Missionary Lampton and Mista Bipi had come over, Bipi hiding his own smirk. He was prepared to forgive Cordingley now he had missed the boat. He shoved the islanders aside and leant over to peer into the District Agent's sand-blasted features. 'Got a nasty bump there.'

Someone else handed over his broken glasses. The sun shot spots off the cracked lenses. Cordingley moaned again.

'Upsadaisy,' Bipi said jocularly under Missionay Lampton's frown. He couldn't hold rancour long. After all the old D.A. was thick as a plank. 'We'll get you under the trees.' And he bent down and tried to hoist Cordingley by the armpits.

Feeling those merchant hands exploring puddles of secret wet Cordingley was dazed with outrage. 'I'm all right.' He tried to focus and his eyes took in a dozen grinning mouths where teeth threatened white on pink in a dark flesh he had always despised. And there was this tradesman . . . 'Let me go, damn you!'

'Okay, old man.' Bipi's ginger moustache drooped blandly. He knew the colonial rules too well to wink at the grinning boys, though he wanted to badly enough. 'Just trying to help.'

Cordingley lurched to his feet, resenting even Belle's arm stuck out for the moment protectively, swayed in a dazed fashion and tottered blindly away from them, as if the flattened folly of his body on the sand would vanish too. His ears only half heard the chukka chuk of a motor-boat somewhere out on blue water. It could have been anything, even the yells of excitement at his back and across them the always too clear sound of his wife's voice calling. Belle's voice was never part of dream. He'd endured its shock-tones too long. Groggily he turned round, scraped away at blood with his sleeve and saw mistily and redly a rubber inflatable nosing cautiously round the southern end of Serua Point.

The mob had lost interest in him and was surging back to the water when the dinghy seemed to hesitate, then gathered confidence and speed, and roared in towards the landing. Standing magnificently erect in the bows was First Secretary Maddock backed by two black police officers with rifles cocked.

'It's like Dunkirk,' a voice said near him.

'Only more comic,' he could hear his wife say as they all watched Maddock reel and stagger against the slap of the water. He heard her giving out that old chestnut about the smell and the people. Even at a time like this, Cordingley thought with rage, she can raise a laugh. Her wrist would have gone campily limp. There were muffled cackles from the Europeans around her, the coarsest laughter coming from Bipi.

Ignoring the lot of them, he strode manfully and obdurately in his agonising shoes down the beach, half blind behind his ruined glasses, jostling islanders rudely aside, and out onto the landing ramp where he began a violent waving.

Maddock spotted him almost at once. He cupped his hands round his mouth and called across the few yards between them.

'We can take about fifteen or so. The *Eurydice* is standing off round the point. Get the Brits, will you? I'm acting under orders.' He lowered his hands and fell heavily against a rifle bearer. The native at the tiller swung the inflatable in a wide arc and Maddock vanished round the point. Within five minutes the *Eurydice* came into view, union jack flapping, and lowered its dinghies.

Cordingley knew a rush of diplomatic corps spunk. He fought back the impulse to go scrabbling through the water and with all his hacked-at dignity pulled tight began giving high-pitched orders to the little white contingent. Women first, he conceded splendidly, then the children. Right? How many? Too many, it seemed. Eleven? He ignored Belle in a moment of spite. Twelve as a mission wife blundered through the press of bodies. Misis Bipi was pulling Belle down towards a second dinghy. Mrs Lampton elected nobly to remain with her husband. There was a tiny, soft and refined argument.

Maddock, safe on the *Eurydice*, was surveying the crowded beach with horror. He beckoned someone behind him and Cordingley saw a hailer handed over.

'All right there.' The voice came bellowing over the water, over the dinghies at the water's edge now packed and ready to pull off. 'Cordingley, you're to board. Orders from Lena. Hop along now. We can still take another five.'

The boats pulled away with their squashed cargo. Cordingley sat very straight near the stern, his blood-streaked face turned into the sun. Belle was somewhere on the other boat. He didn't care. When his feet finally placed their pain on the deck of the *Eurydice* an almost incontinent trembling seized him and someone led him down to the galley for a brandy that bit his stomach like summer. Outside his shaking world there was the putter sound of a dinghy returning for a final load.

'Turned nasty did it?' the First Secretary asked, looking admiringly at the cut across Cordingley's forehead.

Cordingley floated a wisp of a smile.

'Nothing,' he said, 'I couldn't handle.'

He put his glass down and hauled himself up the narrow companionway to the deck. Everywhere people were squeezed down on suitcases and swollen overnight bags. The dinghies were being taken up and lashed into position. The First Secretary became suddenly boyish and was moving among the refugees doing a Biggles. 'Jolly good,' he kept saying, beaming. 'Oh jolly good.' It might have been a wilder cocktail party or the aftermath of a sticky reception. His hair tumbled youthfully above his earnest face. Cordingley averted his eyes from Belle's obvious delight in vacuity. There's nothing going on behind, he could almost hear her say. My dear, there's simply no one at home. Safety made him give a grudging smile at the thought. Well, she was right, really. He forgot his shame, the tiny outrages of the last hours.

As the *Eurydice* headed west down the Channel, out to the heavy waters between Kristi and Trinitas, those who were near the rails began a relieved waving to the crowd still on the beach. Cordingley could see Belle remove her neck-scarf and trail it into the wind. It was baited with a kind of regretful memory. To his vast surprise he found himself waving, too, his arm lifting involuntarily, and to his further amazement, the people left on shore, mainly black now,

127

were waving their despised hands in reply. Waving to him, to Belle, to all the crushing forces of colonial authority.

Korro, the voices called. *Iyo. Ayé.*

They waved. They waved.

Although there were rebels picketing the Boulevard and more along the Rue Dupetit, no one stopped young Salway as he drove out of town by a network of back roads skirting the airfield. He was a few miles from Mataso town near a former American bomber site when the world outside the cabin window burst about him and he saw, swelling above the swaying wall of vine and tree, a thick sock of smoke from the direction of the oil-mill. Leaf cliffs rocked and behind the rocking, shouts and the jungle-crash of running men.

His spongy conscience sopped up the possibilities of devastation. He swung the truck backwards in idiot reverse, bucketing blindly down the narrow track until he reached a clearing wide enough to turn.

Was this the poetry of revolution, this bile in the throat, the shudder-cringe in his belly?

A rifle cracked and there was the splat of bullet on the cabin roof as he sent the truck panic-fast toward the coast road. He tried not to think that the rifle used against him was one of those he had taken to Vimape, but the thought kept crossing his mind along with images of Père Leyroud's tubby shape trying to barricade his entry to this adult world.

He couldn't think. Wouldn't. His foot lower on the accelerator refocused the landscape in green blurs, the islanders' straggling groups along the road to speed-streaks, so that when he finally came down to the coast and the blue thunder of the sea he could only believe he was rushing from disaster into havoc. Slower, heart told foot. Slower. Small villages took shape, copra driers, the white buildings of the Presbyterian mission near Pig Bay, the final emptiness of the road ahead.

After his blood sobered, the pulses dying back, the gut ceasing its contractions of fright, he was kava-numb, driving straight towards a northern sea where islands floated just beyond the hill-top perspective of the trees and far away on his left the towering range of Roy Mata dripped with mist and the gummy silences of leaves. The loneliness of the road encouraged his manhood, made him think of Lorimer alone, too, on his ridge at Mangarisu. For the next ten miles he fumbled towards virtue.

Nengle, Lorimer. Hello. I see you, talking with Lucie Ela on the afternoon verandah, your pipe a steady comfort in your old hand, your voice rumbling on about the porpoise runs at the Bay of the Two Saints or rummaging along Kenasi's sparse shelves, hunting down reading matter or visiting each Christmas in the early years with gifts of fish and skilfully carved wooden fruits and then fewer times as age crept over, preferring to burrow into your own solitariness. 'We all do that,' Kenasi had explained, 'as we get older. It's as if we draw a circle round ourselves and make the boundary smaller and smaller until maybe, one day, we find ourselves at the very centre.'

'What's that?' the boy had asked. 'What's the centre?'

'It might be death,' grandfather had said, softening the word with a smile.

He couldn't bear that memory now.

He drove the truck slowly through the next village, the last before the road fork that would take him to Mangarisu. No dogs barked. No children ran out to stare. Silence wadded itself between thatch and garden. The breath began sawing down his throat, scraping away at his lungs. Last time, last visit, Lorimer had said, 'May I borrow this Simenon?' and 'It's in French,' the boy had apologised to an amused 'Is that so? You'll help me if I get stuck, won't you?' I'll help, Lorimer, the boy told himself driving steadily and scared past the last house, the last yam garden.

Just beyond the turn-off there was a shrine to the Virgin built into the aerial roots of a *nabanga* tree. The truck could have stopped itself at this point and the boy got out, not sure why he was doing this, and walked over to the shrine and, still not sure, knelt down automatically before the sun-faded colours of the statue. The sun wanted to bend him double. He crossed himself and began to whisper over clasped hands, here, exposed on this lonely road in the climate of chaos, *je vous salue, Marie, pleine de grâce. Le Seigneur est avec vous. Vous êtes bénie entre toutes les femmes et béni est le fruit de vos entrailles*, running the words of the prayer like a warm vine among the other vines clambering through the cutting. Even when he had finished with the formality of it, he stayed with his knees rasping appeals into the coral sand at the base of the shrine, taking Lenten pleasure in grinding them more deeply while he said please and please. Placing custom against custom. There were red *lokalok* in the shadowed green and a white star flower gasping for breath amid glutinous succulents. When he rose and dusted away grit and small twigs from his knees he felt foolishly strengthened and protected as if the hazards of his journey could be flicked away by the movement of his hands.

The west coast road rose steeply between swooping jungle that crowded the narrow strip of track. Pigeons rattled across truck racket and parakeets moved like coloured tracers that stressed his isolation. The effects of prayer began to thin under the giant hedges of the rainforest. Although it was cooler in the deepening gloom of the high hills, danger heated him, an apprehension of the saw-tooth mountains ahead and the give-away roar of the truck as it munched up distance. By the time he reached the second junction where the road from Vimape came in, his body was so tense, his feet so stiffened on the controls, he stalled the engine as he fumbled the change-down for the steep gradients towards the *col*.

The truck stopped in the boy's fright.

The rebels had been active here, the southern road blocked by recently felled trees and a rough but effective weaving of branches that rose for six or seven feet. Although prayer had thinned, he grabbed at words, at *sainte Marie, mère de dieu*, the syllables coming in gasps. He looked away from the road-block, staring rigidly ahead with the rigid words of prayer thrusting out like dried sticks.

He got the truck moving again, frightened to look sideways, frightened of the great groaning as he edged off the coral road onto a dirt strip that heaved up the mountain and dropped away from its own terror to the northern coast.

Up. Up. Between noise and silence. Forcing himself more than the motor. He was frozen with his effort, with the insanity of his preseverance. He wanted to run like a baby.

Then ahead the road dived, the world opened out and below him, purple glass, the Bay of the Two Saints.

Its bowl lay between the thumb and closed fingers of the island mitten, the liquid glass licking out towards the Cape whose towering spine dangled cloud. The palm of this glove was sliced by twin rivers that cut through forest out to the bay. It was beyond the first of these rivers that Lorimer's tiny shack teetered in air.

'A natural solitary,' grandfather always described him. 'Lost up there at the delta.'

'But he's not lost,' maman would argue. 'Not at all lost. And he's happy. He happy man same way you happy man!' And she'd laughed, hugging Gavi hard.

Good naturedly Kenasi had grumbled, 'Hypocrite! As if you could tolerate it for one second. I always remember you telling me how you and that friend of yours, Isobel something or other, used to spend whole mornings on the waterfront in Lena, drinking coffee and watching the tourists fall over on that wretched paving. "There goes another!" you'd cheer. You need human disasters all round you.'

Old man, the boy said aloud, I'm coming.

He was sticking scraps of Lorimer together as he drove, knowing whatever order the jigsaw pieces took, they would create a whole. Once he'd driven up here with Doctor Trumble and Rogo on another mercy trip. Père Bonnard at the Port Ebuli mission had found the old man raving in his bunk with blackwater fever and had lugged him somehow to his van and taken him down to the mission hospital.

'C'est un miracle!' Bonnard shrugged his non-comprehension of it as he watched his patient of a week ago, frail but perverse, fight back the nonsense of Trumble's check-up, pocket a supply of precautionary drugs and totter off to the doctor's car. 'He's too old, Doctor, to go back up there. Too stubborn and too old.'

Lorimer had turned at the foot of the verandah steps and threatened mildly with a jaunty walking-stick.

'I heard that. What do you expect me to do, eh? Build me a bamboo cabin at your church door? Eh? Too bloody old!' He turned and went on to the car where the boys were watching, awed, in the back seat. No one got over blackwater, Kenasi said. No one. Père Bonnard and two of the nursing sisters followed Lorimer, hovering as he settled himself in the front seat.

Bonnard stood thin and amused and as Lorimer met his eye began to laugh. The sisters stood, heads on one side, fumbling their rosaries.

Their prayers now licked through the boy's mind and again he saw the old man poking his head out the car window and looking back at the little group by the mission steps as if he were going to cry.

'Forgot my manners,' he had said. 'Thank you. Thank you for everything. *Toute chose*. You'll get your conversion yet.'

Bonnard had given a blessing with his thin hand. 'You have the luck of angels.'

What was old, the boy wondered. Doctor Trumble told him later, 'It is when you cease to try.'

I'm coming, old man, Gavi said.

He remembered the hut. They had driven the old man back. A place of palm thatch and air high above the failed rice paddies and the shallow marshes of the delta where egrets and wild duck fished in shadowy flocks. He remembered the hut. He remembered the stacks of books, the few bits of furniture, the sabre splits in the palm-thatch walls through which white orchids stared and the greenery shifted in the bay wind. The old man had walked all round the room, touching things, patting the friendliness of long-used objects. 'Oh I do love this place,' he had said. 'I do love it.' When Rogo nudged him then, he had turned away, embarrassed for his friend, looking away from everything, especially the old man's joy, and listening to the lonely cries of the wild fowl far below where the endless blue hammered and thrust at the thumb of the Cape.

He heard Lorimer trying out small jokes with the doctor as he brewed them all tea. 'Man is a social animal, I suppose, except for me. But today, eh, with so many visitors, you could almost call me a socialist.'

And the men had talked about Narota as well, words that the boy wished he could remember now. 'Let him be,' he recalled the old man saying. 'We should let him be. He's a good man.'

In his garden, showing them his fruit trees, he had talked compulsively, spending words he had saved for months. And then as suddenly as he had begun his expansive monologue, he lapsed, letting the silence drop round them like silk. 'Oh beautiful,' he had murmured every now and then, his eyes lost on the bay. 'Oh beautiful.' And Gavi thought perhaps that he was the only one who heard.

Who are you, old man?

He knew this. And he knew that. Bald facts starting in England somewhere, the usual way: trader, planter, coming at last to roost his failure under great vaults of sky and in chancels of unending forest. He filled notebook after notebook with his hermit theories on a world he had never really known. Certainly not conquered, he complained wistfully once to grandfather. Oh but he had, he had, Kenasi had begged to differ. The complete and total conqueror. The stout Cortez of Kristi, with poetry and silence and enough food to extend the familiar but varied patterns of his days. He had the lot. 'But no children,' maman had said later. And Kenasi had gone quiet and said to maman, 'Who knows?'

Nengle, old man. I'm your this-day child.

The natives at Mangarisu loved him as a wise man. He had trouble with their dialect but goodwill had its own vocabulary and he refused to use Seaspeak.

'It's offensive,' he would argue, nagging Père Bonnard. 'When you use it, you're treating them as if their language and culture are slum things, nothings.'

'But mine's better,' Père Bonnard would insist unreasonably.

'Let me tell you something, *mon cher père*,' Lorimer had said to him. How Bonnard had laughed when he repeated the story to Kenasi; but he had been affected. 'Just let me tell you something. Your precious culture's in for a wallop. There's a whole new wave of tolerance around. How do I know? I can smell it. Smell it! And you can read about it, anyway. They're flat out trying to preserve local dying cultures everywhere. The motives might be academic promotion but it's happening nevertheless. Salvaging something from the basilicas of Dixie Chicken. That's the killer. The High Mass of Colonel Sanders, offered at a pizzeria in downtown Lena. For this is my body, the Colonel says, with twenty-nine secret ingredients. Take this and eat in commemoration of me.'

Even Bonnard had to laugh. 'You've forgotten to consecrate the Pepsi.'

But Lorimer had persisted, 'You can lay the blame for all this restlessness at the feet of the anthropologists. Or praise them, rather. Nosing around where they're not wanted. But they've done a lot of good as well. They've interested the world in customs other than puny western ones. It's all the same big chap in the sky. We all *stanap long Deo*, as you would say, don't we, eh?'

Energy had drained out of him in the mission garden. 'Come on,' Père Bonnard had said. '*D'accord?*' And had taken him in to the mission house for a glass of wine. The priest house had never felt hotter and more box-like though all the wooden shutters were flung out to welcome the world.

'And what's more,' Lorimer had said with a sly smile as he sipped his wine, 'their culture's older than yours by a long chalk. You bloody *parvenu!*'

What else, old man? Thoughts of Lorimer sustained. The islands were full of characters like Lorimer, men who had drifted in on the spinning tides of adventure and had beached. Coast-watcher, he knew, like Kenasi, pitched lonely for months on end on craggy headlands, nourished by radios and natives' kindnesses. He'd been ambushed once by a party of Japanese who'd landed at the Cape and left him for dead, but lugged all the way, his greenish-yellow stretched out on a bush-pole stretcher, to the mission at Ebuli by villagers from Tsureviu. Real people, then, Kenasi had said to him, stressing the 'real'. It was only in the years since the war that the rot had crept in with go-getting speculators out to make fortunes, cajoling custom owners into handing over land for a transistor radio and a case of canned beer.

Gavi found himself repeating those words: a transistor radio and a case of canned beer. Kenasi and Lorimer were much alike, seeing them twinned in the plantation gardens at Emba, swapping yarns on the long verandah with maman fussing. Two grandfathers, almost, until the old man, refreshed by voices, went back to Mataso, filled a copra bag with supplies and drove up to the high hills that rummaged in his blood.

Old man, Gavi said. I'm coming.

The downhill switchback to Mangarisu was still slippery from last week's rain and the truck wheels skidded or grabbed at ruts, bucking as if its spasms would pitch it straight off this spiral corridor into the tree-heads below. At the bottom of the drop-road a bridge spanned the gully of the coast range. Beyond the bridge, one fork led out to Mangarisu, the other pierced the hills to Lorimer.

The boy swung the truck onto the left-hand track, his whole body aching as the vehicle lurched and fought him around the corner.

Then the fright came back, clawing his guts as he braked hard before the second road-block.

A great pile of axed scrub-trees barricaded the dirt track and stuck all along the withering fronds were *lokalok* flowers, symbol of the rebel Pati.

So close.

He wanted to vomit.

Behind him the road was empty. He could see nothing beyond the barrier. Yet he knew how easily men moved as part of shadow and vine, coming suddenly into a sun-shaped reality. He had no weapon. Once more he found his lips praying, meaninglessly, *sainte Marie, sainte Marie.*

He was shrunken by it. Become small boy who wanted to sit behind eye-rubbing fisted hands and whimper. Every nerve instructed him to swing the truck round, to crash it back and forth between the jungle walls until it was pointing away, away, and he in it.

He thought of Bonser and what Bonser threatened.

He thought of maman and Kenasi.

He thought of Lorimer, alone up there, only a mile or so up there, in his bird-nest house above the delta.

The thoughts came so fast. He's not at risk, he told himself. Everyone loves old Lorimer. Lorimer wouldn't want to run. It was his *man ples.* The generator could go up another day. Lorimer had never run. He was wasting time. There was no way he could talk the old man into leaving his home and heading for the boats. Lorimer and refugee were contradictory terms. Lorimer . . . was Lorimer.

Voices were nagging him: Kenasi's, Leyroud's. The priest's chubby face, crumpled with disappointment, wouldn't leave his head. Oh God, the boy whispered, knowing he *should* go. He couldn't avoid the fact of the barrier and its meaning was two-way.

He found himself dribbling bile down the door of the truck. His retching sounds horrified him in the silent road. Cowardice urged him temptingly to drive back to the mission at Ebuli. Père Bonnard would know what to do but that would mean more talk, more telling and Père Bonnard would despise him as well. The three faces of his conscience stared like faded painted saints from a wall. Their mouths refused the words their eyes uttered.

There was no choice.

The stupendous silence of the hills closed in.

Sunlight patching through the canopy served only to emphasise shadow.

He wound up the cabin windows, got out and locked the truck, standing there vulnerable in his school shorts, his school shirt. He shoved the truck keys deep in his pocket, keeping his fingers clutched round them for the feeling of security they gave. Then he walked up to the barrier.

It took him only minutes to clamber over, knowing all the time that he was being watched, knowing he must not glance round, must ignore the *dark bush* each side of the road. There were men back in it, he knew, he knew. And they were watching.

He was careful not to disturb the *lokalok* flowers.

On the other side he forced himself to walk. Walk, he told himself. Walk. Not run. His body had become dough and putting one foot confidently in front of another was almost beyond him. He barely felt his legs move. If he could have shut his eyes tight and dream-walked he would, but instead he stared straight ahead with the emptiness of the blind, not moving his head in the slightest to either side. He took his hand from his pocket and let both arms dangle loosely, exposing his defencelessness. There was no end to the wisdom of survival.

Two hundred yards. Three hundred.

The hill arched steeply and his breath came in noisy gulps.

Along the back of his thighs muscles sang with pain.

Sainte Marie, he whispered. Walk.

The bush swarmed with men. He could sense them out there, quietly keeping pace beside the road. He knew their ability to materialise from emptiness. 'They're just curious,' Kenasi had said. Swimming – the beach deserted, and when he came out of the water, there they would be, distanced, silent, watchful. He would have sworn there was no one else. Picnicking with maman along the river at Mataso. Only bird noises. The after-lunch nap. And there they would be, standing across the river from them, distanced, silent, waiting.

A short distance away now, the road curved. He strained towards it, to leave the barrier behind, and he couldn't stop his feet moving faster. Ever so little faster despite the breathlessness, the pain. And then the corner was upon him and he broke into a run, his feet hardly making a sound on the leaf-padded track, racing from expected shouts, cries, the crash of broken branches, forms sliding before or behind, an arrow, a shot. But there was nothing except the screech of parakeets far up in the jungle rafters and the thud of his sand-shoed feet running.

The gradient beat him.

It slowed him, stopped him, left him gasping like an old man, like Kenasi, like Lorimer, heart thumping more loudly than feet, hamstrings screaming, ribs cracking. They would have known, he thought, when he first began his dash, that he would soon have to stop. The eyed-bush understood inevitabilities, allowed him to sag, clutching, against a tree, waiting as he waited until his heart subsided and the drumming grew fainter, waited until the trembling ache of legs gave way to mere ache.

Old man, he said.

Nameless as a lizard, dragging slowly along the aisle of this vegetable cathedral, he trudged the last few hundred yards to the crest, plodding through memory to the hut, to where it tottered between water and sky. This last half mile, old man, is twice the journey already taken.

Over the top now and wobbling down the dip.

There was the hut just below him.

Its silence reached up, spread itself into all the other silences as if presence had been sucked out.

It took him two minutes to cover this final distance, less, his feet urgent round by the garden, the fruit trees, the small grove of coconut palms.

The makeshift door was pulled to but already he had begun to call the old man's name as he knocked and then pushed.

Only the creak of palm fronds answered. The wind blew straight up the funnel of the bay and rammed the emptiness of the place at him like a fist.

He would have preferred a fist.

He would have welcomed the bodies behind the observing eyes.

He shoved the door wide and a black cloud rose, buzzed furiously at him, forcing him back. The insect drum dinned round the little room. As the cloud hovered like some ghastly stage effect, the boy could see Lorimer lying on his bush-pole bunk, on the sagging copra sacks, his head turned to the wall.

He moved closer and the flies fought him viciously, enraged when he managed to make himself touch the still figure, touch it and shake and call his name softly again, despite the futility of it. The flies attacked, forcing his eyes shut, driving him away from the bed.

'Oh Jesus,' he said. 'Oh Jesus.'

He was sick. He was terrified. He wanted to run and run and drive and drive without stopping without stopping and get back to Kenasi and maman and the island.

He stood heaving in the doorway staring down at the incredible acres of the sea while the gobbling and nuzzling went on behind him.

This was the worst: there was no worst.

He swallowed a couple of times, then went across the ridge and vomited till nothing came but brownish trickles. He tore off a taro leaf and rubbed his face with it and went back to the hut using the leaf as a weapon, forcing himself across the room against the ripe cheesy stink to where the old man lay with his back to the sea. He closed his lungs against the obscene sweetness, crossing this unending ten feet of space to examine what remained of Lorimer.

I'm here, old man, he thought.

He had never seen a dead man before. He still wasn't sure, couldn't believe, in spite of the flies and the stench. 'Mr Lorimer,' he shouted. 'Mr Lorimer!'

The body lay unmoving under the blanket of flies.

He couldn't bear to touch.

He thrust the thick stalk of the taro leaf at the body and gave it a push, shouting his name again and maddened, like the maddened flies, began slapping at them angrily with the leaf, slapping and slapping.

It was then he noticed it, the hole in the chest somewhere where the heart would be, the great splotch of blood on shirt and bed almost obscured by a black quivering shadow. The body was puffing up already, the features blunting so that it was not quite Lorimer. The pipe had dropped from his hand and smouldered into another black patch on the floor. It was impossible to see the eyes. The blue was lost in flies.

He backed away and the flies sped round him and re-settled.

Somehow he found at the moment that he could reconcile himself to a killing, the speed of it, rather than the slow fever and the lonely death.

He backed away through the door, away from the smell and the flies that followed him and out into the palm grove, looking back at the hut. He found another absence. The little flag, the chain-store union jack that Lorimer always flew from the eaves pole, had been ripped down. The leeched strips of it were scattered among the bushes at the side of the hut.

Why? his mind was asking. Why? He had no enemies. Why? They loved him. Why?

And then, as if the priest were actually there, he could hear Père Leyroud, a morning away, a hundred years, see his eyes mild behind his old spectacles, and Leyroud was saying, 'This is what revolution means. There's no logic to it. It makes men commit insanities without thinking.' And then the voice went on, even more gently: 'Guns can kill.'

Oh my God oh my God, the boy cried aloud.

Pressed by this greater sickness he stumbled back to the hut and sat down on the limestone blocks of steps outside, with the stench, the flies and the incredible beauty of the first days of Eden lying all before his feet, and he wept.

When Hedmasta Woodful was released from Pati headquarters with a memory of native guards all wearing plastic bullet shields, he found the Boulevard d'Urville deserted.

The rebels had gone home for lunch.

There was a steady accretion of comic effects. At one stage during the two hours he had been boxed up in one of the Pati offices, the *yeremanu* had limped through to an inner room, recognised Woodful, taken in the space-age appearance of the guards and had said to him with his wry little smile, 'Don't worry. They're messy eaters!'

Within ten minutes his presence was no longer required.

'Open your school,' they had instructed him.

'You have my school bus.'

'Take it,' they had said. 'It is out the back.'

He had gone to the rear of the building and under the impassive eyes of a crowd of island soldiers had swung into the driver's seat to find the ignition had been ripped out.

Woodful looked out the window at a mass of bland black faces and said in his coldest, most measured tones: 'You have broken it.'

They had stared back, silent, their faces registering nothing.

'You will have to push it,' he said. 'Push it.'

They remained uninterested.

He felt an enormous temptation to scream at them in Seaspeak *'you falla olgeta poussoum'* but the verb 'to push' was so close to the verb 'to copulate' he knew they would start falling about with laughter.

He examined the group of men. There were faces he had taught. He added names to the faces. He gave orders. The classroom timbre in his voice worked.

Slowly, dignified, eyes averted from the straining bodies beside the bus, Hedmasta Woodful was pushed all the way along the

Boulevard to Bipi for repairs. Bipi was closed and boarded up. Planks had been hammered across broken windows against looters. Discarded cans of food lay on the sidewalk.

Woodful stood in the awning shade biting his lip. Then, 'Turn her round,' he said, controlling his fury. He got back in behind the wheel and they moved once more down the Boulevard to the cheers of small boys who had appeared suddenly, and who followed the bus all the way to Bonser's workshop. '*I sarem. He close up!*' voices were yelling.

He left the bus, refusing to thank the pushers, and walked his rage to Bonser's house, surprised at the weakness in his legs, hating himself for having to plead favours, hating Bonser.

But all that was half a day away.

Now he sat chafing in the living-room of the school-house, forcing himself to eat a scrap lunch, listening to news bulletins and planning his own small rebellion. Pati instructions were impossible to carry out. There was no point in re-opening and the classrooms, anyway, were already stuffed with islanders who had fled there for shelter in the first panic and who still had no transport to the evacuation point at Serua. They were a mixed lot, workers from British plantations, workers from British-run stores, ni-Trinitas who had come up from Port Lena to work and were frightened of the rebels. Most of them were too terrified of reprisals to walk the ten miles out to Serua, no matter how he reasoned with them. They sat passive on the classroom floors, their blankets spread over their small bundles in composed attitudes of long-suffering.

At 2, assistant master Coombe brought boyish excitement and news of the loan of another car to help with the shuttle service. 'They've guaranteed safe passage,' he said earnestly. 'All they want is to get rid of us.'

'I'm not being chased out,' Woodful said.

'I didn't mean us,' lied the blushing Coombe. 'I meant – '

'Please,' Woodful said. 'Please. There is nothing I can do now. I have a school packed with unfed islanders, the bus has been wrecked by those madmen. Bonser will take his time about fixing it. I cannot leave these people here without some kind of authority. They're scared witless.'

'Actually,' Coombe said. There were some planters at Pig Bay, he explained, who wanted to get away. The wife was pregnant. Their car had been commandeered and the mission truck taken. 'Don't you want to help?' the young man inquired impudently.

Woodful glared at his assistant. 'I resent that, Coombe. I resent that very much.'

'We can't just sit here doing nothing.'

'I'm not doing nothing, as you put it. Not. I've organised some food for these people. Migo's seeing about that now. Something you could have done, incidentally, when I was tied up this morning. Then he's going back to Bonser's to shake him up over the bus. That's not nothing, is it? Do you want,' he asked bitterly, 'that I go down to the classrooms and organise a *sing-sing*?'

You might have thought *lap-lap*, seeing them all there beneath the flag-pole shyly poking at the rice and vegetables the yardman and his wife had prepared in a copper. The sun had dropped and the only light came from the fire under the boiler in Migo's yard. Woodful felt as if he were at some insane barbecue. His overstrung morning self had subsided into sober concern and a certain hopelessness at the thought of the still unrepaired bus. (A pox on you, Bonser. That should be easy – witty Coombe.) and the realisation that after this meal of sorts, he had to cram them all, the whole two hundred of them, into the buildings somehow and get them settled for the night.

He became schoolmasterly.

Slowly islanders got up and straggled back to the main block. Coombe dragged the sliding doors against the side walls and Woodful found himself confronting a dutiful, terrified pack that jammed the great room and flowed out onto the verandahs.

No smiles, he decided. No smiles. Firmness, kindness, clarity. He would speak slowly and carefully as he always did, certain that half of them would not understand but still refusing to yield to pidgin.

'You are being re-located.' He explained the word. 'When the school bus is returned to us, you will all be driven in shifts to Serua Point where boats will take you to the next island. You will have to wait there until you can be taken to Port Lena. Everything that can be done will be done to make sure you are fed and looked after. Is that clear?'

Not one head moved. A baby cried piercingly.

Woodful, flummoxed, looked about the room. Should he say '*you falla go smôl tai'm. You falla kam bak wat tai'm trabeul i finis?* Should he? The classroom walls shrieked with colonial power. The queen, wearing lots of cargo, a compulsory decoration of *ofisol* walls, turned an uppish profile to the whole proceedings. Beside her the duke looked merely amused. The big wall map of Kristi revealed no turmoil. The large red dot for Mataso town hadn't moved. Pictures of the Houses of Parliament, Westminster, Horse Guards at the Palace and a dated colour print of royal children with dogs dangled mute, without meaning. Woodful had a dreadful impulse to laugh, remembering Augustine Guichet commenting on the little princesses. 'If they had been playing with pigs,' she had said, 'instead of those dreary dogs, the children would have valued them more.'

That's it, Woodful decided, inspecting the scores of baffled black faces. It is all utterly without meaning: this school, my classes, all the paraphernalia of bogus western deals, totally without meaning. We've brought them cars and guns and fast foods and ill health – and an excuse for more servicing – and shoddy consumer goods and poverty. Our sort of poverty. There flashed across his eye-screen a camera close-up of ex-Brother Luke who had worked first at St Pierre, then for him, Tisa Costello, gone so far the other way in the drunken intoxication of the newcomer, he had abandoned first church, then wife, and flung himself with the energy of a copra beetle into local ritual. His new custom wife used washing powder and cake mix. Tisa Costello drank kava and practised native herbal cures. Both Costellos were rejected. The Mataso town cocktailers laughed at them. The natives had made up a song about them, whose words were coarse and unloving.

What was the answer to all this?

He knew the answer. He said, '*You falla go smôl tai'm long Lena. You falla you ol kam bak wat tai'm trabeul ia i finis.*'

Woodful was fluent in French, could find his way round in Spanish and Italian. He got by in German. This was his greatest linguistic moment.

The whole room burst into a grateful babble.

They were so polite. Even when hopeless, they were so polite.

So he wound up his little speech, talking strongly and sincerely about the boats, eschewing Seaspeak once more, using his beautiful and measured English, and only the royal family listened under mould.

Later, of course, driving out to Ebuli, he had time to resent his crumbled resolutions on the purity of language.

Driving over-fast along the faint coral strip between palm-ranks, he turned the darkness into water-sweep. There were few lights along the coast road, an occasional cooking fire from the villages and the pallor of star-shine. He had left Coombe struggling with numbers at the school allowing him – a brief smile at this point – to conjugate the verb phrase 'to do nothing'. In every tense, he hoped.

Père Bonnard was waiting outside the mission chapel at Ebuli, or appeared to be, looking older, thinner, the lines on his face ashed blue, his eyes hollow. He was, in fact, merely agitatedly taking the air and too distressed even to pray.

'Can you take one more?' he asked Woodful. 'It's the Salway boy.'

There were explanations. The priest kept hesitating as if he might discover too much from his own words. The boy had walked in, he told Woodful, late in the afternoon. In the most alarming state. He hardly knew what to do. The priest lowered his voice even further and the words were almost part of the sea's sibilance. Richard Lorimer had been shot. For a man of such definite faith it seemed he could hardly believe this.

Woodful prodded reluctance. 'When?'

The priest made a small face of distaste. Amid grief.

'About a day ago, I suppose. From what I can gather. The boy found him. God only knows what he was doing up there. He told me some garbled story I can't make head or tail of. Guilt. Self-blame. Oh a great deal of self-blame. He had a truck that he's jammed somewhere up in the hills. There was a road-block. Look, I'm telling you all this so you won't ask him questions. You mustn't ask. Anyway, he walked in. It took him half the day. One of the Duchards found him somewhere between Thresher Bay and the mission.'

There was more. 'Be gentle?' Père Bonnard asked. 'Be very gentle?'

The priest's words rose and broke and fell apart against Woodful's mind and shifted it about like sand.

In the priest's house the planter and his wife were waiting with the boy sitting apart from them, tense, beyond exhaustion. Both Gavi's feet were bandaged and shoved into over-size socks. He looked up at Woodful without recognition.

He feels my hand on his shoulder? Woodful wondered. Or accepts my smile? My words not to worry? My promise to get him back to his family?

A wild promise. He didn't know how he could keep it tonight. The thought of three guests loomed. For himself, the living-room couch and suitable insomnia as a penance for gracelessness.

He put the planter and his wife in the back seat of the car and opened the front door for the boy. Bonnard stood with the lights of the house behind him, taller, thinner, more grieved than Woodful could remember holding this moment against others in the last ten years when mischance had visited this forgotten place. The priest leaned towards the car window and spoke softly to the boy in French. Remember, he said, what I said to you. Only remember. He waved them off but it was a blessing rather than a farewell, a sign of absolution from a hand that remained uplifted, Woodful could see in the driving mirror, printing itself on the night air until distance obliterated everything.

The boy was so quiet beside Woodful that the teacher wondered if he were asleep but a brief glance showed him the wide-open eyes fixed unblinkingly on a rush of trees, seeing through and behind them. What could he say to soothe this first shock and amazement of the body? The sense of outrage beside him had the quality of a massive bruise whose storm colour eclipsed the night outside the car. Woodful concentrated on the path of the top beam, the road sliding under, hill outlines and coast where the islands humped black on greasy silver. Though there was nothing to be said, words had to come. Silence was not always balm but he was too conscious of the couple behind and shy for the boy as well as himself.

Under cover of back-seat chatter he said to Gavi, without turning his head, as if he were convincing himself as well, 'This day, Gav, this year, next year and the one after that and even beyond that, they'll all string out like old Lorimer's. No harder, no softer than they are for any of us. Remember that. You'll live through them, as he did.'

'You don't understand,' the boy said. 'I *helped* take them from him.' His voice was so low Woodful had to incline his head to hear.

'Took what?'

'His years.'

That stopped him. He couldn't reply to that, to such self-slaughter. He drove in silence for nearly a mile. Finally, 'I don't know what happened today,' he said, 'any more than you've told me. Perhaps you did, indirectly.' He heard the boy gasp with the pain of accusation. 'Soothers won't help. Soft things. If you did, if that is what you believe, then admit it and accept it. That's the only thing and the hardest. Accepting.' He fumbled around in his mind. Nothing seemed right. 'You'll have learned not to make excuses. That's one of the best things you can ever discover.'

He could hear Gavi crying, not loudly, but insistently as if the tears would never stop.

'The main thing,' Woodful went on, turning the car off the coast road and heading for the school, 'is to be sorry. Beyond that what can you do? Oh it will hurt for a long time, but time does other things besides pass. Sorrow is one thing, Gav. Regret's another. And regret is useless.'

Outside the school-house he switched the engine off and began concerning himself with the planter and his wife. Gavi sat unmoving.

'I can't stay,' he said.

'Just a minute then.' Woodful took the couple up to the house and left them to organise themselves into the spare room. It only took a minute and he was back at the car vexed for this boy who was still slumped in his grief.

The school grounds were filled with moving shadow and men moving behind shadow.

'What shall I do with you?' Woodful demanded. 'It had to be said.'

The boy nodded and now the other two were gone indulged in great gulping sobs, working his head against his arms, while words dribbled out wetly. He asked to be taken to Madame Guichet's. He begged. 'And there's something else,' he said at last, 'I've got something here. I took it from the hut. It's Mr Lorimer's.' He blinked, remembering the family photo on the wall, a mother and father in Edwardian England, the mouldering books of poetry, the unwashed plate beside the make-shift sink. He groped inside his shirt and pulled out a rolled-up notebook. 'It's his,' he said. 'It was the top one. Do you think he'd mind?'

'He would want it,' Woodful decided for him. 'He's part of you now. He would want it.'

'An island is such a small place,' Lorimer had written, 'that we all know each other too well. The *colons*, the traders, the imports, all of us living in this narrow ribbon round the coast. A red white and blue ribbon, two ways. But we don't know the people. Can never know. It's not possible that our imported thrust-on-them bully-a-coon culture can ever connect with theirs or have any meaning beyond combustion engines and canned food.

There's no give and take of the soul.

Should there be?

I sit here and look out over the bay where Spaniards said Masses and failed to connect nearly four hundred years back – and it's no different now. We've failed to connect.

Take us, we say, we order rather, and take our culture.

Work our copra and cocoa and we'll lash you to a punishing God.

We'll give you the right to buy canned peas and cardboard breakfast foods. We'll shove you into the perma-press down-market clothes of our culture. But we don't want to know about yours.

It's ape stuff, anyway.'

There was a drawing then of *man bush* swinging from a liana, his free hand clutching a transistor radio, his ears muffed with earphones and a tin-opener shoved in his loincloth.

There was a little poem under that:

'The woad gave way to chasuble
And penis-sheath to crotch-tight jeans.
Yet Mr Vigors quite forgot
The cod-piece in his Latin screams.'

'High summer,' Lorimer wrote some pages on, 'and I console myself, if that is the phrase, for I love it here, with dreams of ice. Long unploughed slopes of snow flowing over the mountain jungles to the north where the hot green comes in waves. In waves and waves of indescribable sticky, leaf-damp clutching heat. The skin crawls with it.

And yet, believe it or not, it was cold last night, insomniac at two, at three, stuck here on a ledge above the sea with the wind funnelling into the bay through all those lost Masses.'

January, Wednesday. It's another year.

I forgot to put the flag up yesterday.

Duchard, Bonnard – all of them – think I'm a colonial red-neck-England-my-England moron. That isn't why I fly the flag. It's only a cheap kid's one, anyhow, chain-store stuff of reinforced paper for nonsense-waves on *ofisol* days, all the *pikinini* cheering their subjugation. Christ! It's nice to be able to be blasphemous and treacherous on paper no one will ever see.

It's there to remind me that there's an outer world of which we are the jocular rim.

Or the true centre.

It doesn't stand for England. It's a symbol of towns and people and the solace of books, unending ant-lines of libraries down whose supermarket corridors I wheel a trolley loaded with narcotic mementoes of my lost civilisation. Well, *my* sort of civilisation, I must apologise. Long-learnt habits die hard.

I feel such an alien here. Such an outsider, still, having lived in these parts fifty years.

Why don't I go? It's like being in love.

No. The flag is nothing as such. It's Gonzaga's skull. A *memento mori* of all the things I've given up.

Trying to carve out a good sentence. There's little else to do. I might as well give myself up to that.

January 3rd. The reason I forgot to haul up my little piece of cultural irony, my red white and blue irony, was Christmas.

Believing in the Christ child comes harder and harder.

Père Bonnard took me down to the mission at Port Ebuli for Christmas dinner and I sat there eating cold baked *natou*, a sort of wood pigeon, and something the nuns had made called yam surprise. Père Bonnard and I played chess later and drank brandy the Bishop sent for Christmas. I told him, looking at the Crib in the grounds and all the *pikinini* wool-heads goggling at the gilded Mary, about my difficulty – in believing, that is.

He surprised me. 'Do you think I don't feel the same, too?' he said.

For a while the alienation was eased.

February 4th. When there is nothing to write there is nothing to write.

I dreamed of snow again and a glacier so unutterably deep and blue it went through to the other side of the world.

Yesterday Arim Tevi brought me a bamboo flute he'd made. He's *man bush*, not from the mission, and he lives in a little village behind Tsureviu. His people are used to me now. I know a few words of their dialect and I've taught them a few words of mine. *Frari*, they call me. It means Friday in Seaspeak. Now that is strange. What do you make of that, Defoe?

I can't get anything out of the flute except a high-pitched whining sound.

This morning I cut more holes in it, approximating what I remember of recorder positions. Pretty awful, but I can get a tune, now. Or the sketch of a tune. I played the 'Keel Row' for hours.

Like the flag, it's simply a symbol of love, not ownership.

March 23rd. I do miss music.

After the generator collapsed last month I couldn't afford another.

I've been getting by with a kerosene stove and the last time I went to Mataso town a week back, purely to assure my blood, I bought a little battery tape-deck at Bipi. A useless thing when I want great thunder-heads of sound rocking out over the Bay of the Two Saints, and the tapes distort in the heat. Imagine Schubert with mildew. Mozart with mildew. Especially Mozart. All those clear bell-like phrases fogged up with damp and mould. It's not so bad with Schubert, somehow. *Im grünen* sounds better.

April 1st. My day. Don't ask why. It should be obvious. The sweat is running away in small winds.

There's a busy-ness in these hills.

Something is up. Something's going on.

Last week an unpleasant bit of work called Leblanc drove through and down to Tsureviu. He had two boys with him and they had guns.

I'm not sure what he's after. He was all Algerian teeth and smiles. I had the feeling he was trying to impress recruits.

When he went by some hours later, there were six boys in the back of his truck.

The isle is full of noises.

April 10th. I ran out of kerosene yesterday. And reading matter – more important. It forced me out and down to Port Ebuli where Bonnard wisely rations me the few books he has that I haven't yet read. There's a loyal sister in Montreal, somewhere, who keeps him supplied. 'You could die,' he says, 'from over-feeding.' And he shakes with quiet laughter. '*La mort par la nourriture. Un excès de livres.* You know what they say about starving men.'

The nuns invited me to lunch. They are dear hard-working things, one as old as I am. Never a complaint. Perhaps they're as happy to see a different face as I am.

Why do I stay?

I am in love.

So I hate as well.

It is my *man ples* now.

While we were eating, Père Bonnard had a visitor. Tommy Narota had driven down from Vimape with three officials of the Talasa Pati.

What do I think of Narota?

I've known him too long and don't know him at all. It's impossible to know. I see only the externals, despite fifty years. Yes, despite fifty years. Off and on through all those years. Five lens-quick, shutter-quick decades.

Tommy Narota and I have grown our wrinkles together, though he has fewer than I. But then he has fewer years.

Fifty summers.

The hills haven't moved.

The sea always moves.

I stay.

The sea's wrinkles are eternally young.

Tommy is what they call a sweet bloke. That's a western white judgement. He has dignity and humour and is kind. What more can one want? Being a *yeremanu* has given him voyages to Europe and America. Among the people of Vimape he has great prestige. He has seen Australia. I'm laughing. Laughing.

We talk about his family and his rheumatism and his plans for Kristi. Père Bonnard doesn't want to be involved. 'L'Eglise,' he says to Tommy, '*ne s'intéresse pas aux affaires politiques.*' (*Quel mensonge!*) Narota speaks French as well. He speaks our European tongues hesitantly but with a lot of charm. And he jokes. He's a whimsical chap. Would his tribe have a word for whimsical?

Despite Bonnard's unwillingness, Narota talks about secession. He has been talking about it for years, even before he went 'public', as they say. Like the boy crying 'wolf'. I knew him down in Trinitas when he was running a fishing boat at Matapao Bay. Everyone liked him, black and white. And especially women, so the stories ran. White women too? Ah well.

I look at this celibate and polygamist sitting happily together under the allamanda vines along Bonnard's verandah and I have a rush of happiness like wine in the veins; and that distancing, that alienation that so worries me, becomes the shadow of a shadow. Yet I can never think black. Tommy's a *hapkas* after all – he has the genetic worst of both worlds.

Everywhere the *namatal* trees are heavy with pink flowers.

April 12th: I must put this down.

I forget so easily these days. Seventy next month. Wonder what I can do to celebrate?

Last Thursday Père Bonnard was telling me of his days on Ambrym at Sesivi. Poor Bonnard. Deep in volcanic ash.

He was walking along the beach early one morning performing his own mysteries, one finger stuck in his breviary, when he came upon one of the villagers doing an intricate and delicate drawing with a sharpened stick in the black sand. Bonnard asked permission to watch and when the young man finished tried to show his delight and admiration.

'What is it?' he asked, pointing, making question faces.

'*Tanis,*' the boy replied. '*Rom tanis.*'

Ah, Bonnard thought, the Rom Dance, the dance of young men at the time of ripe yams, the dance of quasi-priesthood and power.

Then he held out his hand, palm up, pleading, for the drawing tool and the young man with a smile gave it to him.

Below the pattern of the Rom Dance he drew a chalice with the Host rising from it, like a sun from a cup. Or a half-world.

And underneath he printed carefully

Christus
    Natus
        Est.

The whole thing looked like a flower. And the young man laughed, pointing, smiling with a split of white in his handsome face.

Then a little wave broke and when it ebbed, Bonnard's sand drawing was gone.

Gavi had nearly reached the end of the notebook. Lorimer's dark sprawl of a hand went on for only a few pages more.

He didn't know if he felt better or worse reading this but he knew he had to finish.

April 24th: I'm not sure if the date is correct.

Last week I had a recurrence of fever and lost track of time.

Arim Tevi found me rolling around on my stinking little bunk and he must have walked all the way to the mission for Bonnard was up within the day, I suppose, and hauled me off for some doctoring. When he drove me back he relaxed on his book rationing and I have three *policiers* on my table.

'I'm no good on the *argot*,' I told him.

'That's good,' he said. 'They'll last longer.'

May 4th: The world is very beautiful. I must admit it. I see so clearly these days.

Despite the indifference of nature all about me and the terrifying threat of its power of – what can I call it? – continuance? – I can only sit back gape-mouthed in these early mornings. Words aren't enough. The softness of it all, the draped clouds on the great ranges to the north and west and the Pic thrusting like a needle with the sun coming up, stretching the grey into blue as it comes. The moisture is wonderful then – infinite small glister-bubbles of light that spit colour.

I no longer think of snow at these moments. It's the time of day when I do my small bit of gardening. And then the first cup of coffee. The coffee perfume amid all the vegetable green. And the day stretches before me.

I am making a bamboo flute for Arim like the one he gave me and with holes in it like mine. It's taking longer than I thought to shape the stops.

May 19th: There's been a great deal of activity on the Mangarisu Road. From here on the hillside I can hear the grinding of trucks and an occasional order shouted in French. It must be the toothy

Algerian. Men shout out to each other. But I can't be bothered driving down to investigate. Still feel weak after the fever.

I have taught myself 'Lillabulero' and sit playing my little repertoire of half a dozen pieces in the late afternoon.

The bamboo gives the music a sweetly woody sound and the sounds it makes must carry far down into the delta and along to Tsureviu for as I sat on the porch last night, playing into dusk, Arim came up, a basket of fish hanging from one shoulder.

I gave my concert again and he sat beside me and I handed him the pipe I'd made for him with its holes and thumb-stop and showed him a few finger positions.

He is so quick.

In a week, I swear, we'll be playing 'Lillabulero' together.

I tried to persuade him to stay while I cooked the fish. He had even gutted them for me. But he shook his head and smiled and became part of the twilight.

Protein. Protein. The fish are a kind of mullet and very sweet.

God bless you, Arim, I say aloud. And am surprised at my use of the word. God. It has a nice feeling, that, God catching me in a slip of the tongue.

Happy birthday, old man, I tell myself. It has come one week early.

Gavi shut the stained covers of Lorimer's diary and put his head on his arms and was beyond tears.

Taking hostages was another cliché of revolution.

The Trumbles, father and son, had been taken to Vimape to wait uselessly in Eden for three hours until Narota, returning from Talasa headquarters, greeted his old friend with expressions of outrage and ordered that he be instantly released. Perhaps he could look at his second youngest son first? The boy had fever.

For three hours Trumble had felt cut off, apart, the wrong colour, despite the gentleness that went with his detention. He would never understand the islanders, he admitted, no matter how long he treated their pains.

Dokta, mi sor bel blong mi.

Dokta, mi traout tri tai'm long nai't.

Dokta, mi gat fiva. Hed blong mi i sor.

Oh Rosella, oh Jubilee, oh Solomon, *you takem pill hia, eh? You takem. You sik no mo.*

He was a presence. A voice. He was never reality.

They would take his pills and go away to their custom medicine – and something would cure, he didn't know what. He didn't really believe any longer that there was a point in knowing so long as they got better and the dirty grey left their handsome skins. He felt surer when it was a gash to be stitched, a broken limb to set, something so externally physical neither he nor they could doubt the efficacy of what he did. But in the fever months what greater magic resided in antibiotics than infusions of bush herbs? They were so polite. He suspected politeness rather than a genuine plea for help lay behind their visits. He could have been shouting his cures like some quack pedlar over long distances through soundless lips.

Now, on riot morning, it was political sorcery they wanted, their faces set towards a destiny as fragile as wind pattern on water.

So the Pati rebels released him and his son after three hours, first politely driving him back to the Paddock so that he could survey his ruined dispensary and the wreckage of his house and then letting them go. Mrs Trumble? he asked. They shook their heads and suggested Mataso town. His car had been taken and there was nothing for it but to walk back to Mataso's lunch-time street and begin searching.

Augustine Guichet spared them the long trudge in the heat.

As they walked past her house in the Rue Gauguin they saw her, ignoring revolution, reading at her garden table, unruffled beneath the heavy flamboyants. '*Qelle sottise!* Such nonsense, this riot!' Yet she put her book away, insisted on driving them to the Boulevard and nagged loitering children for information. 'She knock,' one little girl finally admitted at the back of Bipi, pointing along the street to the Dancing Bears. 'She knock and she cry out.'

Now Trumble crossed footpaths to the music of broken glass.

He refused point blank to be forced out.

After he had persuaded wife and son to Serua Point, hauled there in Madame Guichet's dying Citroën, leaving them to wait in the ardent sun for the promised boats, small fragments of the mid-morning returned to stun him into love: a delicate change in his wife, some odd reduction (he could never know that she had whispered shame-faced to the long-late madame of the whore-house on d'Urville 'But I envied you. I *envied* you. We all did.'); Chloe's smokey voice saying something about 'a belief in the next minute, the next hour. *Nothing* can be *something*.'; his subtly altered wife planting a kiss like a sticker on the remnants of Chloe's face; Augustine Guichet watching his boy's straight back as he headed into the crowd at Serua and admitting gruffly, 'I always wanted a son.'

He walked past the Ciné Mangrove where two young men were pasting up Talasa Pati posters – *Independens Kristi Now.* The young men nodded and smiled and said '*goudaftnoun*' echoing his own nod and smile. Insanity, Doctor Trumble thought. On this glassy music.

Outside the hotel there was a group of newspaper men and photographers who had flown in on chartered aircraft from Port Lena. Rebels in battle dress posed with big white friendly smiles. Madness. He spoke to one of the reporters asking when they had got in and was told half an hour ago. 'There's more of us,' the journalist said. 'Another plane load coming in tomorrow. Brits, French, *Guardian*, *Times*, Reuters. This pub's never had it so good.' He lowered his voice. 'What a circus, eh? Like drag night at Rent-a-Dress! Fuckin' amazing!'

'Well yes,' Trumble said. 'Yes and no.'

'You a local?'

'Yes.'

'Got time to tell me about it?'

The journalist was a big good-looking fellow, young, aggressive. Trumble was made more aware than ever of thinning hair, straggly beard, the research assistant's stoop.

'No,' he said. 'No time.'

He went in to the desk and booked himself the last room available.

Le Parc de l'Unité was a few acres of over-bright grass on the edge of the sea, a triangle whose long side was formed by the Boulevard. There were mango trees and an ancient banyan and closer to the Channel those low growing shrubs known as *burao blong solwata*. It had always been a meeting-place and its story stretched back into custom, into the kava ceremonies when men sat drinking in the weighted dark, watching the stones, watching the stars fall. It was a place to *storian*.

Now it was mown and clipped by Le Département de Travaux Publics whose buildings adjoined and whose presence has ruptured the sense of *man ples*. Cars and trucks grind along the Boulevard. Kids punt balls. Some well-wisher has erected swings.

It had rained during the night and Trumble had lain awake on its battering giving wasted worries to his family at Serua, obsessed by the pathos of the grubby bandages about his wife's knees and seeing the dirty lint float like a goodbye bandanna through all the febrile dreams that came before dawn.

He woke to puddles and a greater violence of green.

Through the sunlight, through the greenery, through the morning, people in their hundreds – ni-Kristi, *hapkas*, *colons*, settler sympathisers of Talasa – had come walking, cycling, driving in from villages and plantations along the coast. Trumble stood on the balcony outside his room to watch. Expatriate French wives shoved strollers, native women wore their best Mother Hubbards, shoulder ribbons bouncing, native men had *lokalok* flowers stuck in their hair.

They were gathering to hear the *yeremanu*, Tommy Narota.

To cheer Tommy Narota.

Independens! Independens!

He put his ear to the shell of the day, stunned by the light-heartedness of the crowd, the surge of it, the bare skin and the clad, the white faces and the black, the feathers, the flower wreaths, the *masta* panamas, the loincloths, all, all moving in a slow river to the park.

Outside the hotel journalists crowded under the verandah awning and when he went downstairs there were more in the lobby with notebooks and ant-eater pencils. The young reporter who had accosted him the day before was still sitting over coffee in the dining-room. His eye brightened when he spotted Trumble who tried to slip past him unnoticed.

Trapped. Endless questions about colonial policy, about approaching independence for the whole island group, about Kristi's autonomy. Trumble fenced most of them. How could he speak honestly of the criminality of colonialism, the banditry of planters and trading empires, of the fools of men who strutted on the red carpets of tradition sustained by a bit of coloured rag, centuries of acute class distinction and a belief in their own godhead?

He said, 'It's time we went. We should never have been here. We have no moral right in any of it.'

'Really,' the man from the *Guardian* said. His eyebrows were indescribable arcs while he scribbled notes. 'You really think so?'

'I know so.'

'You don't believe in the empire then? The value of the mother country?'

'Don't make me puke,' Trumble said. 'This island's a motherless child and always has been. You don't really think Britain or France has ever given a bugger for what happened to the islanders do you? Are you as naive as you pretend they are, the ni-Kristi? The islanders know no one has ever given a tuppeny damn. They know.

They always have known. That's what makes the continued presence of these do-gooder brigands so intolerable.'

'I say,' the man from the *Guardian* said. 'That's really interesting.'

But Trumble had taken his coffee and gone back to his room.

He showered and slept again and woke into noon-time, his mouth stale, his eyes gummed in the twilight behind the heavy curtains.

All traffic in the Boulevard had come to a stop and the heaving mass of people in the park pressed out over the railings and along the footpath. Talasa Pati policemen were stalking the crowd perimeters, upright and important, their guns sloped.

Trumble showered quickly and re-dressed in his sweat-stiff clothing. Downstairs he had to shove through a crowd of newsmen gathered outside the hotel entrance to watch the mob across the road. The man from the *Guardian* nodded briefly, still in shock Trumble thought sourly, and followed him with two others out into the sun. One of them came up behind Trumble and said 'Reuters' and 'He'll be coming any minute now. I hope you can fill me in.'

Trumble decided to pretend the other man wasn't there but as he fought his way through the northern edge of the crowd, he was conscious of the journalist panting behind his shoulder. In the crush he caught a glimpse of Augustine Guichet, her face half-blocked out by sun-glasses steering young Salway forward, her head bent as she said something to a face that was grey with distress. It was the most transitory of glimpses. He tried to move across but the reporter pressed closely against his back nudging him on and the weight of the crowd decided their direction.

The whole throng rippled suddenly – Trumble felt the wave pass through him and beyond – with jolting tension.

Coming along the Boulevard from the direction of Pati headquarters, past the markets, the Magasin Lantane, the *mairie*, down to the park entrance and the makeshift rostrum, were two army jeeps and a truck. As the vehicles swung slowly into the grounds, marking languid time in the heavy post-noon, a great sigh – the held breath of expectation – rose from the crowd and lost itself in the trees. The assembly became one animal swooping forward to see Narota, then became a throbbing mass of individuals shoving and pushing as they craned.

161

Narota was standing in the back of the second jeep wearing his Bipi ceremonial wrap like a toga magnificently draped over his chubby chest. He wore a beret, army style, a double circle tusk and an enormous smile.

The crowd began chanting his name, their need for him, their needs for Kristi, in echo-resonance of the *toka* dances the way those voices took up isolated song-cries then swept together a pounding rhythm created from those cries, weaving all the time through and round and over the *yeremanu*'s name.

People waved flags and *lokalok* flowers. Palm branches beat green arcs in the air.

In the centre of the crowd the stamping began and spread in a drum-roll to the rocking edges where Trumble stood. For a moment he saw Gavi Salway stamping with the rest, his face grave and concentrated and Madame Guichet laughing, her head back, her great compound eyes turned like a beetle's into the sun. All of them, all stamping as Tommy Narota limped across the cleared space, soldiers on either side, and began to hobble his painful joints onto the platform.

The roar of homage broke on him like high seas. He loved it. You could see he loved it. He turned his cherubic face to the crowd, his arms raised.

The chanting changed to cheers as he stood on the rostrum, cheers that rose like wind over the running tides of love, wind that beat all about him as he stood there in the shade of the mango trees his great smile beaming out to them, through them, across the Channel.

This will never be my country, Trumble thought, watching the hundreds and hundreds of absorbed black faces raised in worship to this pudgy prophet. Despite the years here, I'm in stranger territory, newly arrived. What was he doing there? Did he really believe he was helping? How had life manoeuvred him into this, a victim of misplaced emotionalism? There was Tisa Sullivan screaming his head off, both hands, both, for God's sake, waving Talasa flags. The European settlers were more restrained but he could tell the revivalist measures of it all had entered their blood.

What do I think of Narota? Trumble asked himself. Why am I so alien, so unneeded by any of them? There's their *marasin*, their medicine, up there on stage, his double circle tusk swinging, his brown hands showering plump benisons. Trumble felt sun-claws ripping into the back of his neck; he was still dopey from broken sleep. What did he think of him, that ageing kindly man he had treated so unavailingly for rheumatism? He'd talked with Narota in his pokey consulting room at the Paddock and had said 'Try this, Tommy, or this or this.' And the pains continued to rack him and finally he'd abandoned Dokta Trumble and his western *puripuri* and gone to a *kleva* and swallowed gallon upon gallon of herbal juices and felt better and then he'd gone to a Tonkinese acupuncturist in Mataso town whose needles discovered cure points. But he still limped.

The cheering would help most of all.

I don't know what to think, Trumble decided. Except to like him. He had endured pain and smiled and brought little presents of lime and papaw from the gardens at Vimape and cried once when he carried in his seventh daughter suffering from measles and after she recovered there was a leaf-wrapped parcel of turtle meat he had caught off Thresher Bay and a woven basket filled with *naoura*, the sweet river prawns. Courtesy. Feeling. Courage. What did he think? I cry for you, Tommy Narota, taking on the *gavman* men. Challenging a system that believes criminal practices are a form of beneficence. I cry for you.

'Listen,' the journalist from Reuters was hissing in Trumble's ear. 'This really is something! Do you know there are chaps here from all over just waiting to hear what the guy's going to say? UPI. AAP. The *Washington Post* came in this morning. Wouldn't read about it, would you? Some tin-pot baboon cage and the whole news world has gone ape!' He had his notebook ready and a little battery cassette recorder hung round his neck. 'There's the *Times. Paris Match.* And at least six blokes from Oz.'

A wind leapt, cracking the coconut palms at the southern end of the park. The military aides were having trouble with the public address system that they'd rigged up with the longest lead in the world stretching back to a power point somewhere in the Travaux Publics. One of Narota's provisional cabinet ministers stepped to the front and took the microphone.

'Tess-ting,' he called in his sing-song accent. 'Tess-ting.'

The crowd beat its hands together. Shrilled. The P.A. system crackled and the cabinet minister began counting: *wan tu tri fo faif*. He looked up frowning, weighed down with importance and then bending to the microphone began again: *wan tu tri fo . . .*

'I say,' the man from Reuters said, 'I don't think they've discovered the mike goes up and down yet.'

Trumble laughed dutifully but he felt affronted, not just for Gabriel Toma, struggling on stage, but for himself. You bloody outsiders, he fumed inwardly, coming in here sneering.

'God I wish they'd get on with it,' the man from Reuters was saying.

Toma moved aside. The sun was plunging in straight from the third quarter. It was like being bombarded by laser. Narota, swinging his robes with a splendid wide gesture, took three steps forward and pulled the microphone up with a flourish. The crowd began its wild cheering again and Trumble heard the man from Reuters say 'touché' and forgave him and the cheering went on and on until Narota, harvesting all this applause like yam, raised both arms in the presidential manner, the benedictus, the victory sign suspended in the hot blue air – and the great black mass fell silent.

Trumble heard the click as the journalist switched on his cassette. Everyone was eye-eating, glutting on the frail packing-case platform and this rotund little smiler who appeared to be having trouble beginning.

The silence stretched.

'Dear people,' Narota said at last in his broken English, 'dear brothers and sisters of Kristi. Today we have become a nation. Today we are independent.' He allowed the crowd to scream approval. '*Tede man Kristi i bos long Kristi.*' There was universal madness. 'Today we are separate from the other islands. I declare it. Kristi is now an independent land.'

Narota waited amiably for the shouts and applause to die away. It took a long time.

He raised his arms again and the crowd obligingly subsided into a listening silence. Papa Yam, Trumble thought, bringing them presents.

'We are a gentle people,' Narota went on. 'We want no violence. *Mi falla i no askem long Trinitas pawa blong sapotem mi falla.* We do not ask the Trinitas government to suport us – *mi falla i askem long tufalla blong no kilim mi falla* – we ask them not to kill us!'

It was delivered with an ironic grin. The crowd loved it. They screamed with laughter.

'Trinitas is Trinitas,' Narota pronounced. His radiance entrapped them all. 'Kristi is Kristi.'

The cheering was crazier than before. People jumped, stamped, flung hibiscus flowers in the air, waved tangled streamers of fern and vine.

Narota stepped back from the microphone and began whispering to Toma, the interim Minister of Public Works. Their heads closed, nodded and moved apart. They stood there smiling at the jumping crowd. The minutes lengthened. The leaders kept smiling.

'Christ,' the man from Reuters said. 'Is that all? Twelve thousand miles for that?'

He was mopping at his face with a sodden handkerchief. His pink British skin looked punished. He glared at the make-shift platform and the men on it and at that moment Narota stepped forward and took up the microphone again.

'And now,' he announced, 'I have this to tell you.' He repeated his words in Seaspeak. He paused. Marvellous smile this time. 'There will be a barbecue at the other end of the park.'

That was it.

That was *it*.

The guards started rolling up yards and yards of electric flex. The Minister of Public Works assisted Tommy Narota totter down the three steps to the grass and the *yeremanu* began to move slowly, painfully but graciously like a royal progress across the lawn to the area near the swings. The crowd struggled forward, wanting to touch but the guards shoved them back. Yet every now and then Narota held out a hand, *was* touched, clasped, patted.

'I don't believe this!' the man from Reuters kept saying. His eyes had a glazed look and they were very red. 'God! I've been flying for thirty-odd hours. Special charter yesterday. Cost me the earth. Well, not me personally, but the old firm. They're making a killing the smart boys here while the blockade's on. Just a killing. And what do I get? Six bloody sentences. Well, maybe seven. *Little* sentences. And then some crap about a barbecue. I'm going off to get pissed.

Want to come?'

'Rain check,' Trumble said lightly and slipped away into the shifting crowd.

He could have cheered Narota too.

Secession is catching.

Little islands around Kristi seceded for company's sake, making their move before the glorious moment of independence and there were further meetings in Mataso town to underscore all previous statements made by Tommy Narota.

Nengle, Narota. I see you. With your fourteen article constitution, your *Dekleresen blong Provisional Gavman blong Kristi*.

Mataso town, deprived of its senses – telephones, transport, food – managed to stagger on with supplies smuggled in at Thresher Bay. The French armoury was left loosely locked. French government trucks sat waiting to be stolen, their keys in the ignition, suggestive exclamation points. *Oué! Oué!*

Rain drenched Kristi for three days, the streets steamed with slush and on the wharves fish and copra rotted. The smell became part of the island's identity. Then the rain stopped as suddenly as it had begun but payback darkened the sky.

Payback came fast.

The interim government in Trinitas organised a joint force of British troops and French *garde-mobile* to act as candle-snuffers for the tiny flame of revolution.

Punitive forces have never had such a welcome.

On a sodden morning less than two weeks after the revolution, Hercules carriers flew into Mataso town, the great clouds swirling across the Channel matching the outpourings of soldiers, two hundred of them, who raced into battle formation, Hollywood attack positions and guns at the ready, all around Mataso airport.

There was a huge crowd of islanders to meet them.

The crowd laughed as the troops sprang threateningly about, thinking it was official display rather like their custom dances.

Then, as one, the islanders rushed forward with garlands of bougainvillea, streamers of fern, and flung them, shouting with pleasure, about the necks and shoulders of the troops. Native women linked by a trailing chain of hot pink bracts wound their way through cheers. The islanders laughed, chanted and sang, and the soldiers, crouching, grinned sheepishly, suspecting some finer Melanesian irony.

'Shit, what is this?' one British marine was heard to say. The world had gone crazy with petals.

'We're not copping any,' the man next to him whispered out of the side of his mouth. 'It's only the frogs!'

The officers of both groups ran in little worried packs, conferring, arguing – flowers and no blood! – and the commander of the British troops, languishing from lack of violence, called his men to attention and, stepping forward into the lonely centre of the landing ground, announced with some diffidence that this combined army of two great nations was assuming control. This presumption of priority enraged the French captain who stepped forward as well and announced the same thing.

The singing kept going on. It ignored both utterances.

Oh Mista Mercet, you trikim! You no tok tru! You gammon!

The islanders had been seduced by Mercet's words given to Narota over Radio Talasa the previous day: the government in Trinitas will have no jurisdiction over Kristi. We understand your problems. The double government will continue in Kristi as it has always done until a solution can be found. British and French troops are coming. They are coming to protect you. They will stay until a solution is reached.

Pauvre Mercet! Poor Colonel!

He hadn't really envisaged a pitched battle on the lush green airstrip of Mataso town but he had meant to defuse something, if only with flowers. At the back of his mind there had been notions of his finest hour, the brilliance of Mercet as diplomat war-time leader, holder of outposts. If there were a faint twinge of guilt as he lied to Tommy Narota during that urgent radio call to Talasa headquarters, he repressed it. It was too late for him to lose face, even to Narota. And funnily enough, he liked Tommy. Yes. Liked. He would hate having to admit at this late hour that the whole seccession plan, the revoultion, the speeches, the dreams had all been for nothing.

Mercet had already been lashed by his superiors in Paris. It was all too much. He would be going in a week, Paris having grudgingly decided to allow him to stay for the Independence ceremony in Trinitas. And then, he knew it, it would be the backwater of some provincial French town with its dusty streets and flies and dried out date palms.

Kohito, Mercet. *Kohito*.

Adieu. Adieu.

So the troops stood bemused under peltings of blossom, peltings of greeting, of singing, of chanting, the Frenchmen busy disentangling gun-barrels from trails of allamanda and finding purple and scarlet leaves clinging to their forage caps and army shirts.

The singing simply would not stop.

The British and French officers in charge were snapping salutes at each other.

'What now?' the Britisher asked.

'You suggest?'

'I suggest,' the other said, 'that we form ranks, get the trucks unloaded from the planes and establish our presence peacefully.'

They both understood euphemism.

The officers formed their men into ranks and marched them stubbornly into a pelted confetti of flowers and smiles. The softest of yieldings.

Then at one corner of the field just beyond the terminal building, a jeep came into view and rolled forward as the chanting islanders made way. The jeep stopped within a few yards of the troops and Tommy Narota hauled himself to a standing position in the back while one of his own rebel soldiers sprang out and stood with sloped gun.

Narota raised both arms. The officers checked the advancing men and the crowd of islanders held breath and flowers still.

'We welcome you,' Narota announced. His smile was gentle and warm. 'We know you have come to protect us. I see you are armed with guns but there must be no violence. I have said that before. It is alien to us. We are grateful that you are here to look after our interests.'

The British commanding officer found himself shaking his head. He caught the eye of his second in command. What the hell was going on, he wondered. Should they arrest this crazy hothead now?

He seemed to have things arse up.

He blinked and tuned in again to Narota's words.

'All we are asking for are rights for our people, the people of Kristi.'

Narota, waving one hand like a pontiff, was driven off in another rain of cheers and blossom; the crowd scattered along roads leading in to Mataso and the idiot troops followed, stepping out precisely through mud.

Rainspeak.

In the serenity of Vimape under rain, in the wisdom of taro and firefly and the numbing force of kava, Narota explodes the fraudulence of Mercet.

Mercet was the flute player of uninterpretable phrases, performing, he imagined, delicate arabesques for a dancing whale. The great animal could only sniffle and whistle agonies of reply, display a quiescent curiousity as it approached the player, its monster body poised in the anguish of response.

Mercet had been wrong.

There were two flute players, one on an instrument of political silver, the other on bamboo, and the mathematical vibrations of their notes were never accordant.

It took only days for Narota to realise betrayal as the foreign troops moved around the town challenging his interim police force, raising the new Trinitas flag in Le Parc de l'Unité and confiscating firearms.

It hardly seemed worth going on.

He was hiding and ashamed. His ministers, his pastor, his wives and children, his ragamuffin rebel army could not penetrate the calamity that had doused him.

Independence day, the unshackling of colonialism, had come and gone in a blaze of fireworks that shook the harbour at Port Lena. He might have heard the cheering and the blooting of car horns all the way to Vimape. Speeches in three languages established the Nabiru government rule. *Aeland* Kristi was to be absorbed. Little *aeland*, he said into the rain, we grieve for you.

Fireworks spluttered into dark. Trembath left after one last cynical bash at the bongos. Mercet was removed within hours of Lemoa's taking over. Leblanc and Mango Wilson had fled Kristi without warning on a lugger bound for Noumea. Although there was sporadic looting, the blowing up of a bridge, the tearing down of the new flag in the park and Radio Talasa's daily broadcasts from the transmitter at Vimape (We will never yield. We will struggle to the end. Radio Nabiru tells lies. *Radio Nabiru tok gammon.*), no one's heart was really in it.

These are marginalia, the current skirmishes and harryings, the mindless carry-on of louts. Mataso town had received the peace-keeping force with a mixture of panic and relief, the town dividing sharply into those who saw them as saviours and those who regarded them as invaders. When it became obvious that the Talasa Pati revolutionary government was not to be recognised, that these were the forces of Nabiru, *colons* began a hasty packing. Some left houses filled with furniture taking only clothes and cash. District Agent Boutin left town even before Mercet.

In the sleepless after-midnight with the crack of falling water on the broad leaves of the banana thatch and the taro, Narota wept a little for a crumbled kingdom. Weep? The doors had been held up only by vines, the floors tracked by ant colonies, the windows the fragile panelling of spiders.

Rainspeak and tearspeak and the river shouting its permanence and his failure from the gorge.

Feelings had hardened. Refugees drifted back and Narota's own troops were attacked by aggrieved returned islanders. A mob of them had gone to Loka Beach near Thresher Bay and beaten the fibro walls of an American tourist resort to death. Wiring was ripped out and plumbing torn up in a vile dismemberment. The wall to wall floated in the bay. Now the sea looked in at the cheap little rooms built by the Salamander Corporation and the rooms looked back with the comprehension of a glass eye.

Tearspeak.

There had been violence. Despite his pleas, his insistence on the gentleness of revolution, Lorimer had died. Rainspeak and tearspeak. Oh Lorimer, Narota said in the unassisting dark of his palm cathedral, the walls enclosing a God he didn't quite believe in, I grieve for you. He wept for forgiveness, for his custom gods, for the re-sinewing of the dream. Only the gorge answered.

Marginalia. Anti-Talasa slogans appeared on the walls of the Ciné Mangrove and the fickle islanders sat in at the renewed screenings while Yankee big-men flattened tribes one-handed, their own *yeremanu* forgotten. *Le Dernier des Mohicans* ran for three weeks, the same audience returning and returning. Letters of expulsion began arriving and those who ignored the letters were taken by police guard to Mataso airport and removed. The Bonsers were escorted forcibly, Lemmy Bonser rising to his feet during the hostie's pre-flight safety instructions, to denounce the Nabiru government to the entire plane. His voice was loud and forceful. It took two hostesses and the co-pilot to pull him down. Bingi and Charlotte Larsen went away in their own boat before they were made to go, sailing straight into the dawn. Hedmasta Woodful had reopened his school and Dokta Trumble worked from a make-shift outhouse at the hospital.

Narota was tired. He was old. He was waking uneasily from dream to nightmare.

'Surrender,' the Nabiru government broadcast daily into his green cavern of leaves. Narota, sitting under his banyan tree at Vimape, fingering his tusk, listened and talked with his appointed ministers and knew he had been abandoned.

The final spasm of a fever.

Nabiru, tired of pleading, wanting finality, acted.

On an early morning of what should have been spring in other latitudes, a combat force bristling with guns, walked unchallenged into Vimape and found Tommy Narota sitting at peace beneath his banyan tree, a white flag dipping from a pole. He was surrounded by his ministers, a few hundred rebels and a tribe of frightened wives and children.

Still dignified, Narota rose and raised his hands in custom greeting, then held them out palms upward to be arrested. What lay invisibly on those submissive hands was his own betrayal.

A great and melancholy wail rose from the crowd about him.

There was silence as the riot police moved in and searched the huts, the *nakamal*, the church building and the yam houses; and then they packed Narota and his cabinet ministers and scores of his rebel army into trucks and drove out of that small Eden by the rushing waters of the Tasiriki down the long road to Mataso town and up to the prison that also watched the sea.

So long in the happening. So quick to tell.

They stripped him of his ceremonial tablecloth, gave him prison fatigues and put him to sweeping the prison yard while awaiting trial.

He was hardly dangerous. *Oué*, Tommy Narota. *Oué*.

And no one came to visit him.

No wives. No children. No supporters.

Certainly not those *colons* who had marched on secession day.

Tommy Narota swept dust, watched it rise into the air and re-settle, smiled at sunlight and waited. He waved to children passing on their way to school. Only some waved back. He winced from his rheumatism and remembered many things.

Tearspeak.

It was such a soft, a gentle yielding.

One week. Two.

Things were returning to normal. Or almost normal.

What is normal? old Salway wondered, coming across to town in the island runabout. The last weeks had jammed together, the corrupting twenty-four hour absence of his grandson hanging over the days like nimbus. The boy had returned, bleached as it were, to Lucie Ela's frantic waiting form by the jetty late on the afternoon of secession day, that damp squib.

All the horror of his involvement, of Lorimer's death, of a retching kind of guilt, had gushed out. Then nothing. Nothing. Père Leyroud had talked to the boy, had offered consolation and love and gentleness and Gavi said nothing.

'Thoughtlessness,' Leyroud had said. 'Your actions weren't thought through. It was folly. God understands folly.'

'You've told me all that.'

'I can only keep telling you.'

'It doesn't change anything.'

'You have to accept,' Leyroud had said, suddenly exasperated. 'You must accept.'

'I'm not sulking,' the boy had said with unexpected energy. 'I'm just wrestling with it.'

Good can come from it, old Salway thought. From anything used properly. He hoped.

He angled the runabout into the shingle and hauled himself heavily out trying to wipe away the vision of his grandson moping along the Channel-front gardens back at the house, refusing steadily to return to school.

'For a while, Kenasi, please? For a while?'

The truck he always kept on Mataso side was returned, shoved into the shelter of the *burao* trees where he always left it. There were gashes in the side and the rear vision mirror was gone yet it barked itself into life after some wheezings and the old man drove steadily along the Channel Road on this first visit after rebellion. Landmarks still stood – mission school, the *relais* no one had ever occupied, Talasa headquarters now guarded by riot police from Lena, the Magasin Lantane unboarded and open for business as usual. On the surface, everything as usual.

On the surface.

The trouble with islands, as he was often fond of saying, is the intertwining of smallness that prevents us knowing where the loyalties lie. Perhaps there is only one certain thing – intruders should go. He was sure of that, had been for a long time. Daily, more and more frequently, he was embarrassed by his colour, his long-ingrained manner of planter-master, out-flanked – that was it – and doubting the validity of his presence. He said 'plize' all the time now; understood he was living there on sufferance and could feel his days numbered, failed uprising or not, though he had never bothered politically one way or another.

'How can you not?' planter Duchard used to marvel. 'At least, old friend, not have *feelings* one way or the other?'

'Oh I did. I used to.' Salway sighed. 'The war took that out of me. I saw rotten things the Japs did and rotten things we did and I saw the poor bloody islanders here jammed in between being used – like New Guinea – and all of us, dammit, all of us – Japs, Yanks, Australians – we just marched in and used their land for our fights as if the owners had no rights, no say at all about their bombed villages, their ruined gardens, no say, and all of us killing off people who had nothing to do with it and it made me sick. Like Vietnam. I knew them. You knew them, too, Georges, and the poor buggers hadn't any idea at all what was going on. I guess I got sickest when the Yanks pulled out. They'd brought in all this cargo, lots of lovely jobs and gadgets and then they took them all away again without a bloody thought about the cultural disturbances they'd cause. Oh God bless America! Well, blacks have psyches too, you know. But not according to us. Only whites get mental scars.'

'Some of the whites were left beached.'

'Like Chloe, you mean? Poor old Dancing Bears. Or Leyroud? Well, it was choice for some of them, wasn't it? Christ, why don't we all pack it in and leave?'

Salway hadn't even the energy to mock Duchard's reply. He knew all the tired old theories: the natives weren't ready for it when what they really meant was there's still a little more we can squeeze out! Everything would grind to – God, he hated that claptrap! Why leave them wide open for some hostile power to move in? The Russians, say. Yes yes. He'd heard that one as well. The Red threat. There'd been the Yellow threat before that. It was so dog-in-the-mangerish – if we don't exploit them others will, so Lord, let it be us. Why had it taken him a lifetime to see the immorality of it? Was Narota's sad little gesture his own moral turning-point?

Why couldn't he admit he stayed for other reasons, as Lorimer had, the reasons many of the others came and stayed for. It was the poetry of the place now, the unscannable rogue ballads that land and water and reef pitched rhyming together, the heart-stopping caesurae of different skins and different tongues. He'd never made much from his plantation. The copra was poor and the market slump just about finished him but still he hung on with a fifty-year-old memory of mango dawns and the salt-drench smell from the Channel and no sound but seaspeak or palmspeak and the long evenings on verandahs in the circles of golden light and moths, the kerosene lamp flicker and the sound of paddles across water.

The thoughts of any wet boy, he told himself.

So things had returned to a sort of normal.

The Boulevard was patrolled by military police, *man solwata* created patterns at street corners watching them. Kristi Motors was closed but telephones were ringing again, the *bureau de poste* had reopened and small army helicopters flew up and down the Channel and the east coast roads and made little sorties over Vimape. The rotting fish and copra had been taken out to sea and dumped but its lingering smell held the odour of war.

Almost normal. There'd been a Mass for Lorimer up at Port Ebuli, the Anglican minister having fled and not yet returned. 'Same God, different custom,' Planter Duchard said who was watching Kenasi Salway haul the accumulated mail of a fortnight from his box. Duchard was full of sad news as Salway sorted through his letters. 'It was an accident, you know. The most stupid of accidents. Some freelancing *man bush* who'd never held a gun in his life. He should never have had a gun – but he had. And he was trying to shoot down Lorimer's flag. *Rien que ça* – the flag. There were others with him and they said the same. I believe them, old friend. It's too late for lies. There was Lorimer roaring out of his shack and trying to protect that foolish bit of rag. And then this idiot of a black panicked, lifted the barrel towards the flag and pulled the trigger. All over in seconds. Lorimer crawled inside and the blacks rushed off and hid. Later one of them told Bonnard down at the mission.' Duchard found he couldn't bear the other man's eyes. 'Narota was so distressed,' he went on. 'The pointlessness. He, too, lost a friend.'

'There's irony for you,' Salway said. He was thinking of Gavi.

He turned and began to walk back to the truck and heard Duchard saying, 'You've got one too.'

'Got what?'

Duchard put a finger on one of the envelopes in Salway's hand. Salway pulled it out and peered at the front of it.

'It's for my grandson.'

Duchard was quiet for a moment and then he said soberly, 'I think you had better open it. I think it really concerns you.'

The envelope was official government stationery. The postmark was Port Lena. Duchard's eyes seemed too close, too concerned, even eager, and Salway hesitated before he tore it open and read the slip of paper inside.

He could hardly believe this.

He fumbled with his glasses and wiped them. They seemed to have misted and the island rocked under him as if earth and sky were splitting. He heard himself asking what it meant.

Duchard's eyes were concerned after all. 'Exactly what it says, *mon ami*. If it says what I think it says. What mine says. I've just been given *congé*, my marching orders.'

'But they can't deport a child. He's only a child.'

'They can do anything.'

Salway read the blurring words again and phrases stood out from the page in frightening slabs.

' . . . in view of your sympathies with the rebel movement in Kristi and your known clandestine operations in supplying aid to the rebel movement in the form of weapons, the government has no alternative but to issue you with this order of deportation to take effect as from the 11th day of September. It is recommended . . . '

He handed it across to Duchard who skimmed through it quickly.

'Much like mine,' he said. 'Except, forgive me, old friend, they didn't call me a gun-runner. That can't be true, can it, what they say?'

Every second of Salway's age rose up and swiped him. The explanations he pushed through were a vine-maze: stupidity, Bonser, hot-headed notions of loyalty, idealism – he didn't know, couldn't get it out of him, he –

'It's his age,' Duchard interrupted gently. 'C'*est les kalos. Les couilles.* He was trying for manhood, perhaps.'

'What a way!' old Salway said. He sensed tears squirming at the corners of his eyes. It is just a weakness, he thought. It will pass.

'Fifty years,' Duchard was saying, 'in this place. Both of us. Fifty years. *Pour rien.* Nothing nothing nothing. I'm guilty too, you know. I backed the wrong horse.'

'You mean Narota?'

'No,' Duchard answered. He shifted his aged panama and wiped his forehead. 'He backed the wrong horse too. I mean Mercet. *Sans kalos,* my friend. *Pas de kalos.*'

They stared out across the changing blues of the Channel. The air was ripening into its early summer with smells of succulence flooding the little town. Overhead two helicopters were spinning down the Channel like fever mosquitoes.

'It must have been time,' Salway said. 'It has been settled for me. It must have. I've been feeling that for ever so long.'

It was the end of his world.

Or the beginning.

So much was falling apart or coming together. He saw Lucie Ela in this very morning's sea-light waving him off at the jetty. 'Take care, papa,' she had said. She had called him that several times these last months. 'Papa.' Perhaps it was what any son's wife might say but he knew he would never ask.

It was too late for almost everything.

The trouble with islands is that the world beyond the island is forgotten.

The island is the whole world.

The island is its own planet.

Seas beyond can boil with bombs, war, carnage. The island remains . . . the island.

Kenasi, old Kenasi, wanted to unlearn the rooms of fifty years, those large airinesses he had known by heart down to the last warped transom, stain, split louvre.

He wanted to unsentimentalise himself. Which was itself an act of sentiment.

He wandered backwards and forwards through the house, from verandah to dining-room to bedrooms to kitchen to verandah, surprising memories on the edge or dissolution, seeing faces which, when he addressed their smiles or frowns, moved tantalisingly away and faded, voices that became dumb upon his greeting. Along verandah to the run-down tennis-court and the – was it? was it really? – the smack of tennis balls from long-played games always lost to Duchard who slammed him all over the court until he was glad to escape to the terrace and Callie and Victorine Duchard languid with their drinks in the shade and dinner still three hours away. Walking in the garden afterwards, after too many whiskies, rum punches and the whole place under moonlight mellow as papaw, catching the scent of jasmine with the flowers unnaturally white in the moon against black puddles of shadow, their own shadows stretching far across the moonlit grass straining to dip in the Channel, the shadows of the palms lying down like tired animals on the lawn and music coming from the boy house, someone with a mouth-organ sketching tunes and a voice crooning in the dialect that floated as the moon floated.

Leaving plod-prints like some forgotten film-star through the cocoa gardens, the sun catching him and clouting the back of his neck with a chop that made him buckle. Would he ever get over missing the heat? It was addictive: he hated and needed it. And Lucie Ela has said 'papa' and it didn't matter any more, his urgent secret and his world exploded in one. They'd be gone in less than a week now, had to be gone, with cocoa still drying in the bins and the burnt-out smokehouse unrepaired and the boys to be paid off.

He'd miss them too. He'd always liked them and now, his feet uselessly printing themselves on a place that would have forgotten in a day, regretted those times he could have been kinder or less demanding. It was years before he'd said 'plize'. 'Not too many "plizes", Salway,' the old-timers had warned when he first arrived, while smacking their own children for not saying it. To them of course. Never to natives. 'They'll think it a weakness.'

Foot after foot down the plantation slopes at the back of the house, old bones giving it up when he reached the court again, the balls still smacking and shouts flying up from the sidelines of cracked bitumen, aching old bones through the narrow garden paths, the coral crunching under foot, limping to the boy house with its shutters always open to the Channel wind.

They all knew he was going.

It was a funny thing about this place, this green mitten that was the whole world. You didn't have to say. They simply knew.

He leaned against the open doorway, adjusting his eyes slowly to the shadows and called his grandson. There was only Eroni who kept the kitchen garden going, poor Eroni, too old for plantation work, his family long gone. He hadn't been worth his keep for years but Salway couldn't bear to see him go. It would be like ripping up a page of his own history.

Eroni was lying on his bunk simply staring at the sky between the shutters.

Salway asked in Seaspeak for his grandson and Eroni turned his head and struggled to get off the bunk shaking his head *no kam i no kam* and Salway crossed over the room and gently pressed the other old man down onto the copra sacks. You stay, he said. Stay.

Sori you go, Eroni said then. *Sori.* His smile showed gum. A crumpled black hand pointed in the direction of the jetty. '*Long bot*,' he said.

Gavi was sitting at the end of the jetty gazing into nothingness, his fingers knotting and unknotting a piece of rope.

He looked at his grandfather coming unsurely down the steep path, stumbling a little on the uneven planking of the walkway and got up suddenly and went towards him with a smile. It was, thought old Kenasi, the first smile in weeks.

'It's right we go,' the boy said without preamble. 'I've been thinking about it. It's right. I'm sorry about you and maman, but it *is* right. It *is* time. Maybe when I'm older I can come back. If the island will have me. When I've learned to – well – have myself.'

'That could take a lifetime,' Kenasi said.

He felt ashamed and old and close to oldman tears.

The Channel had never looked more beautiful and more dangerous. The deadly blue was littered with the broken crusts of waves indifferent to the two of them standing there. St Pierre slept behind mango trees and east of it, the merest glimpse of the first white roofs of Mataso.

The boy nodded. He kept smiling despite the difficulty of it and his eyes were solemn, untouched by that smile.

'I know,' he said.

They walked slowly back to the house.

There was only the wind.

The shutters.

The long lines of the palms.

Last goodbyes.

Tiavar. Korro. Tawarro. Ayé.

Goodbye Ebuli. Goodbye Bay of the Two Saints. Goodbye Pig Bay. Goodbye Mataso.

The big house on the little island across from Mataso town is open to the wind and the Channel blue. They are leaving the furniture and the furniture stands uncaring.

Solomon runs them across the last stretch of water for the last time.

Don't look back Kenasi, Lucie Ela, Gavi. *You no kam bak. You no louklouk.*

The shutters are closed like eyes but one has worked loose and winks in the wind. *Ayé.*

Palms wave broken fingered hands.

There are so many goodbyes and so few – for though this is the world it is an island.

There are Père Leyroud and Père Bonnard and all the sisters and Dokta Trumble and Madame Guichet and Hedmasta Woodful and Planter Duchard who will be leaving as well and even Chloe Dancing Bears and all the shop-keepers. All. All. Goodbye.

And even then there is a hitch that mars the tempo of farewells, drags out the inevitability. The plane is delayed until the next morning. They stay at the hotel in the Boulevard where they must try not to look across the water at Emba.

It is sad, this goodbyeing. People call. 'I am too old to throw out,' Madame Guichet says, frightened. 'They do not know I call my dog Big Charlie. That is a joke.'

It is sad. Wine is poured. Hands are clasped. Kisses exchanged. Promises made that will never be kept. *'Il est nécessaire,'* Madame Guichet says. 'It is what is required.'

Gavi is close to tears. My dear one, he thinks, my little island, I love you and I've lost you for the three of us. Four, he admits, remembering Lorimer.

'Cry,' orders Madame Guichet when she catches him mooning near the hotel stairs. 'Cry. That is also right. It also heals.'

Their plane will be leaving at 9 in the morning. They will catch it. They will all catch it. Already Mista Bipi who has returned from exile has arranged to drive them out to the airport.

But Gavi has something he must do on that last morning, something that has been biting at him through the last sleep he will ever take on this island, threshing about on the stuffy upstairs bed with the air conditioner not working, the pillow crawling with memories.

He is out of the hotel before 7 and only the house-girls see him go. And he is half walking, half running along the Boulevard and up the Rue Gauguin along the back streets to the prison on the hill behind the town. Already the children are trailing in to school, walking or riding their push-bikes down to Hedmasta Woodful, down to Ste Cécile, out to the mission at St Pierre. They, too, are early in the blazing morning.

It is a long walk but he has walked farther. So he goes up the Rue Gauguin into the Avenue Février, past the sprawling gardens of Ste Cécile and along the shady side of the Rue Picot, not once looking up, just watching his feet as they take him steadily up the hill road to the tiny prison that watches the Channel.

He is there, Tommy Narota, paramount chief, *yeremanu* from Vimape, and he has been sweeping the prison yard, sweeping up the fragments of his splendid fourteen articled constitution of the republic of Talasa and his Declaration of his Provisional Government, for his broom is propped against the side wall of the cell block. Hello Narota. *Nengle.* As he nods and smiles to a group of little boys who are staring wide-eyed at him through the iron-barred gate.

There are guards, Gavi can see, but the guards are *man* Kristi and not very interested and are smoking cigarettes.

Narota's back is hurting. He bends slightly and rubs his kidneys, rubs his hip joints, nodding, all the while, nodding and smiling to the group of children. Some are silent and simply want to gawk at their fallen *yeremanu.* Some giggle and want to be rude. And suddenly, one boy bigger that the rest, yells out scornfully. Gavi cannot hear what is said but the tone is translatable.

He pushes through the smaller boys, big-eyed at the back of the group and thrusts himself past the older ones, the rude one, and wedges himself close against the uprights of the gate.

Ayé, Tommy Narota. Goodbye. He shoves one hand, two, through the bars and waves them, holds them still. They are palm upward and begging. They are pleading with the prisoner.

Narota blinks at the babbling that has broken out beyond the gate and he sees the hands and that they are empty and full of requests, and he limps over to the gate to take them even as the hands' owner is tugged and wrenched by the other children. And then there's a voice calling from the struggling figures by the gate, a voice that goes with the hands. He has heard the voice, he knows, stirring memory, stirring all the lost years. And it becomes clear, clearer, like the river rush at Vimape. Recognition trembles at the edge of his mind.

'Metuan,' Gavi is calling. 'Uncle.'